FLORENCE

Mistress of Max Gate

A Novel by

PETER TAIT

THE SUNDIAL PRESS

FLORENCE Mistress of Max Gate
First published by The Sundial Press 2011

THE SUNDIAL PRESS
Sundial House, The Sheeplands, Sherborne, Dorset DT9 4BS
www.sundialpress.co.uk

A CIP catalogue record for this book is available from the British Library

Front cover image: 'Max Gate, Dorchester, Dorset' by John Everett
© Dorset Natural History and Archaeological Society

Back cover image: Portrait of Florence Hardy by William Strang
(drawn at Max Gate, September 1926)

ISBN 978-1-908274-08-3

Printed in Great Britain by the MPG Books Group
Bodmin and King's Lynn.

For Sarah

CONTENTS

PREAMBLE

Poor Florence. When she died the best she could manage by way of an epitaph was that of "helpmate of genius". Her life had always been measured in relation to that of her famous husband for whom, as she lamented, she was neither muse nor (as she complained to Siegfried Sassoon) the first-called. She inspired little of Thomas's poetry and, as she later acknowledged, quite the best letters he ever wrote were not to her or even to Emma, but to an earlier subject of Hardy's affections, Florence Henniker. Her other close friendship in the years leading up to her marriage was with another married man, while the only person that she said she truly loved died when she was only thirty-two.

Florence's presence at Max Gate, both before and after Emma died, and the secretive nature of her relationship with Thomas, aroused the suspicions of the servants and the townsfolk of Dorchester, as well as the animosity of the Gifford family. Within a year of their marriage, she had been betrayed by her husband's public declaration of affection for his late wife. Dull, gloomy, dreary, neurotic: these were the epithets used to describe her. Why did she put up with it? And how did she endure the humiliation that Hardy's writings visited upon her?

There was a letter. It was one Thomas had written to Florence on the eve of their wedding in 1914 after he had read Emma's diaries. It remained with Florence until her death when, under instructions, it was burnt by her sister Margaret. And with it died part of the secret, the secret that helped explain Florence. For, as Thomas found out to his cost, there was more to Florence than was evident from their first meeting. And so began their trail of deceptions, first of Emma, then of their friends and, finally, of us all.

Chapter 1

FROM HER LONELY HUSBAND
WITH THE OLD AFFECTION

So she was dead. It had happened unexpectedly that morning, the note said, in her small attic room. She had felt unwell and within minutes, before her husband could get up the stairs, she was gone. It was so typical of the woman, Florence thought, to make her exit at such an inconvenient moment. She repressed the initial reproach that crossed her mind that it was, in fact, something she had once willed to happen, folded the note neatly in her hands and placed it beside the bed. She turned, as if to compose herself, to say something, but not finding it in her to offer a solicitous word or two merely lowered her head and nodded. The maid, who had delivered the telegram, mistaking her reticence for grief, went out with a rustle of skirt, closing the door behind her leaving the poor woman to her sorrow.

Florence sat unmoving, her breath drained out of her, her thoughts caught on the premiss of death. The word numbed her, as did the mere contemplation of bodies moving from one element to another. But then she had always found the act of dying terrifying. This was especially so when she thought of the last expiration, the gasping for air (and what terror must be felt when the lungs collapse like sponges wrung of water), of that precise moment when the heart stops pumping. She thought too, in a wave of billowing sadness, what is lost in death, any death – the sounds, smells, language that are peculiar to the person, and the irrevocable fact that they are no longer present, in any realm. Every death of someone she had known in her life punched a small hole in her already dark universe, and sat upon her as a precursor of what was to come to her too. Florence shuddered and pulled her shawl tightly around her. Of Emma she did not

1

know what to think and because she feared she might not be charitable, chose not to think at all. She would rather abstract the death, for while it brought it closer to her own, it was preferable to straying where her thoughts did not belong.

She thought of Thomas last of all: Thomas, who had told her that the death when it came would only confirm an earlier bereavement, that being his marriage, which had been put to bed years before. He had said to her that the Emma he had married, whom he loved once, had died some twenty years before, if she had ever existed at all. Would he be thinking that now? How much rawness would come out in this finite act, the dying of the person he had known for so long?

She knew she could do nothing. She could not go near Max Gate, not yet. Her letter of condolence that she must write that very afternoon would be carefully crafted, and while it was another opportunity for Thomas to see her skill as a wordsmith, it must say all that was necessary and no more. She must mourn in just the right measure and when she saw Thomas again, she must be properly solicitous. She must appear unaffected although she was not, for the universe and the natural order of things were changing and she knew, with a sudden start, that she would have to change with them.

It was prescient, she thought, when she read the telegram again, that she had been on the train to Weymouth at the very time Emma had died. Florence had not been aware the older lady had been ill, although she remembered now that at their last meeting she had seemed vexed and anxious, her face flushed and coloured as if she had been labouring over a hot stove. Emma had always seemed like a much older woman, too old for Tom. When Florence had last seen her, she saw that the once prominent jaw line had started to sag, the face was more lumpish and blotched, that her deep-set eyes, once a feature of her visage, were rheumy and withdrawn beneath her deep overarching brow. She had noticed folds of loose skin gathered about her jowls and that her face was made stern as if by her constant chewing of the cud. She did little to help herself, or more importantly to help Tom, by taking little care over how she appeared to others. Her manner, likewise, was little better and did nothing to appease her appearance, and her agitated and inconsequential ramblings either irritated visitors or made her appear an object of pity.

Florence could not bring herself to feel any sympathy for her, however, even in the abstract. To do so now seemed wrong, as she tried to tell herself, for Emma would hate it, but she knew that was not the reason she could not. It was because the old lady had taken so little account of Tom, had disparaged the very privilege of walking beside his genius; it was because of how little she did for him and how often and cruelly she demeaned him. This did not make her deserving of pity in Florence's eyes. Yet she was Tom's wife, his chosen, and while she was unpredictable and given to volatile and impolitic comment, Florence had learned to live with her foibles, had even sought to be of considerable assistance to her so that Tom could see, or imagine he could see, a close communion between the two. But then he only saw what he needed to see. To succeed, Florence had learned to feign consideration and concern, play the role of a good listener, and to keep out of her way when prudence suggested it to be the right thing to do.

When Florence stayed at Max Gate, she had tried especially hard to befriend her, not at all unsuccessfully, and indeed it appeared as if Emma and Thomas at times competed for her attention when she was with them. For some two years they had even been friends, to all intents and purposes, a fact that pleased Tom, although both women never dropped their guard or opened up with each other. Recently she had sensed an indifference on the part of Emma that had troubled her. She recalled a time some eighteen months back when, walking with her in the garden at Max Gate, Emma had begun one of her frequent indiscreet railings against Tom and his family, how she had married beneath herself and that without her Thomas would have achieved little. Florence, rather unwisely she saw now, had been moved to defend him as she felt she should and had sensed the error too late. 'He was a bricklayer's son,' huffed Emma, 'and he had no business thinking he could escape the fact. As for thinking he could have gone to university, well!'

And she wondered, always wondered, after that what Emma thought of her, what she knew of her, the way she looked at her so intently with her eyes almost opaque, as if her sight was failing, as if there was something else there to look at beyond the mask of her face.

These moments of self-doubt made Florence's normal sallow complexion redden, not unattractively, although she did not feel it so, and she wondered at her being part of this ménage. How had it all happened, this strange place she had found herself? There would be time enough for wonder at such things, but the fact was the old lady was gone and these shadows would fade and for that reason, try as she might, Florence could not bring it upon herself to feel sad, not properly so, or carry the pity that any less knowing heart would feel.

Florence had come to Weymouth to see a dramatization of *The Trumpet Major*. She had also harboured hopes, not without expectation, that Thomas would come to Weymouth too and that they would have some time there away from the Hardy household, or perhaps, failing that, she could also call on them at Max Gate, but only reluctantly as she knew such visits were full of compromise.

Later, Florence walked from the hotel across the street to the beach and sat looking out across towards Osmington and further round to Durdle Door. The day was clear and pleasantly mild for late November, although the wind off the sea reminded her that all was mutable. She pulled the large shawl tighter around her, and adjusted the smaller paisley headscarf that covered her hair which was pinned and tied into a neat dark bun. She leant forward, her head looking straight out to sea, like the carved prow of a boat, her hands on her knees, rocking herself gently, and considered what it would all mean for Tom and what role she must play now. It had been seven years since they had met, since she had ingratiated herself into his life, and she had not properly considered the likelihood of what now had happened. She wondered why she had not done so, for there must always have been a chance that life could turn out like this, but she simply had not. Their time together over recent months had been too transient, too unsettled for such thoughts to have ever taken root. Moreover, she reflected, the last two years had been so very difficult coping with the loss of Alfred and then Thornley, and she had simply not thought of her and Thomas as an entity, for he had not allowed it. Nor had she any idea what would come next, or what she could do to influence anything that may happen. She wondered whether Tom, free from the yoke that he had so often spoken to her of, might want to be free from her too.

She would go home she ventured, in a day or two's time, and wait, just wait for something to happen, as it must, she told herself. With that passive thought in mind, she returned to her hotel, took supper in her room and read until her feverish mind had stilled and she was able to sleep.

4

The next morning, before she opened the copy of *The Times* that had been delivered to her room, she stiffened herself for what she thought would be written about Emma, the unnecessarily nice things people say at such times, even when they are palpably untrue. Eventually, she found what she was looking for in the lower right corner of the second page under the headline ***Wife of Famous Novelist Dies***. She read it slowly, not bothering to sit, instead balancing herself by leaning against the back of the chair that was beside her.

On November 27th 1912, Emma Hardy, wife of the eminent writer Thomas Hardy, passed away at the couple's Dorchester home, Max Gate. The Hardys had been married for 38 years. Mrs Hardy died of heart failure and impacted gallstones and had been unwell for some time. Mr Hardy spoke of his intense sadness at his loss.

There it was in four curt sentences. Thomas could say what he wanted, she thought, now, today, using his penchant for romantic fiction, but the bald fact of the matter was that the tribute, thankfully, was less than she feared it would be. Of course the paper wouldn't say the two had been estranged, that Thomas had suffered her solecisms, her sullen and erratic behaviour stoically, that while naturally sad it was as if a pair of hands had been released from around his creative neck. That he was well-pleased to be rid of her she was sure, but no one, not even he, would utter such a heresy, although that did not stop her thinking it. She smiled a grim smile to herself. Thomas in his brief tribute, as she had expected, wouldn't risk saying anything that might alter the public view of him, although she knew and he knew and others knew what had been brewing inside him and that his "intense sadness" was a mere euphemism for a deep sense of relief. Surely that was the truth of how he felt, surely. She read the lines again, more slowly now, and felt a shimmer of resentment at the amount of time and energy Emma had consumed with her eccentricities and demands, time that Thomas should have used for his writing. But she bade patience and instead amused herself by thinking how Tom, who had renounced his writing of novels in favour of his beloved poetry, would react to the headline. And then, ashamed of herself for thinking such a mixture of unkind thoughts, she tied her hair in a black satin ribbon that should have softened her but had the opposite effect, so tightly did she pull her hair back. She sought out a pen, her special pen, Tom's pen that had been gifted to her, to write to her eminent patron and protector, Mr Thomas Hardy Esq.

The letter of condolence that she wrote and sent on that same day was a model of propriety and she was proud of it, saying as it did all that was necessary and expected, shorn of any ambiguity, righteous enough to stand up in a court of law and soft and comforting where and when it needed to be, able to be read by any of his kith and kin, those that could read, without suspicion.

Leaving the hotel, she walked along the esplanade towards the post office where she bought a stamp, and having licked it and prepared to pass over the envelope, paused momentarily to recall what she wrote and whether it would be enough or too little. She hoped Tom would be the first to see her hand and would decide against sharing it with the others (although it was perfectly respectable for doing so), that he would choose to keep it to himself. She wondered what would happen to them now, with Emma gone, whether her role would change, whether his need of her would diminish, whether he would require her in the same way as before. The promise of the next day's train journey weighed upon her, for she wondered if by going away, by establishing a divide between them, she would still inhabit the same place in his life as she had assumed or be cast off as she had once been abandoned by another. She was always full of wonder, although her horizons were grey and her hopes never more than modest, especially in this matter.

That evening, being her last night in Weymouth, she decided, after all, to go and see the production of *The Trumpet Major* at the theatre in nearby Dorchester. Thomas had let it be known that the performance could proceed as planned, as he explained to the local newspaper, for 'Emma would have wanted it so'. But after the curtain went up and throughout much of the first half, Florence's mind drifted, assailed by doubts, distracted by feelings of guilt she could not properly rationalise. On stage, meanwhile, the heroine Anne Garland was being pursued by three suitors before eventually settling on the dull and lightweight Bob Loveday over his altogether more admirable brother; a choice Florence put down to Anne's vacillations. She was too weak, thought Florence. How differently she would have handled things. In her own situation, she reflected on how bereavement had taken away any such choice for her, with the loss of her two dearest friends, either of whom could have offered her the opportunity of another life. Just perhaps. But now there was no choice, thought Florence, not unless she wanted to move back to London and start her life over again. There was just Thomas.

Chapter 2

ALL'S PAST AMEND

Florence need not have worried. As soon as the funeral was over, a letter arrived from Tom urging her to come back to Max Gate. She took little time in agreeing that she would do so, quickly packing her suitcase and making the necessary arrangements. It was early December and the journey to Dorchester was not straightforward, involving as it did two changes of train, first at Woking and then at Chichester. But when eventually she arrived at the station, he was there waiting for her. A cold wind was coming from the north-east and a damp fog was starting to settle in the air and he had, most sensibly she thought, wrapped himself in a long overcoat with a fawn tartan scarf wrapped tightly twice about his scraggy neck. She saw as she alighted that he was wearing his black hat that rode high on his temples, covering his thinning hair, with the effect – no doubt desired – of making him look taller than he was. She smiled inwardly at his vanity, and how his head was more like that of a petulant bird and how much older he seemed to be than she remembered. Death, even a welcome one, must age one, she thought. It was not an unkind observation although she knew she was not beyond harbouring ill-feeling, but only what she earnestly believed to be so.

'Tom,' she said. 'You could have sent someone else.'

'My dear,' he answered holding both her hands, 'I would not allow anyone else this privilege.' He smiled weakly. 'It is so kind of you to come to help an old man in his time of need.'

She looked at him. His hooded greenish-black eyes were dull, vulnerable, set, it seemed, deeper into his face than she remembered; his head appeared to have shrunk so that the skin that once fitted comfortably no longer did so, settling instead in loose folds around his jowls. He appeared limp and tired, in need of being looked after.

8

Much of the journey back to Max Gate was conducted in silence although he held her hand tightly. Only as they neared the house did he tell her that Emma's family had been meddling and that his sister Kate and Emma's spinster niece Lilian Gifford were encamped inside, and that he was being driven to distraction by their constant interference and was growing ever more fearful of the arrangements that they had in store for him. Grief, if it was anywhere near the surface, was eclipsed by the impending domestic crisis and all the arrangements that had to be sorted out. He was irritable, scared of how to cope despite having ostensibly done so for so long. Emma had been a hindrance, an impediment to his writing, and now he had someone who understood the process of writing, who would work for him, not against him, someone who would allow him one last great hurrah, one final flourish, for at seventy-two years of age he felt it tempting the Immortals to plan too far ahead.

At the house, Lilian did not come out of the kitchen and when Florence appeared at the doorway, she greeted the newcomer with a surly nod and a hello without pausing from her needlework. Lilian had the same broad face and ruddy nose as her aunt but, as Florence observed, without any of the odd mannerisms that gave Emma the quaint charm espoused by some admirers, even though this was lost on her. Florence looked at Lilian's stout back and doubted to herself if the woman had even read Tom's books. Undoubtedly she would have been better suited to a dairy, even if she was a Gifford, than here in the company of her famous relative, strutting about as if the misalliance of her aunt entitled her to this.

After a cup of tea, Florence was shown up to her room and had just picked up the copy of the *King James Bible* placed on her bedside cabinet when Lilian appeared at the door, informing her that supper would be sharp at seven because, she added curtly, 'Mr Hardy likes it to be so.'

Florence laid down her bag and coat and sat on the bed end, hands in her lap, staring intently at the wall. The room was cold and no effort had been made to heat it, even if just by the act of leaving the door open a little to let the heat from downstairs climb and mingle. There was a fresh flurry of rain starting to fall outside and she felt miserable, the resolute mood that she had carried with her from Sussex ebbing away. What was Tom planning to do with her here? Could he not see how unbearable it would be for them all?

She made her way downstairs and was heartened that Tom's sister Kate was not so indifferent to her presence. She greeted Florence with a gentle hand laid on hers and said quietly, 'It is good to see you again, Miss Dugdale' – careful, though, that she would not be overheard in doing so.

The conversation over supper was strained, covering as it did her trip, the weather, the garden, the cats, but never once Emma, despite Tom's attempts to jolly all along. Lilian was happy to allow Kate to prepare the meal and to clean up afterwards and it was evident she did not see herself being there to help in any manual way, but rather as family, as Emma's living shadow. Later, when they moved into the drawing-room, she placed herself opposite Thomas and talked at him about Emma, about Cornwall, childishly mimicking her late aunt and excluding Florence and Kate from the intimacy of the subject matter.

It was therefore with some relief that it was decided that all should turn in soon after the meal and Florence, glass of water in her hand, walked up the first flight of stairs to her room. Putting on her nightgown and dressing gown, she made her way to the bathroom and was almost through with her ablutions when there was a knock at the bathroom door. She opened it cautiously to see Lilian there, nightgown buttoned firmly to her neck.

'You should not have come,' she said, fixing her grey eyes upon Florence.

There was a pause as both women looked directly at each other, measuring the other's countenance as pugilists would in a ring, looking for signs of weakness.

'You might say that, Miss Gifford, but Tom asked me himself to come and stay and be a help to him. And so I came.'

'He's a fool. And he's a grieving fool too who doesn't know the rights and wrongs of what he is doing, let alone the workings of his heart. He's brittle is Thomas and has always liked a younger woman around him. But I know, and others know, you shouldn't be here. It's not right.'

Florence met the gaze of the older woman with an expression that exuded self-assurance and equanimity, though it was far removed from how she actually felt. She paused, considering her next words.

'Then I will ask the master of the house if he wants me to stay. I'll let him decide whether he needs me here and whether it is right that I remain. He will want to write, if I know Tom, and I can help him. And he wants me to work with him on his new American editions. What do you know about writing, Lilian Gifford?'

Lilian glared at her.

'I know what's right and wrong, Miss Dugdale, and I know without the help of my aunt Mr Hardy would never have become the famous writer he is. I know of you and your family and where you're from and I know it's not right that you be here. Remember it is the Giffords that made Thomas respectable and Emma who inspired him and was his companion as a wife is supposed to be. That's what I know. And I'll bid you good-night for I have said all I meant to say for now.'

Florence sat for several minutes on the edge of the bed. There was so much accusatory venom in the other woman's voice, so much vitriol. She picked up the Bible that she had placed on the edge of the eiderdown and noticed a torn corner of newspaper, leading her to a page that was itself folded over, reinforcing the urge to open it at that chapter. Having given in to the enticement, Florence's eyes rested on the verses from the book of Exodus and noticed the heavy scouring of pencil under the seventh commandment. She felt herself go weak. So this is what they thought? This woman who cares not a jot for Tom but whose family won't just go away now that there is no call for them, this woman who presumes to pass judgement, though her sister and her family did nothing for Tom except interpose and obstruct. She felt a mix of anger and trepidation, not knowing what the morrow would bring, but not caring either what they knew or thought for she would not waver under their censure. Slender and diminutive she might be and gentle and frail she might appear, but she was steely also, as they would discover.

The next day was warmer and while the air was a little strained, nothing more was said of the previous night's conversation. Breakfast was conducted in a more cordial manner and Lilian quickly absented herself leaving Florence on her own with Tom. After she had finished, she decided to go into the garden to take some air. Emma's cats, all four of them, were mewing about and their mess was everywhere. They seemed to Florence to be like spiteful reincarnations of their mistress, protecting their territory. Folding her arms across her and pulling her shawl to, she walked across to the garden seat under the loping plane tree that anchored the garden, carefully watching where she was placing her feet.

The tree was bare now and without its leaves afforded little shelter and while the day was not particularly cold, she shivered involuntarily. She took out her sketchpad, for she liked her hands to be doing something, and fancied she could sketch the side of the house from here, but had only been there for a few minutes when Kate joined her. She sat down with a sigh, leaning back and splaying her legs in an altogether rural manner, or so Florence thought to herself by way of explaining away her demeanour.

'I know how you feel, Miss Dugdale, wanting to get outside. The house can be too much with Miss Gifford shuffling around making everybody feel not wanted.' She paused. 'I do hope she doesn't drive you away as she'd like to do with all of us. Do you plan to stay long?'

'I don't know.' In truth, Florence had thought only of the coming, not of the leaving, and she realised, yet again, that it would be what Tom wanted that would determine the duration of her visit or even whether she spent a now imminent Christmas with her family or with Tom and the two spinsters.

'How is Tom?' Florence asked, for though she had spoken to him the past evening, she knew there were things a sister sees in a brother, some part of life's familial rhythms that only siblings can discern.

'He's well enough in himself although he has been acting a little queer at times. He found some diaries and notebooks that Emma had been keeping and I know that in one of them in particular she savaged him something awful and blamed him for treating her so bad, and even of being ashamed of her when visitors came and trying to hide her when it was she they wanted to meet too. He never did, though. I'm not saying my brother was always proper, but he did right by her. Knowing Thomas, though, he will use it all to write another book or one of his scraps of verse for that seems to be all he has in him now.'

Kate smiled a grim smile, her lips pursed, her eyes flat and bodiless.

'He's an odd one, is Thomas,' she continued. 'At times he seems as hard as flint, doesn't want anyone fussing over him, hates even being touched and then he comes over all maudlin. I think it's all for effect, at least the most of it. I can hear his mind whirring sometimes, asking what can I make of this, as a carver would with a piece of wood. I assume it all ends up on a piece of paper somewhere. But he likes you being here, Miss Dugdale, that I do know.'

'Thank you, Kate.' Florence was touched that Tom's sister was so open with her. She said nothing for a minute or more, grateful for the company and for it making no demand upon her.

'These diaries. What do they say?'

Kate hesitated before replying.

'He won't say much, but apparently she wrote down all the things she didn't like about Tom over these past years and why she thought she was wrong to have married him and how she had let her family down, them being somewhat better than the Hardys. Her father never forgave Tom, you know, for presuming he was good enough for Emma. He called him "a lowborn churl" he did, and that's how the Giffords saw all us Hardys, not good enough for their high and mighty ways.'

'But that's nonsense, Kate. Tom is a great writer and that is far more than the Giffords ever were or shall be, I dare say. What has Tom done with these nasty books?'

'He has them in his study as far as I know. I saw them there when I took him a cup of tea a day or so back. He was very upset. I know he was badly shaken when he discovered them the day of the funeral and did not want to believe it was really Emma that wrote them, but it's her hand sure enough.'

'You've seen them too?'

Kate paused and picked up a large piece of variegated bark off the ground, and picked at it before replying.

'Briefly, for I had to see what was upsetting him and why he was so morose and gloomy. It was she alright, her peculiar scrawl, full of poisonous thoughts and nasty words. It makes no sense. He was so good to that woman despite her peculiarities and her letting him down as she did so often.'

'So why doesn't he just destroy them?'

'Because he can't do that, not now. Because it's all too much for him, awash with guilt and longing and the like as he is. He will burn them in time, I am sure, for he would not want them to survive for others to see. As I said, he's a strange one, my brother. And now we've got another Gifford in the house, all high and mighty too, and not welcome either although he hasn't the heart to tell her so. He sees her now as tied to that he has just lost. That's Thomas. That's how it always is with him when remorse takes hold and naught we can do about it, but stay it out.'

The sun had gone behind a cloud and Florence stood up to go inside. The wind had a chill in it she hadn't noticed a few minutes earlier and it no longer seemed sensible to sit out in it. She was unsettled by what she had heard, unhappy that what Emma had written in her own vituperative hand mattered to Tom, that it could affect the manner of his grieving. He had told her that Emma was no wife to him, had not been for many years, that she was an embarrassment, a yoke, a hindrance to his writing. So why did he suddenly feel anything, she thought to herself? Why did he care about someone he spurned and who had spurned him? And now, now, she asked herself, why do the words upset him so? It is his caring that upsets me, especially now that the obstacle has gone and we can be who we talked of being before all the subterfuge.

Inside the house, Lilian had been busy talking to Tom about settling the costs of the funeral with the undertaker, acknowledging the choir and the vicar, and about the need to respond to the many letters of condolence. She would go into Dorchester that very afternoon, she suggested, to have cards printed that he could sign with a brief, personal comment. Tom had listened and suggested that this was a job that Florence could do, being well-read and knowing the sort of verse that would be right for Emma as she had been a great help to Emma with her own insubstantial writings.

Lilian sat up, her eyes angry at the suggestion.

'But she is like you, Thomas, a non-believer. A non-believer should not be asked to choose a verse of scripture in memory of your late wife. You forget that while you saw fit to abandon your faith, Emma strengthened hers throughout the life you allowed her and it provided her with a comfort when you were so heartless. She has told me what it was like, having a godless husband, one who thought he could fly in the face of the scriptures.'

Lilian broke off her diatribe and raised her eyes towards heaven in a gesture of supplication before continuing.

'While you might want otherwise for her now, you are forgetting her upbringing and who her father was. What you propose is disrespectful to her memory. To suggest you ask a non-believer to choose a verse for her and especially one such as she, who is here because you are weak, Thomas, weak and pliable. It is not right.'

Thomas stood up, visibly shaking with anger.

'That's enough,' he retorted. 'Florence is my guest and is here to help me with my work. You know nothing of what she thinks or is capable of. I will not have her spoken of in such a way.'

He paused and leaned across to adjust the window.

'And you are wrong about her. It is true that I have seen enough of

14

churches and the folk that inhabit them to steer clear of the faith myself, but she sees the spirit of God in many things and I dare say could even see the good in you, although that's as may be. Churches are interesting as buildings, that I know, but the people who gather in such places, in my view, are too inclined to pass judgement on others and sound narrow-minded, Lilian Gifford, as you do now.'

Lilian scowled at Thomas and was about to respond in kind when Kate and Florence came in from outside. She glared at them both before disappearing up the stairs, holding her voluminous skirt firmly in both hands as she did so.

Relations were strained for several days before life settled to a routine. Florence arranged for the cards and oversaw the checking of the list and the sending. Increasingly, it was she who Tom turned to for advice and who read to him each afternoon in between helping with the editing of the new edition of his novels. Kate came and went, as cheerful as ever, while Lilian filled the house with her brooding acerbic presence, running the domestic arrangements without doing any of the work and never missing an opportunity to belittle Florence in front of the servants.

Christmas was an altogether trying occasion. Florence chose to stay on with Tom, at his urging, rather than with the Dugdales, although she felt the simmering resentment all around her and regretted the ceremony of the day and wished it would end. At church, she was conscious that many of the congregation, mostly folk from around Stinsford and Bockhampton, were looking at her in an unfriendly way and she knew it had been a mistake, even if it had been what Tom wished, although he appeared unwilling to tell others she was there at his bidding. Afterwards, she and Tom went to the old cottage at Bockhampton for the last time before the family relinquished their lease on the property, ending a 112-year tenure. Thomas's other siblings, Henry and Mary, like Kate, were welcoming of her, as they had always been, and she enjoyed a pleasant hour or so with them before returning with Thomas to Max Gate and Lilian's waiting scowl.

Her time alone with Tom was never long enough and there were always others about, prying and listening. It hurt her so to see how he was suffering and yet she found him increasingly withdrawn and uncommunicative on the subject of Emma. He was proprietorial towards her and while she felt the relief of not having to play a role anymore, others demanded it of her, at least for the moment. She often found herself asking what she was doing there, but could find no pressing reason to leave. Yet she knew she had to do so before too long as she had left her lodgings unattended, while her mongrel dog, deposited with her cousin several weeks before, had no doubt worn out the lukewarm welcome it had received.

'What are you feeling, Tom?' she would ask. 'Why are you so solemn?' And he would answer that it was the suddenness of Emma's leaving that haunted him, being so unexpected and not at all planned for, and that although he was not unhappy in himself, he regretted things he had said.

'She said awful things about you, Tom,' she would remind him, 'she didn't love you,' but he would brush them to one side and answer, yes, that was as may be, but it didn't affect the propriety of it all or the fact that people had said he had neglected her and he couldn't prove otherwise, not now, or make amends.

She pushed him about the diaries, but he would say little other than that Emma was clearly not of sound mind when she wrote them, that she had not been well. When she asked if he still had them, he demurred, saying he would not be keeping them although he was not ready yet to rid himself of their complaints for he needed to find a little joy in them too.

It was not the answer she wanted to hear, but she bore the comments, and the company, with stoicism.

The winter, when it eventually arrived, was cold and bitter and by early January Florence was ready to leave. Tom had tried to persuade her not to go but was ambivalent in saying so, although he did press her on the promise that she would come back soon for he needed her help sorting out his correspondence and the like. Lilian had gained a stranglehold on the household staff and with Kate coming in for only a few days at a time, Florence was finding the atmosphere increasingly unpleasant. Moreover, she was unsure what Tom was thinking. The last year had been difficult for them both and while she was now more independent financially, and not bound by other attachments, somehow she felt more bound, more compromised than ever. Was it the passing of the years? The aftermath of the twin calamities that had befallen her? Fear of being left on her own? Somehow, what she felt about Tom had crystallised, had become more deliberate and consciously decided. She held to the promises he had made and the inveterate kindness of his heart, but she was troubled by his ambivalence and the uncertainty of the moment, and felt that she needed time away as well. She wondered, too, whether he might write of her and make her recognisable as his muse as well as the beneficiary of his gentle, caressing words, spoken to her in the few quiet moments allowed them.

Chapter 3

THE VOICELESS GHOST

From the moment she boarded the train at Dorchester, Florence started to shiver, not visibly so, but palpably nonetheless. The melange of emotions that had run through her since the funeral had been difficult enough to cope with, particularly Tom's invisible dependence on her. She felt hurt by his muted failure to acknowledge her presence as being what he wanted, and was disturbed also by his obsequiousness to Emma's high-handed and judgemental niece who saw herself as the protector of past slights. She had always felt as if she was being watched, that Lilian was looking for her to say or do something wrong, that somehow she suspected something amiss, for she had the face of a judge.

Whatever her doubts and misgivings, Florence had not been back at her home in Enfield for long when the letters and entreaties from Tom began, saying how he missed her and pleading with her to return. He sounded lonely, lost, and she felt her heart stir. His words of affection gave her strength and confidence, adding to her own resolve to cope with the politics of Max Gate and not be cowered by Lilian's brusque manner and acidulous asides.

She did not want to rush, however, and instead travelled to see her sister Margaret, of whom she was especially fond, and to spend a little time with her parents whose knowledge of their chameleon daughter had become more blurred and indistinct. Florence told them little about her role at Max Gate, for what was there to tell, and had distanced herself from the family roots in Wareham although when with family she played the part. But as the letters continued and, as she acknowledged to herself, it was Tom's company and approbation that she most wanted, she began to waver. Eventually she made arrangements to return to Max Gate and, having booked her seat, sent a telegram to Tom to give him her arrival time in

Dorchester. On this occasion, Florence took a little more time than usual packing, for she had no idea when she would return. That decision she surmised, when it was needed, would again rest with Tom and she would accede as she always had. The cousin who had agreed to look after Wessex chided her gently not to abuse his kindness for taking in her mongrel, having already been more than tolerant of a dog that took readily and gave nothing in return.

'There are enough dogs that need a home without putting up with one as cantankerous as this,' he complained to Florence, but her mind was elsewhere and she smiled her quick smile and lifted her dark eyes upon him, dark within dark, and he could do little but smile weakly back at her, enthralled as he was by the most mysterious and remote of all the Dugdale girls.

The day was cold, as would befit early February, perishingly so, when Florence alighted at Dorchester, her hand luggage clasped in one gloved hand, an umbrella in the other. There was no Tom this time and when she saw a local cab driver hail her, she realised that it would be a different welcome than before. He collected her luggage for the short drive across town and while she was pleased to have been gathered up, she felt uneasy that she would have no time to glean the mood of Max Gate, to feel what was going on at the house or Tom's state of being. His absence ate away at her on the short drive from the station even though she would have told him not to bother coming himself.

She was particularly worried that it would be Lilian who met her, but thankfully it was Kate who opened the door. She had moved back to Upper Bockhampton now and only came to see Thomas on odd days, but had reasoned Florence would want a familiar face to greet her. Lilian was busy preparing tea in the dining-room and paused only briefly to greet her with the same impassive countenance and lack of warmth as she had employed in saying farewell to her some five weeks previously.

Florence could see, however, that the niece had made good use of the time since she had been left on her own with Tom, for she had retrenched, as if settling in for the duration. There were subtle changes in the décor, in the ways things were arranged, in the colours and the smells and the synergy of the house, changes that disturbed Florence. She could feel the fresh optimism she had garnered on the journey start to seep out of her.

They took tea, and half way through Tom joined them, looking much as she had left him, dapper still with his braces and cuffs and squat ink-stained fingers, the little hair he had seeming thinner and more unkempt than ever. He welcomed her warmly, but made no apology for not meeting her and Florence sensed that he was more distant than his letters had led her to believe. He could not settle, in gaze or word, upon her and again she wondered what he wanted of her and where was the heart and hand that wrote those letters, begging for her to return. She thought, not for the first time, that he loved her more when she was away from him than when he could reach out and touch her, as she had once yearned for him to do. Now that she was here, in his domain, perhaps he felt he could relax. His discretion, subsumed in his written words, was emerging again. He was one for appearances she knew, and words were meant to say one thing, but perversely when faced by their subject, he was disinclined to accept their authorship. Perhaps later, if they were alone, allowed to be alone, he would say to her how grateful he was that she had come, how much it meant to him, how much he needed her, but whether the right words would be said or not, she had no idea, so she had to be satisfied by imagining them said instead.

After supper that evening, an opportunity did arise for them to talk in private, sooner than Florence had imagined. Tom took Florence into his study to show her the first proofs of his new edition of *A Pair of Blue Eyes* and although it was Florence's least favourite of his books, she agreed that it was finely printed. He sat on his chair, Florence leaning over his right shoulder, her left hand gently resting on the other as he showed her the new preface and then a bundle of new letters, asking favours of him, commiserating with him on his loss and inviting him to various soirées or lunches with those in society who courted eminent men as a means of embellishing themselves. She noticed also on a further perusal the small heap of notebooks – five, maybe six – and the inscription on the top one that read 'What I think of my husband'.

'Are those the wretched notebooks that Emma wrote?' she asked.

There was a pause. Tom reached slowly across his desk as if to protect them.

'They are.'

'Why, Tom, why, why keep them if they make you so unhappy and miserable?'

He looked down at his desk. Clearly, he was finding it difficult to answer and when he did so, he spoke more slowly, more deliberately than she could remember he had ever done so to her before.

'Because I needed to know what went on in her mind, what soured her so.'

She could see he was troubled, disturbed even by the subject and was determined they should not continue to haunt him in this way.

'Promise me, Tom, you will destroy them when you are finished with them. They have no place here, not with us.' She paused again, blushing at her own choice of pronoun.

'I will my dear, I will, but I needed time. It was a dreadful shock you know, the suddenness of it.'

He looked old and frail and she wavered, momentarily, almost excusing his sense of loss before continuing to admonish him further.

'You didn't care for her anymore, Tom, for you told me so and that was the premiss for the understanding between you and me. There was no other. You are a sentimental old fool sometimes, Tom Hardy, but you need to get over this, for I am not here to listen to things about her that you and I know are not true.'

For the next few days life slipped into a regular pattern. Tom had been busy sorting through Emma's papers, taking what seemed to Florence an inordinate amount of time poring over the scrambled pieces of prose that his late wife had written and that she herself had typed in her efforts to ingratiate herself with the woman. It had been decided to leave her room largely as it was and to disturb it as little as possible; it was a decision Florence found ghoulish and unsettling. To get out of the house, she went for a walk each day and as the weather was unseasonably kind for late February, found early shoots of spring in the nearby woods that ran from Bockhampton to Puddletown. She usually walked alone, for Kate was always busy now with her family and Lilian never ventured from indoors. Her relationship with the Gifford retainer, as she thought of Lilian, was no better and the caustic comments that dripped from the latter's tongue continued to irritate rather than wound her. Yet she knew she was in some ways dependent upon Lilian who had enthroned herself as the lady of the house, with Tom's apparent acquiescence. The servants, likewise, were cordial but little more and for some reason that she ventured had its source elsewhere, even Kate started to grow more distant and less engaging towards her.

When, at the end of February, Tom pushed his papers to one side and looked up at her, she felt that this may be the moment that he would say something about them, about *them*, Tom and Florence, and would snap out of his gloom and despondency. But she was mistaken. Instead, he told her of his intention to travel down to Cornwall, to 'exorcise his demons' as he put it, and to organise a memorial for Emma at St Juliot's; to revisit old haunts, to wallow, as she saw it, in the memory of that woman.

She riled at his intention to further sentimentalise Emma's death and stared at him angrily.

'Why did you bring me here, Tom, to treat me like this? What am I doing here in this miserable house with that woman making my life a misery while you pine for another? What of your promise?'

'Please, Florence, please be patient.'

'Patient. Patient! I would need the patience of a saint to put up with you in these moods. You go then and exorcise this demon, for that's what it is, and I will go away until you are ready to receive me as promised.'

'Florence. That's the thing.' He paused momentarily, as if girding himself in order to deliver what followed. 'I don't want you to go away.'

He looked pleadingly at her.

'I want you to wait here, to look after the house, to protect my papers, to make sure your presence doesn't fade altogether – please!'

Florence turned on him, eyes blazing.

'You want me to stay here with that woman? For God's sake, Tom, do you know what you are asking of me? What of you? Who will accompany you and look after you?'

'I will travel with my brother. Henry has already agreed.'

She stared at him.

'So, it is all arranged. And you think I will agree with you, this time like every other?'

'I hope, my dear, I hope. That is all. It is what I most want. I want you to be here when I return. I want to rid myself of one life and start anew and so when I return, it is to you.'

'And do you promise, Tom, if I agree to this thing you propose, living in this house with that horrible woman, that you will do just that?'

'That I do.'

'And why not take her with you, back to where she belongs?'

'Because it is not that easy.' He sighed and his shoulders dropped in exasperation. 'Nothing has ever been that easy with the Giffords.'

And so it was decided. She would stay in the house while Tom and Henry would set out in a few days' time for Cornwall. Ostensibly, the reason given was to organise the memorial in the church at St Juliot's, although she suspected Tom also wanted to explore old haunts and to assuage his grief. Still, she reasoned, if he was to make this pilgrimage, best it was done now and was out of the way so they could realise the promises made so long ago.

Tom and his brother set off two days later, leaving early in the morning, travelling first to Plymouth where Emma's father was buried. When Florence heard of this detour she was incensed, for his father-in-law had never said a civil word to him throughout his marriage. She wondered what it meant, this familial pilgrimage, and how Tom would weather it. It made no sense, she thought, thinking again of those poisonous diaries which should have lessened the sense of loss he felt, but had somehow had the contrary effect. Even beyond the grave, she could sense Emma's formidable presence and trembled, hoping that the trip would lay to rest the memory of the late-departed. She shivered when she recalled the assistance she had given Emma two years before, when the old lady was writing of her childhood, and wondered if, at the same time, she was writing her diabolical diaries.

The atmosphere in the house was fraught. Kate hardly appeared and when she did she was rather curt and distant as if her mind was elsewhere. Her only comment on Tom's absence was that it would do no harm, although she did not know or would not guess at Florence's innermost feelings. Her cursory comment that 'as long as he doesn't come back with another Gifford' was said without malice, but maligning Tom's whimsy as it did, made her anxious. Little was said, one to the other; skirts rustled brusquely as they passed each other, eyes averted, jaws set. The servants were watchful, mute, making themselves scarce whenever possible.

Despite the underlying tension, Florence felt that the truce would hold until Thomas returned from his miserable pilgrimage, but it was not to be.

In the early evening, only three days after they had left, Florence was sitting in her room when Lilian suddenly appeared in the doorway.

'I think we should talk,' she said and without waiting for a response walked into the room and partly closed the door behind her.

Florence looked at her, taken aback at the suddenness of the intrusion. 'What about, Lilian?'

'You and Tom. I want you to tell me just what you think you are doing here?'

'Why I am here is clear, surely. I am here to help Tom with his papers and to read to him when he requires me to do so.' She paused. 'I think I also provide a little companionship.'

'Companionship!'

Lilian stared at her and Florence could feel her hackles rise.

'He will not be getting that from you, Miss Gifford, regardless of how well you order the house and interfere with the normal running of things.'

She bit her lip, knowing she had overreached herself.

'That is not an appropriate comment, Miss Dugdale, especially coming from one such as you.' She stared at Florence who visibly blanched at the effrontery. 'Tell me, what are your designs on Tom?'

Florence looked directly at her and answered with considerable equanimity.

'I have no designs on Tom.'

'Then why are you here when he is not?'

'Because he asked it of me.' She paused, then added by way of explanation, 'As I have told you, he wanted me to sort through his papers.'

'And my aunt's diaries no doubt?'

'That is none of your business.'

'Oh but it is, Miss Dugdale, it is. Someone has to look after Tom and I doubt, from what I've read in those notebooks, that it should be you.'

Florence coloured. 'What do you mean?'

'I would suggest that you take some time to read some of the truths my aunt tells. Mad was she? Bitter was she? Not of sound mind? I think there's more than that. She told me once you were a good friend of hers.'

'And that I was.'

'For a purpose, Miss Dugdale, for a purpose. I think you should read a little of them yourself to see if you can identify the scheming woman that I see now, your claws into our Tom.'

'How dare you. "Our Tom?" When was he ever "your" Tom? You hated him, the lot of you. Get out.'

Lilian rose and walked to the door where she turned, a snarl on her face.

'I would be a mite cautious, Miss Dugdale, if I were you. There is no one to listen to you here and provide you with companionship, not now, until he comes back at least.'

24

And with that she pulled the door to and descended the stairs, her heavy leather soles clipping each step in turn.

Florence sat frozen to the bed, paralysed by the outburst. What was she to do? What had the woman read? What falsehoods had been written and had now entered the head of this vile woman. Who else had she told? Kate? And had Tom read these ramblings too? She knew that in the morning, against her judgement, against her natural instincts and sense of probity, she would go to the study and take the diaries and read them, for she needed to know too.

In the meantime, sleep was impossible. Tomorrow she would go into Dorchester and find an extra lock for her door. She would look to protect herself until Tom returned and put things to right.

Four days later a letter arrived for Florence and she withdrew to her room to read it. It was from Tom and he sounded, she thought, properly miserable. He had been to Boscastle, to Tintagel, to Pentargan Bay and the rectory at St Juliot where he had first met Emma some forty-three years ago. He said he had found the whole experience exceedingly painful. 'What possessed me to come?' he wrote, telling Florence how he had regretted his decision many times while on the journey and how he longed to be home. The whole idea of his pilgrimage to Lyonnese as he had colourfully thought of "Emma's Cornwall" had been a terrible, terrible mistake. He had done nothing during the whole time but long for Max Gate and her company.

Florence folded it neatly and tucked it into her blouse. Tom's words warmed her, but she knew they would not protect her, and so did not deter her from her plan to walk into the centre of Dorchester the next day.

It was a cool day and she enjoyed the solitude. There were a few clumps of early daffodils on the side of the road and the wind, while brisk, was not unduly cold. She knew no one in the town although she suspected some knew of her, thanks to her adversary.

Her first stop was at the gunsmith's where her request for a revolver was met with some surprise, her being so small and demure, although her explanation that there was a fox which was killing the chickens seemed plausible enough, at least to her. That done, she sought out a locksmith to see if she could find a new padlock for her door, before she returned to Max Gate, her mission achieved, with more determination, more bravado, than she had left with some hours before.

Occasionally her mind wandered, her resolution wavered and she would think of Alfred, of Thornley, and of her family back in Enfield and wonder at her being here at all. She paused to wonder why Thomas had done this to her? And the longer she dwelt on the question, the more obfuscate became the answers.

Tom arrived back two days later. He looked tired, Florence thought, and old; older than before, his face pale and strained. It had evidently been an exhausting journey, both physically and emotionally, and he had not stinted on the walking as well, around the old haunts he and Emma had frequented when they were courting.

She waited for him to confide in her, but he was not forthcoming about any of the time in Cornwall other than to say it was mistake, but that it was best done than left undone and had helped lay some ghosts. That was as may be, thought Florence, but there were plenty more ghosts she had found from her rummaging through the diaries, ghosts that she could hardly yet speak of or comprehend, ghosts of a wounded and embittered wife that he, Tom Hardy, would have to make peace with before she was finished with haunting him.

Chapter 4

THE UN-STILLED VOICE

The first few days back were not easy. Conversation was strained and everyone moved about the house more quietly, more discreetly than was normal. Tom had caught a chill and took to his bed. Lilian and then Kate, who had arrived full of concern when she heard he was ailing, took it upon themselves to look after the patient. Between them, they took him up his meals, fussed over him and helped him with his ablutions. After a few days, when he was starting to feel a little stronger, they helped him downstairs so he could sit at his desk and spread *The Times,* commenting acerbically on anything that he took issue with, while they plied him with cups of tea and cake. During this whole time, Florence was pushed to the periphery, reading to Tom on only one occasion, for only once did he ask for her to do so, at least in her hearing.

With so little call for her from Tom, and with so little warmth towards her from the others, she spent more time in her room or walking along the criss-cross of paths in Puddletown Forest. Now that Thomas's three siblings had left the old family home at Bockhampton and had moved to Talbothays, the new house that Thomas had purchased for them at West Stafford near Dorchester, there was no one she knew in the vicinity. Walking alone, however, was never likely to lighten her mood and Florence fell to convincing herself that she was not welcome at Max Gate and that if she was not required either, for any purpose, then she should leave. But she needed Tom to say it to her for it to happen.

In reality, there was little for her to go back to elsewhere. There was no companionship at the house, it was true, but she had few confidants elsewhere, nor anyone in Dorchester she could talk to about her writing or her feelings, about anything. Her closest friend, Florence Henniker, had gone for an extended trip to the continent, while the Stoker family had

27

cut off all contact with her, no doubt at Bram's instigation. Nor had she ever been good at ingratiating herself with people, something she readily accepted, and was used to being treated with reserve, even at times, suspicion. Once when she was at school, another girl, her best friend she had thought, told her classmates in a slightly barbed jest that she thought Florence had the air of a witch about her, with her frequent moods, her dark and brooding nature and the tendency in her stories for the morbid, and that it was the portent for something far darker than the rings of shadow that circled her eyes. It was a joke, soon forgotten by all, except by the subject of the joke who used it as a pretext for retreat.

Florence remembered it even now as a recent wound and used to agonise over how people saw her, what they felt when they looked upon her visage. And with such thoughts running through her head, she had pulled her hair back tighter to her skull, shrunk further into herself and learned to trust fewer and fewer people. It was a great handicap, she felt, that she could not talk easily with others, could not just join a conversation without a preface and while she knew that the fault lay within her, she did not know how to change herself. She was aware that men were attracted to her for they had told her so in glances and by occasional compliments. It was, she deduced, because she was dark and petite and that her reticent and often pensive nature appeared in some way as mysterious to them, but although she preferred the company of men, she did not know how to turn this to her advantage. She hated that she was seen as not being warm for she desperately wanted to be so. If only people walked with her a while, they would get to know her and they would come to like her; they would see she had spirit, for she was good at playing devil's advocate with herself. But why should they bother, as she gave them no encouragement to do so?

Tom knew her best of all, to the fullest extent she allowed, but she was one for her secrets, knowing the world was full of people who blurted everything out and then regretted it. She was most definitely not one of those; she kept herself to herself, firmly under lock and key and could not change, for that was her nature.

When she was called by Tom to help with a new edition of *Under the Greenwood Tree*, she went resolute in her determination to inform him of her intention to leave. But as she sat down to work with him, proofing page after page, as he told her how much he depended on her, how much he valued her comments, her skill, her critical eye, her sense of literary perspective, and as she realised with a little modest surprise how important he felt she was to his work, she could feel her resolve begin to weaken. She did well, therefore, to keep her equilibrium long enough to initiate the conversation she had intended, to tell him she planned to leave before the end of the week. When he protested that she should not desert him now that he was better, she didn't cower as she was wont sometimes to do, but became more forceful in her opinion.

'Tom,' she said with some feeling, 'there is little point in me staying while you vacillate. I cannot live in a state of limbo, especially as you know that "she" in the next room doesn't care for me being here. I was perfectly happy, you know, with my work in London and being closer to my own family. I don't need to be here anymore, nor do I know why you want me to stay for you don't tell me. I have my own rooms to look after and a life to lead and would be quite happy elsewhere.'

She paused, wondering to herself about the veracity of her last statement.

'I cannot see why you wanted me to stay here all this time, except to punish me, when all your daily needs are being met by family.'

'Not all, Florence, not all. They fuss about me and keep me alive and think that that is all important, but it is not. What matters is us. It is your company I want and crave for. You must know that.'

Florence stood up, her scarlet velvet dress pulled tightly to her. She walked to the window and looked out, before asking, 'Then why, Tom, do you allow that woman to stay on, knowing what she says about me, making my life a misery? Your family I can abide, as you know, but not Lilian. Are you prepared to tell her to go, Tom, for my sake – for our sake?'

She turned to face him, prepared to wait, while he squirmed under the directness of her gaze.

'I can't do that, Florence, not yet. She is still family. What's more, I believe, she means well. It would be churlish for me to say go and would, I suspect, rebound on both of us also for the time is too soon to do so. The truth is I don't cope very well on my own and with you here as my secretary, as we mean you to be, I need someone to look after us. If she goes, I would need someone else, for Kate could not manage by herself. While you keep threatening to leave to go back to Suffolk or to London for one thing or another, at least they are constant. What do you think the folk in

Dorchester would think if you and I were here alone? They would not be forgiving. People around here tend not to be. Just give it time, Florence dear, give it time.'

There was a long pause before she answered.

'I'll give you time, Tom Hardy, but I'll not give it to you here.' She looked directly into his pale eyes that were fixed on her. 'Mrs Henniker has asked me to join her at her house and I will do so before I go onto Southwold for the summer. If there is anything you want of me, then send it on. Perhaps when you are properly better, you will think more of us and show a little more courage in deciding what you want.'

Before he could muster an answer, she gathered up the pages she was working on and walked from the room, leaving Tom looking down at his desk calendar, fixed as it was, ominously, and irritably to Florence, on March 7th, a date he had hallowed as the day he had first met Emma.

There was one solace in the days before she left. Thomas, assisted by his handyman Maxwell, lit a bonfire at the end of the garden and for much of a grey and portentous afternoon, Florence watched as sack load after sack load of letters and notes along with the hateful diaries were opened up and fed to the flames, consumed in a fire that became so hot and venomous that its ashes scarred the circle of ground beneath as black as a devil's heart.

Florence departed by train at the end of the week. There had been a slight easing of the oppressive atmosphere that had hung about the house after she told the others that she was leaving, and for the last two days she felt her relationship with Kate was almost back to its most cordial, as they chatted about Tom and his writing. Lilian, however, was a different matter and she never wavered in her animosity towards her. Even when she went out of the door, bags in her hand, she was given no more than a churlish good-bye.

For three weeks or more in the company of Mrs Henniker, she received a number of letters from Tom appealing for her return. She noticed, however, her hostess received an equal number of missives from him and she felt jealous that somehow she was not more special, that there was nothing that set her apart in the eyes of this household either. She knew that Tom and her namesake had long corresponded and she also liked her hostess very much, for she was their mutual friend, but she wondered if Tom's extra letters were not part of a smokescreen, an attempt to distance him from her in the eyes of others.

Florence returned to her family home and to her ill-disciplined dog. Not surprisingly, her cousin was irked by the length of her absence and was pleased to see the back of the "little terror" that had lived up to its belligerent reputation. She reflected on how precious little time she had had to herself since Emma's death. Only the year before, her book on baby birds had been published and she remembered vividly how excited she was, so secretly proud. Now, after the strain of recent weeks, she was keen to get back to her writing and doing those things that constituted the norms of domestic life, even the chores of preparing food, cooking and cleaning and fitting back into her old familiar life.

She did not feel inclined to return to Max Gate as things stood. The recent experience had scarred her and left her emotionally brittle. She needed some quiet, she reckoned, and quiet she would have. But Tom was not of a mind to let her be. After a few days of persistent entreaties she weakened, and when he told her he was travelling to London, ostensibly only to see her, she agreed to accede to his request. A further letter, both grateful for her acquiescence and contrite for having not been more attentive towards her of late, arranged for her to visit him at the Albert Hotel in Battersea where he was staying.

When they met, Florence was wary, reserved and finally irritable and the time was not successful. It was only when he had left that Florence found a bunch of flowers from him with a note attached. She undid the bow, opened the card which he had carefully dated April 16th and read it slowly: 'My dearest Florence (for so I have always thought of you). Do not abandon me now we have come this far. Love always, Tom.'

Florence took one of the flowers from the posy and pressed it inside the copy of *Jude the Obscure* she had with her, placing the card on the following page. The rest of the blooms she took up in both hands and breathed their scent deeply before placing them upon the table. She was surprised at the realisation that he was capable of stirring such emotions in her. Perhaps, she felt, it was a hint of promise, of something in the ether that had not been there before.

In June, having tired of her own company and unable to settle to her writing, she left for Suffolk where she had been invited to stay at the home of Edward Clodd in the coastal town of Aldeburgh. Edward was a contemporary and friend of Tom's, and as well as being a banker, an anthropologist and a writer was one of those colourful people who delighted in entertaining his many social acquaintances and contacts.

Tom had first introduced Florence to Edward at Max Gate several years earlier when he came for a lunch that dallied on through a whole afternoon. It had been scintillating, she recalled, the playful cut and thrust of conversation of the two men and had quite entranced her at the time.

Since then, she and Tom had stayed at Strafford House several times, invariably in company, meeting a number of writers and amusing raconteurs at his literary luncheons. Florence had come to see Edward as a confidant, someone she could rely on for his sagacity and his discretion and counted him now as something of a friend, someone she could turn to for a comforting word or hospitality, and it was clear that he harboured a soft spot for her and Tom alike. It was in conversation with Edward that Tom's own ideas relating to the theory of evolution had grown as they sat together, dissecting and unravelling their faithlessness and talking about the righteousness of Darwin instead.

Florence hoped that the lure of the Suffolk coast and the promise of such similar profundities between the two men, assisted by her own inadequate presence, might draw Tom away from Max Gate. She felt the longer he stayed in Dorchester, entrapped by the pettiness of the house and the tedious regime imposed by Lilian and the other Giffords who had now taken to visiting their distinguished relative, settling like ghouls on the place, the less likely he, and therefore she, would ever have that which they had long promised each other.

June was proving unexpectedly warm although the brisk easterly wind that peeled off the North Sea regularly each morning meant that a shawl was necessary for the daily walk along the shoreline. She spoke to Edward at great length, sharing with him what had happened and how ghastly life had become at Max Gate and he, who had never seen Emma as anything but an impediment to Thomas, took hold of her hand and reassured her that all would be well if she were patient. He had always been kind to her, she thought. She recalled when she had written to him three years before saying how good Mrs Hardy was to her, 'good beyond words and affectionate too', he had written back some cryptic letter, the essence of which was caution, that Emma was not all she seemed, and more certainly cleverer than she appeared.

Florence was bemused but forewarned, and she gently pulled back into her own space where she felt herself safe and impenetrable. She remembered later feeling grateful for the advice.

The letters that had come to her at Florence Henniker's continued to seek her out at Aldeburgh. The entreaties to return to Max Gate had stopped and instead Tom was talking about coming to meet her and writing disarmingly, as if the whole world was reading his letter over her shoulder, that the sea air would be good for him, as if little else there would be.

He arrived on the last day of the month, directly from Cambridge where he had been awarded an honorary degree by the University and made a fellow of Magdalene College. He had enjoyed being entertained and fêted and at the dinner held in his honour at Trinity was at his mischievous best, telling guests that Cambridge had made amends for Oxford's treatment of poor Jude, if by a somewhat circuitous route, and that he was mightily pleased that it was the "other" University that had accorded him the honour.

Edward was delighted to see him and congratulate him in turn, and Florence had to wait for the male bonhomie to wane a little before stepping forward to welcome him, and was met by an unexpected kiss on her cheek, an action in front of another, even one as complicit as Edward, that brought a quick blush.

He settled quickly into the spirit of the home, and once he and Edward had got over their initial banter he was soon the focus of visits from literary friends of Edward's from London. H. G. Wells arrived one day, and George Gissing another, while Florence waited in the wings, polite and deferential as ever. She was invariably introduced as Thomas's secretary and as such her role in the house was defined, while Tom slipped comfortably back to his old self.

Their rooms were in the same corridor they had always occupied when staying at Aldeburgh and so the opportunity for some privacy was afforded them.

On the first morning, Florence had knocked lightly on Tom's door and on hearing him call 'Come in' had gone and stood at the side of the bed where Thomas was busy correcting a page proof.

He looked up at her, wistful and eager.

'I am pleased to see you here, Tom Hardy, with a little colour to you and away from that viper's nest.'

He reached out and took her hand, laying down his pencil and papers.

'Hush, dear, you mustn't let yourself get so bitter. Don't take all they say so personally for they – she – means well, at least to me. And it's you I've come here to see, Florence, you, and not for talk of others. Here it is just us as it always was. We have always been happy here and Edward has been very good to us, you know.'

Florence sat down beside him, her hand still captive in his.

'I know, Tom, but you must see I cannot go back to Dorchester, not while things are as they are, if that is what you propose.'

'I know you've been upset, Florence, and we will talk, we must talk, but you must remember too that it is a little over seven months since Emma died and that I would be expected to still be grieving.'

'Grieving? What for?' Florence stared at him. 'For her? For your sham of a marriage?'

She dropped his hand and stood up abruptly.

'Florence, be quiet. We are not alone in the house and it would not be proper for anyone to hear voices, or to think you are in my room. The expectation would be normal, for others did not know and to say so now would be graceless and seen as bitterly cruel.'

'You and your propriety, Tom, you and your appearances! I sometimes wish the world knew about us and that you and I had to flee somewhere, to an island in the Mediterranean where I could grow olives and you could write without all this subterfuge.'

'Florence, you are talking nonsense. I am an old man who writes poetry. What would I do on an island?'

'You might love again, Tom Hardy, as you once professed to do or so I thought of you. You might see me as worthwhile, the subject of another novel perhaps, someone who meant something, just once.'

She picked up the empty glass that sat beside his bed and walked out the door, almost colliding with Edward who was coming along the corridor. If Edward was surprised by the purpose with which she strode from the room, there was no sign of it and being as affable as ever he merely asked how the old boy was and made the comment that the day looked stormy and was one for staying inside.

The following morning was more settled and Tom and Florence walked across the road and down to the beach where they sat on a large tree stump, looking out at the sea which was still running high. They had not said much to each other since the previous morning and there was an air of solemnity about them both that provoked more caution in their movement and words than usual.

After looking out across the North Sea in silence, Tom reached over and took Florence's gloved hand.

'I am so sorry that this has been so hard for you, my dear. I have not handled it well, I know, and feel more bereft than I would have thought likely. It was not that Emma did anything much for me, but her being there meant that I did not have to bother much either. She has gone now and I'm glad of it for she was vexatious and not of sound mind by the end. It was the timing, you know, that's what it was that affected me, her dying on the very day I was to join you in Weymouth. It pricked my conscience too, if truth be known. It's foolish, I know, to dwell on such matters now, but that's the truth of it.'

'And now?'

'Now we should make plans, you and I.'

'Plans? And what plans might they be?'

'Plans for us to marry, my dear. Did you not read that into my note to you?'

'Not in so many words. I have wondered when you would return to what you always promised in the hypothetical, Tom Hardy, but what makes you feel such a thing is possible now, or even desirable? I may have changed now that you are available. I might think the gap in our ages too much. Perhaps what I needed once, I have less need of now.'

He was not sure of the seriousness of her answer, but answered earnestly.

'I don't know, dearest, I don't know, but I hope.' He took hold of her other hand and saw her as she was, her dark brown hair pulled off her face, her serious eyes and tight mouth, pretty still and half his years.

'I know what I ask is presumptuous. But I wish it anyway.'

'Are you asking me to marry you, Tom Hardy?'

'That I am, but just not yet. We need to wait.'

'So it is a conditional proposal. And for how long, pray?'

She allowed herself a small smile.

'I was thinking next summer.'

'By next summer those two old maids will have taken over the running of Max Gate with you as their house guest, so long as you behave, while I ...' – and she paused for effect – '... I won't even be allowed to cross the threshold. If we are to sort things out, Tom, it should be done quickly and not be allowed to unravel like a bolt of cloth. Take me at my word, Tom, I will not go back as things are nor will I return with you without a firm resolution on your part.'

Thomas looked at her intently. Her spirit, seemingly invisible to others, stirred her blood.

'Then let us look at early in the New Year, for by then another Christmas will have passed and folk will think that more seemly.'

Florence didn't answer directly, as if building the moment.

'Very well then, so long as you make it clear, if I return to Max Gate before then – if, mark you – who is in charge.'

'I will talk to my sister, Florence, I promise.'

'And the other?'

'And her too.'

She looked at him and smiled softly.

'Well, if this is the best proposal you can manage, then I will consider it most carefully. It is not the most romantic proposal, Tom, especially coming from a famous wordsmith who has used the King's English to woo old ladies and upset the church and all else. I might have expected better.'

He looked a little startled at her sudden mirth, ostensibly at his expense. His reply was delivered with an unexpectedly serious air.

'I am sorry, dear Florence, I should have thought of a better way to say what I meant. I have been a little clumsy, but I wasn't sure of how this conversation would go and I did not prepare. Sorry, my love. But please take time to consider what I have said.'

She lifted his hands to her lips and kissed them both, one after the other.

'I will.'

For the rest of the week at Aldeburgh, Thomas visibly relaxed and his mirth and good humour were noted by Edward who commented so to Florence.

'There is reason for that,' she said, 'but I should not tell you yet.'

'But you must,' he countered, and Florence, who needed no extra persuasion, told him of the offer of marriage. Edward was not surprised, but did draw her to one side.

'I can see what is in it for him, to have a pretty woman like you looking after every need, but what of you, Florence, what of you?'

'I would be happy enough, Edward. He is not as old or decrepit as he makes out and I am easily contented. I do not see myself as pretty or desirable. He needs me and I like most to be of use, and for who better? Besides,' she said, 'it is where my life has arrived and it seems right now, right and proper that I give back what I once took without thought.'

'What do you mean?'

'I don't – mean. I don't mean anything. We're both wounded soldiers, Tom and I, both scarred by life. I just trust that we will be able to write, both of us, and even perhaps be happy.'

'My dear, you make it sound like a marriage of convenience.'

'All marriages are marriages of convenience, Edward. Successful marriages, anyhow. I think everyone looks at matrimony as a ledger of credits and debits even if they never admit it. You could say that the best you can hope for is to have the balance showing in your favour at the end of your life.' She smiled grimly at him. 'Perhaps because I never expected very much I can be happy enough with that responsibility.'

'That is a bleak outlook, Florence, for one such as you.'

'Not really. It is just realistic. We all compromise endlessly in life, so why should marriage be any different?' She lowered her voice and turned to face him. 'Edward, let's be adult about this. We are not talking about some sort of romantic love, rather companionship, affection, perhaps, a mutual interest. And that is enough.' And she shrugged, looked up and smiled a wan and lifeless smile.

Not long after returning to Max Gate, there was a brief parting of the clouds when Sydney Cockerell, the director of the Fitzwilliam Museum in Cambridge, visited. He had first done so in 1911 while Emma was still alive, to persuade Thomas to gift his manuscripts to the museum and various other national institutions, a task at which he had been very successful. More recently, the two men had met at Cambridge on the occasion of Thomas's honorary degree, for which Thomas accorded Sydney much of the credit.

They arrived on a warm Friday afternoon in early July, Sydney accompanied by his wife Kate and the painter William Strang, whose sketch of Florence now hung on Thomas's study wall. The group proved to be jolly company, quickly dispersing the gloomy air that had pervaded the house with their energy and animated talk. For Florence, with Lilian safely away in Cornwall, it was an opportunity to play the hostess and she revelled in the role. Sydney warmed to her immediately, sensing (and tacitly approving of) her relationship with Thomas, and the weekend that followed was one of the happiest the house had known. There was much laughter and banter and Florence delighted in the company and in discharging her obligations, organising the tea and supper and waiting on the fringes of the discussions that were lively and wide-ranging, and more than occasionally irreverent.

On Sunday, there was no inclination amongst any of the guests to attend church, but instead they chose to walk in Puddletown Forest before returning to Max Gate for lunch. The afternoon's revelries were a little more subdued as their host tired, but the whole weekend and the few days that followed before the guests finally left were, most certainly to Florence, a resounding success.

This was the role she wanted, this was what she could do so well, serving her master and entertaining visitors. But this was not meant to be an end in itself, this display of quiet, obsequious devotion, for she wanted Thomas to notice how significant she was in his life, how her words, when offered into the mix, were apt and thoughtful, how he depended upon her. Moreover, she wanted him to see her as someone to be properly recognised as an observer and author of human foibles and follies, a writer in waiting. For this to be so, she must rely on him for his patronage, for him to say a quiet word in the right ear when required – and, she thought belatedly, as it all depended on this, for his continued interest and affection.

Chapter 5

THE COMPACT OF MARRIAGE

Thomas left Aldeburgh for Max Gate at the end of the month, his pending departure having been the excuse for a particularly noisy and jolly dinner party the night before at which he was fêted as the guest of honour by his generous host along with several eminent guests. Florence enjoyed seeing Tom in such good form and being accorded the respect that she felt he so richly deserved. For once, he appeared completely at ease with those he usually spoke of darkly as his "betters", talking authoritatively on the poems of Rupert Brooke, the unrest in the Balkans and the tragic and nonsensical protest of Emily Davison amongst other subjects and exuding a confidence that suggested he felt he could say little wrong in their company. As he spoke, stretching himself upwards on the balls of his feet to maximise his diminutive stature, his moustache bristling with pride and shoulders pushed back, he looked to all intents and purposes like a strutting rooster, with his beak-like nose and wrinkled neck. But Florence saw none of this, ignoring the vessel to focus on the effect his words had on those listening expectantly in the room, ready to dine out on some *bon mot* or other that he might drop.

The next morning, however, Thomas was more subdued, especially in saying farewell to Florence. Their union established (for she had coyly acquiesced to his proposal the previous evening in his room), it was agreed that he would send for her when he felt the time was propitious for a return to Max Gate.

In the meantime, as Florence stressed to him at their parting, he needed to be more assertive with his family in order to prepare the way for her.

'You must tell them, Tom, you must,' she said. 'You need to impress upon them what will be my new status at Max Gate. You have to make my role plain to all at the house, family and servants.'

Thomas looked at her gently and went to kiss her cheek.

'No, Tom, listen to me. You must be properly assertive for that is the only way it will be possible to dissipate the ill-feeling whipped up by "that woman".'

He demurred, succeeding in kissing her and seeing her away, yet without making any such undertaking.

On this occasion, Florence was in less hurry to travel and chose not to do so while the Indian summer continued through September. She reasoned that, once at Max Gate, the summer would be over for her whenever she decided to go and so held off the onerous trip to Dorchester until the first real signs of autumn were in evidence. This time, she had packed for the winter and possibly, it seemed to the household when she arrived by car, for the spring as well.

The first shock to the gathered company that met her, including Tom, Kate, Lilian and Maxwell, was the appearance of the scruff-necked terrier, Wessex. He promptly dropped off Florence's lap as she alighted and announced his presence by chasing one of the two remaining cats at Max Gate out of the drive and then proceeding to yap throughout the first night. Lilian, who had appeared to be trying to be civil to Florence on the first afternoon, had lost all goodwill by morning and cursed the dog over breakfast for pulling at the covers on the sofa and tearing one, for digging up a corner of the garden and for the noise it made. Her disquiet was compounded by the discovery that her dislike of Wessex was reciprocated by the dog, who barked and nipped at her when she came near.

'It is nothing like Moss,' she exclaimed, raising the spectre of Thomas and Emma's previous dog, 'and won't do for the cats.'

Florence's own arrival, by contrast, was rather more subdued. She slipped in quietly under Wessex's distracting cover and had completely unpacked her suitcase before being called down to tea. Again, she was disappointed to discover, it was Lilian who presided over events, with Tom the dependent host. She waited for some sign from him that he had promoted her niche in the household, in advance of her arrival, but there was none forthcoming.

The next day she asked Tom directly what he had said to Lilian and was met by an awkward shuffle and a convoluted reply which gave her no encouragement that the wrongs previously cited had been addressed let alone righted.

Later that day she tackled him in his study, before they settled down to the correspondence that seemed to be more voluminous than ever.

'So tell me, Tom, what you have said?'

The old man shuffled again uneasily. 'I have said that I have asked you to move here, as my secretary and as a companion.'

'And nothing more?'

'Florence.' He looked at her pleadingly. 'Please understand that I am trying to do what is best for us, to protect you too. We have each other's company. We have the promise of our agreement. In time, they will see they are not necessary or failing that, one day and not too distant, they will find you are mistress of the house. But please don't ask for more, don't stir up trouble where none brews.'

Florence looked hard at him.

'This is not what we agreed.' She stared at him defiantly before answering further, her voice cold and curt. 'Alright. I'll abide by your wishes. But if it goes back to what it was, then you will have to make a choice, Tom Hardy, for if I go again, I will not return.'

Throughout October Tom settled down to his work, writing occasionally when on his own, but pushing any writing to one side when Florence appeared in order to work on the revised edition of his novels required by his publishers and to chip away at his correspondence. He was being harried for a new collection of poems and had started to gather pieces together, although these he kept to himself. At other times Florence took herself into the garden, gathering up the broad, crisp leaves from the plane trees into bonfires before lighting each and then presiding over them, rake in hand, as they shrank to a pile of red ash, watched as she did so by the gardener, Maxwell. During the same time Emma's last two cats had disappeared: one had fled and the other was found dead under a hedge. Wessex, it appeared, in a matter of weeks had staked his territory rather more successfully than had his mistress.

Florence dreaded the anniversary of Emma's death and was right to have done so, for Tom descended into a period of mourning all over again. He wanted to go to the grave in Stinsford churchyard and Florence offered to go with him, but he declined her offer, preferring to go alone. Her fury when she found that, instead, Lilian had accompanied him, knew no bounds.

'Why, Tom, why can you not see how divisive it looks, you and her going off, and me, once Emma's friend, left here?'

'She is poor Emma's niece, my dear, her kinswoman, or do you forget that too? It is a natural order of things for a niece to want to pay her respects to her aunt, blood being blood and all that.'

'You mistake her, Tom, for someone other than she is. She should not be here any longer.'

'And has she not been civil to you these past weeks and tried to make amends?'

'For you she shows this side perhaps, but for me, I know otherwise. I do not trust her, Tom, despite the words that tumble from her and the appearance of friendship.'

'Then I must say you are not giving her a chance. Try harder to forgive, try harder to be a little more tolerant and don't always think she is there to spite you.'

And Florence would try to avoid Lilian, but she could not shut her out for the woman seemed determined to prey on her nerves. So each day simmered, but thankfully, for a period at least, the lid stayed on.

The moment that Tom had feared came one afternoon in mid-December when Florence returned from Dorchester, puce with rage. She burst in on him as he was napping in the chair in the corner of his study.

'That woman. That woman goes or I go.'

He held out his hands to her, but she brushed them aside.

'Hush, dear. What has brought this on?'

'Do you know what the shopkeepers in Dorchester are saying? They are saying that I am a gold-digger, that I am unfeeling to your family and do nothing to help about the house. More, that I have particular ways, that my family are too ordinary for the likes of you, talking of when we were in Wareham which no one knew of and it's all come from her.'

'And what makes you say that?'

'Because that is what Adelaide told me at the gallery, that Miss Gifford has been spreading rumours about me over town. If you don't act, Tom Hardy, I am packing my bags.'

With that final utterance, her face flushed and animated in a way he found most becoming (though this was surely not the time to say so), she left the room.

Thomas's talk with Lilian was not an easy one, although the gratitude that he expressed to her for her care did not completely fall on deaf ears. This was, in large part, due to the caveats he offered in the form of financial help for the family back in Cornwall and a promise that she could come back in the New Year, if she so wished. As he explained, he just needed time to learn to cope without his calling on family. He would employ a housekeeper immediately and Miss Dugdale – at whose mention, Lilian's brow arched and darkened – would be about to assist with any menial jobs he required.

Lilian did not feel inclined to disagree, having grown weary of her position in the face of Florence's unremitting presence, but hedged until Thomas agreed to settle an allowance upon her. A widow from nearby Bere Regis, a Mrs Miskell, was employed as live-in housekeeper and the week before Christmas Lilian left, without so much as a farewell to Florence who watched the goings-on from an upstairs window as the horse and trap collected her nemesis and drove her through the gate and away.

It was a cold and sombre Yuletide. After church, Tom and Florence joined with Mary, Kate and Henry at Talbothays to celebrate their first Christmas in the house. A few well-wishers called on them, mostly from out of the area, while they maintained a seemly distance from the town and the townsfolk. On New Year's Eve, to see the old year out, Kate, Tom and Florence went to Emma's graveside to pay their respects. Florence had her black coat on, with muffler, scarf and gloves, her grey eyes entrapped in dark circles. Her cheeks were pale, her face dull and tired, and Kate was moved to observe how wretched she looked, standing so forlorn beside Tom. The very features that rendered her attractive, she thought, now had the opposite effect, making her face seem sour and melancholy; indeed, she felt she had never seen a more dismal or miserable critter in all her life.

The year had aged her, had taken what little joy she had and wrung her out, and it was only the hope of a promise that sustained her. She was exhausted, but felt that 1914 would be different, would see the realisation of the decision taken at Aldeburgh and that that would change everything.

With Lilian gone, Florence turned her attention onto the marriage. She wanted, she hoped for, a marriage of some ceremony although not, she thought to herself, at Stinsford, with those memories to disturb Tom and the grave promised him only a few feet from the walls of the church. Tom, however, was adamant.

'We cannot celebrate in such ostentatious style,' he said, 'for as it is, believe me, people's tongues will wag anyhow. I don't want to go through a church revelry and a wedding breakfast again for I have done that and as I no longer believe in a lord and maker, it would make a hypocrite of me. I am sorry to deny you the trappings of marriage, but you will, I promise, know the reality of it. We don't need a gathering of people who don't have anything in common, my folk and yours, and all those others who would come, and those from the newspapers, talking of our age difference or who you are to me, and where this courtship came from. Present the fact of marriage done and the gossip will cease. It is for us alone, Florence, this marriage and I tell you a little discretion will not dampen the occasion for us. That you knew Emma and befriended her will mean, in most people's eyes, no rupture to continuity and it is best like that.'

It was with a heavy heart that Florence gave way and then only on condition that they did not marry in Dorset. It was an inauspicious way to start, she knew, yet she could not countenance his arguments for she sensed that, in this instance, he was right to be wary.

The arrangements for the wedding were conducted with a measure of subterfuge, a process that again upset Florence considerably who felt besmirched by all the secrecy.

'It is no way to begin our married life, Tom, to be so clandestine even with our families. What are you afraid of?'

But Tom would only continue to try and soothe her in his cloying way, telling her it was for the best and that they could celebrate on their first anniversary when any fuss ('What fuss,' asked Florence, 'do you expect?') had died down.

The night before the wedding, he arrived, quite unexpectedly, upon the doorstep of her parents' house. Hearing the knock, Florence answered the door and reluctantly let him into the hallway, but no further, chiding him for the inappropriateness of his visit.

He stood solemnly before her, undeterred by the coolness of the welcome, and thrust out his arm.

'I've come to give you this,' he said, holding out a long envelope.

'What is it?'

'It is a letter you should read and keep, my love. You may wish to open it after the event, although that might not be so wise. It is just that I am feeling nervous about what we are committing to tomorrow and feel we must be prepared to wed together our nuptial understanding with a proper confessional.'

'Must do? What are you talking about? I'll be doing no confessing tomorrow, Tom Hardy. You'll be confessing on your own.'

'Then I will confess for you.'

'It will count for naught, for I will disown it. Go, you're being ridiculously emotional and unseemly. Go and get some sleep.'

After he had left the house, Florence fingered the envelope before opening it. She read it with dread, presuming its contents already, and having finished, placed it in her bag and wept long into the night.

The wedding took place at the unseemly hour of 8.00 a.m. on February 10th, 1914, at St Andrew's, Enfield, the Dugdale family church, with no pomp or ceremony and only her father, Henry and Florence's youngest sister Margaret present. Thomas was dressed in a formal dinner suit with its waistcoat fastened high on the chest by a battery of mother-of-pearl buttons, a white shirt with rounded Edwardian collar and light-coloured tie. Florence wore a sombre travelling costume and heavy felt hat, plum-coloured, plain and severe, and had a small posy of flowers given to her by Margaret who was both bridesmaid and half the congregation.

They had told no one except for their closest family and so when the news appeared the very next day in the national press, someone having taken the liberty of informing them of the event, they were faced with the delicate task of writing retrospectively to their friends and family to explain what had transpired and why they had acted as they had.

Thomas tried to gloss over the reasons. He wrote to his family and his closest friends immediately, asking for their understanding as to the need for secrecy, explaining he had wanted to tell them each by letter, but that somehow the news had got out sooner than he had expected, necessitating this retrospective correspondence.

He had been most concerned to write to his dear friend Florence Henniker, explaining that if he had foreseen the slightest possibility that she would have heard from another source he would have written to her beforehand, but saying by way of explanation, 'We thought it better in the circumstances to inform nobody, not even relations.'

Florence Henniker clearly did not think so and rebuked him for not telling her first, to which he responded apologetically while conveying his own mild astonishment that the news could have been anything other than expected or welcomed.

'I am rather surprised,' he wrote, 'that *you* were surprised at the step we have taken – such a course seeming an obvious one to me, being as I was so lonely and helpless. I think I told you in my last letter that I am very glad she knew Emma well, and was liked by her, even during her latter years, when her mind was a little unhinged at times and she showed unreasonable dislikes. I wonder if it will surprise you when I say that, according to my own experience, a second marriage does not, or need not, obliterate an old affection, though it is generally assumed that the first woman is entirely forgotten in such cases.'

The furore soon died down and the transmogrification from secretary-cum-housekeeper to the person of the second Mrs Hardy was soon accepted by those who knew them both and by their families who realised that, once marriage was involved, there was little use in protest. For Florence, however, her new nomenclature and the whole lead up to, and aftermath of, the betrothal had been galling.

'Why did you put me through all this, Tom? It was all to no avail, for folk talked just as you feared they would, but you made us look so guilty.'

'I am sorry, my dear,' he replied, 'I thought it for the best.'

He looked so sad, so down in the mouth, so defeated, she thought, that she let it go. Thomas the husband might be little different from Thomas the suitor. They would work out the rules by which to conduct their lives and enjoy having so much to share after the turmoil of the past two years. She was ready and as prepared as she could be to accept the responsibilities for the next stage in her life, as dutiful mistress of Max Gate and protector of her husband's literary reputation.

Chapter 6

VESTERIS VESTIGIA FLAMMAE

It was a cold winter, which as far as Florence was concerned was a mercy, for by the time she and Tom ventured out of their house and into the town, the news of their marriage had faded somewhat. She and Mrs Miskell had spring-cleaned the house at the end of March and it had more of her about it, although they had left the attic room that Emma had used very much as it was at the behest of Thomas.

Helping him in his study one morning, she recalled the notebooks that had sat there for so many weeks before they had been gathered up and burnt.

'Do you ever think of Emma's notebooks, Tom? All those hurtful, untruthful things she wrote about you?'

He looked at her. 'Rarely, my dear. But hurtful they most certainly were at the time and, sadly, not always as untrue as I would have wished them to be. I prefer to think of them now, if I think of them at all, as some aberration, the ramblings of an unsettled mind.'

With that the topic was dismissed, although she could not so easily forget what she remembered reading, scarred as it was on her memory. Nor could she forget what Emma had said of her in particular, and of them both. She wondered what Tom made of Emma's suspicions and the awful things she had written against her. And she wondered too what Lilian had read and told others of what her dear dead aunt had observed about the pair of them.

Florence quickly immersed herself into the running of the household and the garden. She enjoyed tending the flower-beds when she had the opportunity and sitting on the lawn under the silver birch, reading. She had started writing again, but Tom had not been happy with her doing so, much to her chagrin.

'Tom, before we were married you were so encouraging to me, but now you seem impatient whenever I want to write. Do you think I have no talent in writing, Tom? Be honest with me.'

He never felt comfortable when she confronted him directly, preferring conversations that travelled in a circumlocutory route.

'It is not that, my dear. It's that I am getting on, you know, and all things being equal you will have years after I've gone to write to your heart's content. Perhaps before then I can give you something to write about? I need your company, Florence, and your help at times as well. It is possible I might be worrying unnecessarily because of the trouble Emma caused and that may be, but I think you should rather concern yourself with your responsibilities to me.'

'But that is selfish, Tom.'

'It is, I know, a little, but it surely will not be for too many more years … although' – he added, after a suitably impressive interval – 'of course, my dear, I hope I may be the exception to the idea of mortality being absolutely necessary.' He chuckled quietly to himself before turning to her, and taking hold of her hands said earnestly, 'Write then, if you must, but why not concentrate on filling notebooks, collecting ideas, garnishing thoughts, writing what you see. Look and listen, Florence, look and listen, that's the writer's craft. All that you gather then is the food for later, when you'll have the time to expand and embellish. Perhaps you will also learn a little from me too. Look and listen, my dear.'

He smiled at her, placing one hand against her cheek as he did so, which made her blush. The outcome was that Florence put her notebooks to one side, picking them up in the evenings occasionally after Tom had turned in, but her thoughts and confidence had been diminished, nonetheless.

The escalating crisis in the Balkans in July and the outbreak of war in August cast a pall of gloom over Max Gate. Tom was less optimistic about the prospects of a quick campaign than the national press would have the people believe and feared a long and arduous time ahead. Meanwhile, he and Florence had settled symbiotically into an uncertain state of existence, slowly growing used to each other's foibles and nuances, finding their own spaces and character within the collective identity of their marriage. Florence, however, was frustrated when she tried to talk to him about alterations she wished to make to the house and garden as he would have none of it, preferring things to remain as they were.

Visitors were not uncommon and Florence, though shy by nature, was keen to act as hostess. One regular visitor was a cousin of Tom's, Frank George, who called by often and soon become a favourite of them both. Frank was from his mother's side and had grown up knowing of Thomas and Emma, having lived nearby in Bere Regis. He had started working in banking before being called to the bar at Gray's Inn in 1912 where he had qualified as a barrister. He had never married and seemed to shun the city whenever he could, preferring to spend time back in Dorset, either with Tom and Emma or with his widowed mother. It was noticeable that he had started to call more often after Florence had become a regular visitor at Max Gate, encouraged in part by Thomas, who felt that Florence would appreciate a family friend of a similar age to herself.

His career that had started so promisingly, however, was now to be curtailed as he had signed up amongst the first wave of volunteers, enlisting with the 6th Gloucestershire infantry, much to the disappointment of his cousin.

'You'd have been better off seeing how things went and waited till they came for you, rather than going to them,' Tom had told him, but Frank, with the impulse of youth, had replied he was afraid he'd miss the whole show if he waited.

He had taken a shine to Florence from the first time they had met when she was staying at Max Gate several years previously. Although not a Hardy by name, Thomas had installed him as his favourite relative and had followed his career with great interest. On his visits to the house when Thomas was occupied with his writing, he would walk with her in the woods near Bockhampton or even as far as Puddletown. Florence loved his talk of the goings-on in London and his cheerful banter and endless enthusiasm, as it made for gay company.

'Frank, you are an enterprising one for being of this family, for sure,' she would say to him, and he would chuckle and hold onto her hand as if that was the most natural thing in the world.

One day, they had been caught in a heavy thunderstorm and had sheltered under a copse and Frank grew strangely quiet before speaking.

'Florence, do you mind me asking why someone as young and pretty as you should want to marry my cousin? I know he's a very considerable writer and I love the old man dearly, and I see that he's terribly fond of you, but did you not want for anything other than being an old man's chaperon?'

Florence looked at him and smiled.

'You're wrong, Frank. First, I am not as young as you would think me and nor is Tom so old. We have an understanding, as do all married couples, I'd venture. He needs someone to look after him, to answer his needs, to help him keep writing while I, I get great joy from looking after him, from being his companion and helper.'

'That may be so, Florence. But you could have done better. You are a dear, dear woman and I do care about you, you know, and I am quite sure that others must see the kindness and devotion in you too. Tom is a lucky fellow having you about to look after him.'

'You are a sweet man, Frank, and I thank you for saying it. But we're happy enough, as happy as either of us deserve to be, I'd venture.' She paused. 'You know, there was another one for me too once, as with him, but he's gone now and so we are two sad old things really.'

She smiled at him. 'But I'll bear you in mind should my circumstances change.' And she gave a cheerful laugh, pulled Frank by the hand and said, 'We should be getting back or your Cousin Tom will wonder about us getting caught in this rain and think us drowned.'

Tom doted on Frank and on his frequent visits that summer the two men would become engrossed in deep and earnest conversation about the unravelling situation in Europe, while Florence made tea. Afterwards, as they relaxed on the lawn, she would sit on the periphery and listen to them talking about nothing and everything. She enjoyed the enthusiasm and wit of her husband and the curiosity of Frank, pumping the old man with questions. At times, she was aware of Frank's eyes on her and felt self-conscious, but if Tom noticed he seemed not to mind.

One day, after Frank had joined up and was in training on the Salisbury Plains, Tom shared his fears with her.

'This war,' he said, 'will put paid to young men like Frank. They won't be quite as carefree as they are now when they come home.' He paused. 'Florence, there is something I mean to say to you. I have been thinking about what will become of you after I'm gone. I know you don't like such talk, but you must remember I am the ripe old age of seventy-four years. Anyhow, what I wanted to tell you was that you do not have to worry and that all that is in hand, for Frank has said he will take care of you in such a circumstance.'

Florence started. 'What do you mean?'

'Just what I said. Frank likes you as we both know and recently he told me that when I am no longer about, he'd look after you. He is a good man and I have decided to fix my will on him when the time comes. I thought it very generous of him, being a kind thoughtful chap with no other attachments, being prepared to make such a commitment.'

'And what did you say to him?'

'That I appreciated his kindness, that to have another of the family looking after you means I do not have to concern myself unnecessarily over how you would cope once I've gone.'

'And don't you think you should have consulted me about this ... this arrangement?'

'Pah, it's nothing so formal as that. It's just that he'll make sure he's there to make sure that you will be alright, that's all. It is a weight off my mind, Florence, for who else is there for you?'

'I have my sisters. There's Mrs Henniker, now she's on her own. I have other friends.'

'Frank is family. Frank is dear to me. He is like a son, Florence, like a son and he would be good to you.'

'How?'

'That depends on when I go, surely. He has offered his friendship and made me a promise and I am grateful for it. Don't let's dwell on it any further for you may be an old lady by the time he has to honour his promise to me.'

Florence was shaken by the nature of the conversation and blushed deeply the next time she met Frank, who appeared nonplussed. What Tom had said was so ambiguous, so typically ambiguous: was he to be her guardian, her legal advocate, or was more expected? Surely not, surely her days as a companion had passed by now, especially in the company of one even younger than herself?

The death throes of summer coincided with the first serious exchanges between the Western armies and the central powers. More significant, however, was a battle about to be waged closer to home which would change the map of her heart forever.

The first missive was harmless enough. A parcel had arrived from Tom's publisher that Florence had opened, to find inside an envelope marked "Confidential" which she ignored, assuming there was nothing of Tom's that she should not know. The letter confirmed the upcoming publication of a new volume of poems and questioned his punctuation in a poem which she had never heard of, entitled 'Looking at a Picture on an Anniversary', that she noted was dated March 7th, 1913. Florence read on with a sinking feeling, her eye caught by the final paragraph:

'Mr Hardy, I understand your reluctance to put these poems into print, but I can assure you that they are the finest you have written. While you might worry about their effect on Florence, you are wrong to do so for she shall see them as they appear, a tribute to your late wife and also, as I understand it, to someone who was a close friend of hers. You concern yourself unnecessarily for I am confident that the poems will be very well received by your expectant public when they appear later this month and will enhance your considerable reputation as the leading man of letters in your preferred literary form. Yours etc.'

Florence read the attached verse slowly. He wrote it, she quickly discerned, just after his pilgrimage to the West Country earlier the previous year, dated as it was to the anniversary of his meeting Emma some forty-three years previously. The words stung her as she read:

> *But don't you know it, my dear,*
> *Don't you know it,*
> *That this day of the year*
> *(What rain-bow rays embow it!)*
> *We met, strangers confessed,*
> *But parted – blest?*

"Blest?" He had not been "blest" by Emma. She had been a millstone about his neck, a useless, selfish, unstable human being who did her best to destroy him. "Blest!" She felt the anger rise in her, that her Tom could have been writing such a thing, especially when he had left her at Max Gate against her will and then had told her how much he regretted having done so, and how miserable he had been.

She wasted little time in accosting Tom, whose attempts to defend what he tried to argue was a personal letter to him were futile, swamped as they were by her rising wave of indignation.

'Personal letter? Since when has it been right to receive a letter that betrays us, Tom? What else have you written? What other surprises are in store for me? Why, oh why, did you not share these with me so I could have advised you what to do?'

He apologised for the perceived slight, but as his editor had suggested, he tried to explain that the line did not reflect on them; indeed, it was *because* she was now Mrs Hardy that he was able to publish a poem written in the storm of his grief more than eighteen months previously. Florence was far from appeased, but the matter was allowed to drop. Thomas was more reluctant than usual to discuss his writing for some time thereafter and avoided the subject whenever Florence alluded to it. His nervous disposition, however, was not lost on Florence who was determined to see what else the foolish old man had committed to print that might embarrass them both.

The publication of *Satires of Circumstances* in November 1914 was to prove her worst nightmare. The section of poems devoted to Emma was swooped upon by the reviewers of the book and praised as the best poetry he had written thus far, one of the greatest elegiac sequences in English literature, all of which added extra salt to the wounds. Each poem Florence read caused her an acute mixture of embarrassment, anger and resentment, and she determined that she would confront Tom on every cloying sentiment he had committed to paper and made public, but only, she decided, when she had picked the poems over thoroughly, painful as that would be, to best gauge his meaning and also to prepare an armour for herself for the inevitable questions that would come her way.

Tom was very aware of the storm that awaited him and knew that what had been published would appear, even to his friends, a travesty of the truth as he had described it to them and a considerable act of disloyalty to his bride of less than ten months.

'Why, Tom, why? Did you not pause for one minute in all your wallowing to think of me? Just once?'

She had just read 'The Going' and was still shaking with anger and hurt. 'The "great going"? What great going, Tom? She died, that's all, and you make it sound like a tragedy. "Seem like a dead man." I was there when you wrote that, Tom Hardy, sitting at Max Gate with that miserable niece of yours. "Undone" you, has it? Pining for the West Country when you never bothered to take her back there when she still lived and then shambled off there to write this stuff? It is all mawkish nonsense and you are the lesser man for writing this and lesser still for showing it to anyone. What will people think of you? Guilty, that's what, for there is guilt in each of these poems. "Haunts" you, does she? Well, let me tell you, she haunts me too and this will not rid us of the spectre any more easily.'

He tried his best to hold the flow of invective.

'Florence, listen to me. These were my feelings at the time and I have said to you that going back to Cornwall was a mistake, but it happened and I felt what I felt and writing was my way of purging myself. Other men drink at such times and it passes them by, but I pick up a pen and it stays with me, long after the feelings have changed. I won't deny her death, coming as it did so suddenly, was deeply affecting and, as you know, it was unexpected. Can you not show a little clemency in the matter?'

Florence was not in the least disposed to show any clemency.

'"Frailly follow her thin ghost" do you? Still, Tom, still? "Loved without measure" was she? By you? Not so I saw, Tom Hardy.'

'Florence, you need to see these poems for what they are. They are a signing off, that's all. Do I not say "I shall traverse love's old domain never again"? And nor I shall.'

'And why cannot I believe you, Tom Hardy? Eighteen elegies to Emma, nearly two years dead, written behind my back, published for the world to read. And they will ask themselves, "Didn't the old man just marry someone, his secretary or the like, what of her?" And they will wonder about what I am to you or whether there was some impropriety in our courtship and marriage, coming so soon after the event. Perhaps if I threw myself off Beeny Cliff or Durdle Door, I would get the same treatment. Why is it you only desire what is distant or unobtainable? Emma is dead, Tom, and so was your marriage for many years before that. Why should she call for you, Tom, for you weren't there?'

She pulled at his jacket sleeve. 'Was it guilt, Tom? Was it remorse? Is it that you've been wrong about us and regret what has happened? What is it, for God's sake, that made you do this?'

He could not answer, nor could he deal with Florence in this mood, and whenever she started to hold forth he left the room without attempting to pass comment, knowing it would still be there the next day and the next to deal with, but hoping always that the passing of time would make it less so.

Within a fortnight of the poems' publication, she received a letter from Edward Clodd in which he addressed the matter of the poems directly, as if anticipating Florence's hurt and distress, or possibly prompted by Thomas.

'Dear Florence, I have known Thomas for many years now,' he began, 'and this outpouring does not surprise me at all. He is emotional and maudlin always, and writes with his heart on his sleeve whenever the occasion presents itself to do so, and, yes, he feels guilty about how he treated Emma, and with some justification – but you should not. He was shabby at times, but you must remember, so was she. I suspected she may have got wind of something in particular that may have distressed her in those last months and while we might both guess what that was, it is of no lasting consequence and I suspect it explains that what we see in Tom's poems is more guilt than grief. I have read and re-read them carefully and they are not all that they seem. You must not let them wash away or erode what I know he feels for you, Florence. He is angry with her, that much is clear, and while his anger takes on an occasional romantic tragic hue, his writing about her is full of negatives too, and you cannot help but notice words and phrases that betray a sense of blame and irritation. Tom wasn't in control of Emma's death and found it precipitous, but he is a writer, Florence, and a great one and he will drain every action, every event, every incident for his tuppence worth of versifying. In the end, as Tom points out, Emma is "past love, praise, indifference, blame." He acknowledges that for Emma "good-bye is not worthwhile" for they had said good-bye long before you met them both. The Emma you read about is frankly not real, Florence. She is a creature not of Tom's heart, but of his imagination. Do you see anything of Emma, as you knew her, in this "West-of-Wessex girl", this creature he parades before us? No, for she didn't exist and nor did very much of the Emma these poems describe. Be patient and kind to Tom, if you can stand it, for he will be grieving more for you than she at this moment, I can be sure. Please write if I can be of any use or comfort. Your dear friend, Edward.'

Florence was moved by the letter which went some way to appease her, although it was Tom who eventually brought the whole unhappy chapter to an end, writing a poem declaring his love, his past mistakes, his future hopes that she folded and placed in the same envelope alongside the letter that he had given to her prior to her wedding. And as she wrote to Edward by way of reply to his kind missive, she knew she had been closer to Tom than Emma for several years before her death and that there had been no competition between them, that once having foolishly wished her rival gone, and then having befriended her, she had come to realise that former lovers are the worst of rivals for they cannot be confronted and, worse, that in the matter of love, and the appendages and remnants of love, for that was how she saw Tom's poems, death bestowed upon them a very considerable advantage.

Chapter 7

THE UNRAVELLING

In the months following the publication of *Satires of Circumstance*, Florence withdrew more and more into her shell. She made it clear she did not welcome visitors at Max Gate, yet the occasional interloper still turned up to see Tom on some pretext or other and was welcomed warmly by him, oblivious to her feelings on the matter. Even the restrictions on movement around the country because of the war did not dissuade the more persistent, and so she bit her tongue and adopted the deference of a handmaiden.

She had been deeply wounded by Tom's poetic philandering, as she saw it, and yet knew that she had no claim to sanctimony, that her hurt was more pride than jealousy. His betrayal was not intended, she could accept, but it was little solace to her; by writing as he had, he had allowed himself to hide behind his writer's mask, subverting propriety and making a fool of them both. He did not feel anything for Emma, of that she was sure, but he had filtered her memory through his writer's sieve and produced this mish-mash of poetry.

What hurt was that she counted for so little, was apparently unable to inspire anything in him. The thought often crossed her mind that he would have written about her too, as his muse, had she resisted his overtures and been more remote. Had there been some vague allusion to her, some public affection, however subtle, she would have been uplifted, but there was none. In the same way that she had so dispassionately met his needs, so, surely, could he not meet hers? She thought about him weighing up his favours. He had not been honest with her. Why could he not be more clinical also? She should have stayed single, she knew, and kept some allure, and maybe then he would have written about her: poems of longing and desire that would have given her legitimacy. But he had not done so. Or even – and she hardly dare think it – may not have been *able* to. She hated that it was not the Emma of his marriage that lay at the heart of his poetry, but some subsumed romantic memory, pre-marriage, pre-the awful mess they became. Emma was just a convenience, a coat-peg, of that she was sure, something to hang his guilt on. Marriage seemed to strangle his poetry, with Emma and now with her. Courtship, wistful longing, memory abounded, but domesticity sat hard upon his genius. What was her marriage worth now? She had an urge to write that compelled and confused her, but failing that she wanted his words in print, about her or inspired by her. But these confounded poems out there were about Emma – how they would look to others!

She felt degraded and resolved not to forgive him easily. Whatever happened now she determined would take some effort, some concession from him to put right. Part of her, that weak part she recognised in herself and did not like, wondered whether this was his revenge for being cast as second-best, revenge for Thornley and his ilk, for the Irish, for Alfred, for her desperate family, even for her own talents that he now seemed to want to disparage. But she knew it was not so and that she could not will it otherwise, even to appease herself.

She considered that they would manage this phase in their lives as they had weathered the flurry of gossip after their wedding; they would live through it all and re-assert themselves again. Their interests were ultimately mutual and complicit. But it would need time. Time, she thought, and the recognition of their literary nomenclature as *the* Mr and Mrs Hardy. That, she well knew, depended upon an acknowledgement of her as being *good* for Tom by those who were watching her now. She could sense they were looking to see how she would protect and care for her husband and deal with the public rebuke he had delivered her. And she would do so, would show them that she was deserving of him. In return, they would give her the approbation she craved and provide the social glue for her and Tom to co-exist, for their own glue had become dry and brittle.

Marriage, their marriage, she had later darkly noted in her diary, had arrived on the back of a hearse. It had all happened so quickly, Alfred, then Thornley and Emma all dying in rapid succession followed by her decision to marry, to commit herself in such a public way.

What a fool she had been. She knew that Thomas would be difficult, cantankerous, demanding, for he would not know how to be otherwise.

And while it might only be for a few years, by the end of him what would be left of her? She felt indignant; he had promised her, on one visit to Aldeburgh when this was all first mooted, to protect her and to introduce her to a different world, a world giddy with writers, not bury her alive in Dorset. But then it was all talk, for he had no idea that Emma, strong as an ox, would predecease him. Their marriage, she saw, would circle around his needs, vulture-like, but only devouring her. In turn he would become shabbier and more dependent, for that is what happens to old men. If she had once thought their marriage would be the means by which all her desires, all her feelings of self-worth and charity would be realised, she knew now she was sadly wrong. Fool. Fool. The pair of them had simply decided to travel the years ahead in each other's company, but she had not anticipated that she would have to define herself in relation to another or what it would mean. That it may have been nothing more than the fear of being alone (and how temporary, she thought, that fear need be) which had driven her into this unreasonable state now made her shudder; that, and a fear of what Thomas could say about her if she were to leave, how he could undo her, possibly destroy her. In her mind, shaped now by duress and disappointment, she had sought the sanctuary and the sanctimony of matrimony. It was not what she would once have written, she thought, as she put down her pen, not when Alfred was alive. But his departure and that of Thornley had changed her thoughts as it had changed her expectations. She had to cut her cloth accordingly.

The war was not going well and, as Tom had predicted, it was evident that it would not likely be quickly resolved, one way or the other. She and Tom found great comfort and enjoyment in Frank's regular letters and looked forward to the arrival of the mail each day. Frank had been attached to a division of the Midland Cyclist Company, which amused Thomas, with his own penchant for cycling. He had kept them amused with his letters regaling them about life in the army and although his visits to Dorset were less regular now, he was clearly enjoying the bonhomie of army life.

In the spring of 1915 he was offered a commission in the Dorset Regiment which he accepted and was posted to the 5th Battalion stationed near Blandford. The consequence for Tom and Florence was that once again, for several short months, he became a regular visitor at Max Gate.

As before, he and Thomas sat in the garden, Frank leaning forward intently in conversation, pipe in hand, talking over the situation in France, the early setbacks and the promotion of Winston Churchill as First Sea Lord, while Florence waited on them, hovering patiently in the fringes.

She and Frank would always find time for a walk whenever he visited, setting out from the house on one of the small pathways past Kingston Maurward to the nearby woods and heath. As they walked, they conversed in a quiet, intense way, never about the war or Europe or anything sensible as she recalled later, but occasionally what lay beyond it. As a matter of course now, he held her hand in a way that seemed natural and relaxed when they walked, as would two dear friends, which is how Florence, at least, saw them. They had grown very comfortable in each other's company and despite (or possibly because of) the arrangement that Tom had told her about, on such occasions when they were alone she was as cheerful, joyful and fearful as she had ever been.

As 1915 progressed life at Max Gate took on a routine, starting with a breakfast of tea and toast before they settled to work. Since Tom had received the Order of Merit, the increased volume of correspondence and number of invitations had led to Florence spending most of each morning helping him. Then, after a light lunch, she would leave him alone to his writing, although often, when she would come into the study in the late afternoon, he would be asleep at his desk with Wessex curled up about his feet. An occasional visitor disturbed them, but in the large part their life took on a pattern which they were both comfortable with.

In late June came the news they had been expecting, that Frank was to be posted overseas. With only a week's warning there was little time for the information to be absorbed before he was gone. During the three days he had with his widowed mother nearby he managed to make a short visit to Max Gate, but time was rushed, compromised and conversation stilted. Words were left floating in the air, thoughts were weighed down by futures and the little that was said in parting, as Florence reflected later, was vacuous and wasteful.

'Are all partings like this,' she wrote later in her diary, 'a skirting of what matters for the things that are really of no consequence? Is it because we would rather not say anything that may precipitate a sense that the parting may be anything more than temporary that we are so neglectful of the little time we may have? I wish we had not avoided talking more directly. I wish I had said more. I wish that I had told him we would pray for him.'

The war continued to dominate the news and the household conversation, and in particular the ill-advised landings at Gallipoli for which Churchill was being roundly criticised. It was, said Tom, all wrong, what they had done, that any damned fool could see that, and the result was just more young lives needlessly lost.

The news that reached them on August 23rd descended like a shroud over Max Gate. The wire read simply that Second Lieutenant Frank William George of the Dorset Regiment had been killed on August 22nd on active duty at Suvla Bay in the Dardanelles. There was no other information provided, no explanation, no comfort, no apology. The words were naked and brazen, defying challenge and contradiction, as if death in its starkness needed no elucidation or explanation.

Thomas reacted with the desperate grief of one who had lost a son, as to all intents he had, and while he felt anger at what had happened in the Dardanelles, that emotion was swamped by despair, a deep gnawing sadness about the brutality of life, its utter meanness. Florence, meanwhile, withdrew to her room and came out several hours later dressed in black, in which colour garb she remained for a full month.

An obituary, hastily written by Thomas that afternoon, was wired to *The Times*, appearing the next day under the headline ***Thomas Hardy's Cousin Killed in Action***. While Florence could not bring herself to read it, Thomas was incensed by the implication that, even in death, Frank's name could not stand alone, without being subsumed by his, as if it was only that connection which warranted it appearing in the papers at all.

Frank's death had a significant effect on life at Max Gate. Florence's dark hair began to turn grey at an alarming rate, her face became more drawn, her prominent grey eyes damp and diminished, all of which began to rapidly age her. She shuffled in her movements about the house, partly as she had started to wear slippers unless venturing out of doors, and her mannerisms slipped almost imperceptibly from those of youth to premature middle age. She had taken to wearing a succession of dark velvet frocks despite the heat of summer and chose not to leave the house for several weeks at a time, except to take herself off for long walks with only Wessex as company.

Thomas tried to put his thoughts into an elegy for Frank, which he called 'Before Marching and After' but which he knew failed to represent the well of emotion he felt now that the "marching was done". The formula of writing abstractly about a fallen soldier was not appropriate for Frank who had been so dear to him. Somehow he had become trapped by the genre and admitted to himself, for once, that poetry was no longer enough. Thereafter, the effect on him showed itself to be more profound as he sank into a depression that continued unabated throughout the remainder of that year and into the next.

Tom's grief was compounded in November when his sister Mary died from emphysema. She had been sick for some time and yet during her recent illness he had shown little inclination to call on her. Florence recalled Thomas telling her that, as children, he and Mary had been paired up by his mother as the closest of all the siblings, the most alike in spirit and temperament. That may have been so, she thought, yet over recent years he had been so absorbed in the magnitude of his own life that Mary had simply faded from it. Her death, thought Florence, as with that of Emma, affected him only when it was too late to make amends, the cord of family having shrivelled beyond any fear or chance of regeneration. And typically, only when family were finally at rest did Tom himself become restless. Only then were they of any use to him. It was chastening to think she would likely succeed him so would never get the treatment he reserved for the dead. Perhaps, also, she told herself, it was simply that Mary's death gnawed at him as the death of any younger sibling would do.

They went to her funeral but it was a miserable affair.

'Why did you bother even going, Tom, when you never concerned yourself with her these past few months when she was ailing? You never had her to supper or even suggested it when I wouldn't have minded in the least. She was a meek thing for sure, but she was your sister.'

'She was happy as she was, dear. She didn't like all the fuss being made about me just from my scribblings. It embarrassed her.'

'What nonsense. We could have done something for her, a meal or two, invited her for a visit.'

'She'd not have come. She didn't like dogs – had always been scared of them.'

'That's nonsense, Tom, you always had dogs round when you were young.' She paused. 'You're a cold fish, Thomas, with your own kind. Everything is about you. It's your satisfaction, your pleasure, your writing, as if nothing else matters. What do you give?' She glared at him, giving her next words extra gravitas. 'Just what do you give back, Tom?'

'I gave her and Kate and Henry the house they live in, for God's sake. Is that not a brotherly thing to have done?'

'Yes, it was, but it was a thing, Tom, a thing, not a piece of you.'

He went to say something, then drew his lips together and sat quietly. He looked sadly at Florence, meeting her concave grey eyes with his own, knowing how rheumy, tired and nondescript they looked. What was he thinking? He noticed how deep her eyes had set and how the sockets and rims had darkened and that she had changed, was more like a raven, that she was treating him not as Thomas Hardy, but as a rather senile and pathetic old man, which he most decidedly was not. He looked down at his hands, old hands now, sun-marked and venous, lifted himself up and shuffled from the room, the ability to walk or even answer her diatribe seemingly stripped from him.

Since the death of Emma less than three years before, the whole world had changed. Gone were the laughter and confidence of Edwardian England and the optimism and bullishness of the early years of George V's reign. In its place there was an apocalyptic vision of the world to come, a vision that had inveigled its way into human consciousness where it had taken root. Nothing ever would be the same. People would look back and remember the pre-war days, but it would be memory, nothing more, the past being a dead man's house, a useless chattel, an empty chorus of voices. War had altered everything.

At Max Gate the effects were just as traumatic. At the start of 1911 Florence thought that they had passed their nadir, that the worst was over, only to have that happiness dashed before some lesser hope temporarily took hold again and then was crushed as an impertinence. She looked at the passage of the past three years and knew that doors had closed, that life's options had narrowed, that what lay ahead was her life's residue, the remains of other lives that had crossed hers and had vanished.

It had not always been so, she reflected. Even her contract with Tom had promised more, but had been undone by circumstance. She re-read his pre-nuptial letter often now and his curative poem, written under duress, which she knew was less than his normal fare, and felt nothing other than regret. She thought of Frank occasionally, of Alfred and Thornley increasingly, and of Tom only by default and always with a sense of duty and forbearance.

Occasionally, she would read through Tom's poems to Emma, punishing herself in a valiant search for some reference, some allusion to herself, although she knew none existed. She read and re-read his letters to her and then laboured through the copious notes she had made from the diaries when Tom had been away, purging his soul. And she felt, increasingly, emptied of joy and hope.

What had led them here? This was the question to which she so often returned now, but it was so trite, so self-indulgent. She knew better than to attempt an answer, for life had no logic, no direction. After all, everyone posed for themselves the same question dressed up in different guises throughout the course of their lives and then withdrew to deal with the consequences of what had been visited upon them. As Tom would sometimes say to her, moustache twitching and eyes twinkling, understanding's natural place was always after the event, life never went to plan, and that, that was the plan.

She wondered at the justice of it all. Tom with his mad wife. Thornley with his mad wife. Alfred with his consumption. Each situation came with its own poison, its own weights to drag her down. She had learned – had had to learn – to be a companion, a handmaiden, to listen, cajole, assist, to offer comfort and relief, for that was what she had always been expected to do. It was such an amicably duplicitous thing to have agreed, this negotiated agreement between them, the horse-trading of favours and obligations. Afterwards she had learned to love him a little, fitfully, daringly, she thought, but had never succumbed to anything she didn't keep firmly anchored in her head. And nor had he. They had not really moved beyond – and she shuddered at the words – "an arrangement", an exchange of part-lives, a barter of skills and connections, a game of bluff and counter-bluff, each meeting their match in the other. But wasn't that always so? He would keep her secret and she would keep his. That was what they agreed in settling the thing. They were to be good companions. We fool ourselves, she thought, if we ever think we can know another person, for everyone is, at heart, unknowable. Like two circles that intersect there is a sliver, an ellipse where commonality of thought and purpose reside, but most of the circles are blank. And that's where we live, alone and largely unknown, pretending it is all otherwise.

These two years had aged her and she could not understand how she had ended up quite as she was. It was not what she had hoped for, not when she had been with Alfred, neither in imagination nor in the flesh. Her marriage was, like everything in life, she knew, a compromise.

Chapter 8

AFTER THE VISIT

She had first met Alfred Hyatt in Reading not long after she had started working as a trainee teacher at her father's Church of England school in Enfield. Leaving church one Sunday in the company of her family, her father had stopped to talk to the young man, eventually drawing Florence and her sisters into the circle. Edward Dugdale introduced him as a former pupil of his who was now a successful journalist, a description to which Alfred politely demurred. Brushing his modest protestations aside, her father turned towards her.

'My daughter, Florence, who is also a scribbler.'

With these words, Florence found herself face to face with the shy young man who, while slightly abashed at finding himself walking beside her and behind his former headmaster, did so, intrigued as he was by her grey eyes and dark pensive beauty.

Florence was seventeen years old. Alfred was six years older, a journalist, a fledgling poet, gentle, intense, without means. Of medium height and with a short, wispy moustache, he wore a heavy tweed suit and brogues and carried a hat and writing folder that sat loosely in his hands and which he explained away, stammering awkwardly as he did so, as intended for making notes on the sermon. Florence, so shy and retiring, listened to him intently as they walked along the road, feeling increasingly comfortable in his presence, so that when he called the next day to ask if she would like to accompany him to visit the nearby gardens, neither she nor her father objected.

Their first walks were tentative undertakings. Alfred was very aware that he was physically weak and unprepossessing, dogged as he had been with poor health, and that any attraction he held for Florence would be at best cerebral. But he saw also in Florence someone who was interested in what he was interested in, that being writing and literature; as well, he saw in her someone shy and demure and yet strangely attracted to him. The latter he could not readily understand, but he accepted the gift of her company as just that. He was of independent means, if that meant capable of eking out a meagre existence, bordering on subsistence, was intelligent and interested in people and if she felt he was one with her, then that was his very good fortune.

Through their ensuing conversation, they found that each family had been aware of the other for many years. Alfred's father, the local fishmonger, had always been a familiar presence in the town, as had his family, and Florence was aware she had known of them in some vicarious way. She was sure that she and Alfred had crossed paths somewhere although she suspected there would have been no reason for the recognition, one of the other, to be etched into either memory. He would have left school before she had even started although the likelihood was her father would have mentioned him, for no other reason than the deeds and misdeeds of all his pupils were given a good airing around their dinner table. His being a few years older than her made it easier, she felt, not harder to converse and a lot of the nervous embarrassment that accompanied the pairing-off of young people escaped them. For Florence, Alfred was not only older, but wiser, considerably so, and she revelled in the confidence he gave her.

Alfred, in turn, fed on their shared interest in literature and journalism and made it the common ground on which they made those first cautious inroads that first pricked them and then got beneath the skin. Alfred professed himself keen to foster her literary pretensions, seeing that as the most immediate claim he had to her attentions, and she glowed with pleasure at his gift to her. When she started to write, he helped her to get a story published in the *Enfield Ensign*. After that they met daily, whenever time allowed, always with something fresh to talk about. Alfred had regularly been producing a children's column for the paper and they were soon spending many hours sharing their views and opinions on writers and their tomes, becoming increasingly familiar with each other's thoughts and tastes as well as their whims and mannerisms, growing more dependent on each other.

Through Alfred, Florence developed an acquaintance with his widowed mother and siblings and when, in 1902, Alfred's sister Elizabeth was appointed as an assistant at her father's Church of England school, sharing the teaching of the standard one class with Florence, it strengthened their association and extended the tendrils of their relationship further into their earth.

Florence found in Alfred a reflection of her own literary ambitions. They shared what they were writing, talked of poetic form, of metrics, of allusion, of their desire to be published. This conversation led invariably to the difficulties of doing so, of their provincialism, of their penury, and very occasionally their fledgling dreams. Alfred spoke of the difficulties for people such as them to ever have the opportunities afforded to others, floating the idea of ensnaring a patron, for that way they could be released from the tedium of needing to work and, given time, their talents would find an outlet, one or other or both.

Their friendship had deepened, by the time Florence was in her early twenties, into a close and mutual accord, grounded in their literary interests and ambition. Alfred, who often cut a romantic figure, resplendent in his dark green cloak and large felt hat, still lived at home, but like Florence yearned for more independence. For both, the expense involved in finding their own keep elsewhere mitigated against taking such a step. In Alfred's case, the situation was exacerbated by regular bouts of illness which meant spending considerable time at home receiving the ministrations of his devoted mother. All in all, thought Florence, it was no easy task to fly the nest. She had wanted to write, she knew, since she could remember, but she had to earn a living, as she was frequently reminded. Her father could not support her with four other sisters and a wife dependent upon him. While she found the boys at the school difficult and reluctant to learn, it was, as she frequently reminded herself, a living.

She had started writing – dabbling, really – when she was a trainee teacher and had first begun to talk of herself as a writer. But even though she had an article published celebrating the beauties of nature, entitled 'A Summer Leave', her literary pretensions were gently pushed to one side by her father, although kindly so, and he insisted that she put the word "aspiring" in front of "writer" if she wanted to talk about such things so as not to give the impression she was something that she was not.

While she received little support from her father, he refrained from active discouragement. Rather, his frustration with her was because of the frailty of her health that necessitated her being away from school so much and her lack of any sense of vocation. Her mother, on the other hand, was neither dismissive nor encouraging, just bland in her indifference. With so many daughters to listen to, her maternal affection had been thinly spread. Of her sisters, only Eva showed any interest in spending time with Florence, who craved an audience for her stories. When they were younger, it was Eva, likewise, and Constance, less so, who would sit transfixed, eyes and ears on Florence, who created gently undulating worlds for them both with prosaic word pictures. She was not unhappy, but she felt her job and her family, collectively, were an entrapment from which she needed to escape.

Florence soon felt confident enough to share her family predicament with Alfred. Each walk took on its own pattern, limited to a few gentle and engaging phrases before both relaxed enough to talk more freely.

'I am never able to be myself living at home.'

'Why not?' Alfred retorted gently. 'Your mother and father don't seem to be too protective of you. They've let you walk out with me knowing what a subversive person I am, being a journalist! I like them both.'

'I know,' she continued, with a little more weight in her words. 'I'm not ungrateful to them. But it's ten years since I started as a trainee teacher straight out of school. I've not had any other life, you know, and I find no joy in my job.'

'But what you do is important. Why belittle it?'

'I don't belittle my job, it's just that it is not what I want from my life. I don't enjoy it. I don't like that I am so passive, just going along with what is expected of me rather than what I want for myself. I feel I belittle myself for not having the courage to jump, that's all.'

'So what do you want, Florence? You don't have to stay anywhere if you wish for something else. But it won't happen *for* you unless you see what it is you want.'

'It is to write, you ninny,' she would say, trembling as she did so.

And, having said so, Florence would stare past him and let her hands droop. He felt for her situation, but did not see why it curtailed her. Even so, Alfred knew to say nothing, but when no one was looking he would pick a flower (on this occasion, it was a soft rose bud, luminous white with peach-coloured edges) and slip it into her hands with such care and delicacy she would feel a warmth she never knew existed within her.

Often they walked in silence, as now, not speaking for several minutes before Florence felt she was ready to resume.

'It's not that easy, Alfred', she countered. She hesitated, gathering her thoughts as they walked on, matching pace for pace. 'I was only fifteen, you know, when I started in the classroom. Contrary to what my father might say, I did try hard, but it was just not what I wanted to do. Now I have grown to dislike it. The children seem rude and uncouth. They always want of me and don't seem to have any reserve or consideration when I want some quiet. It makes me ill being in front of them all day. I just wish I was invisible at times, instead of being measured by their beady eyes in everything I do. I hate the smirking. I do. The truth is,' and she paused, 'I'm just not very good at it.'

With that admission, she stopped and looked directly at Alfred. 'You see. I can clearly see it's not for me, so why can't father?' She was saying more than she had meant to, more than she had even told her mother or any of her sisters.

'It is never so easy for fathers, but if your writing goes well, I am sure he would support you. He seems a reasonable man.'

She twisted the stem of the rose he had given her until it started to weep. Turning to Alfred, she said quietly, 'You know, Alfred, all my life I have had to answer to my father, whether at work or at home. I fear he does not have a very high opinion of me.'

Alfred reached out and took her delicately by the fingers.

'Then he must see you as you really are. One should only be judged at doing what one really wants to do. He must decide for himself you are not for teaching. Let me talk to him.'

Florence hesitated. Alfred's way of speaking in aphorisms sometimes made him sound wise, at other times like this, just pretentious. She shuddered that she might so easily find fault with him when he was, as she commonly felt, her panacea, always doing his best for her. He was her one true and loyal friend.

'That would not be a good idea, Alfred, at least not yet. It's not that he isn't a good man, but he can be intolerant. He has his position and he thinks he is doing the right thing by letting me teach in his school, but it's good to know that *you* know it's never been right for me.'

Alfred, sufficiently stirred, had no difficulty being solicitous towards her, and even with his stammer and impoverished air, he felt comfort that it was him that Florence turned to and confided in. That she looked on him with favour touched him deeply, while his own affection for her was at times so overwhelming that he had to struggle to prevent her realising the well she had tapped.

When not absorbed in talking over Florence's feelings of being trapped in a life and work she longed to escape, they enjoyed each other's company immensely. They would go to the Town Park off Cecil Road where they would sit on the circular seat at the foot of the giant sequoia and look at the formal rose gardens. Alfred was knowledgeable about the flowers laid out in the various raised beds and would enjoy sharing his botanical knowledge with this intriguing and seemingly curious young lady. They would spend many hours in the early summer of that year walking around the gardens and beside the ponds, talking about a rich mix of anything.

Alfred spoke always with a sense of urgency, passion even, about all sorts of issues. He wanted to defend Oscar Wilde. He thought the Boer War had been wicked and wrong and the only people who benefited were the big financial houses, and was fearful about what was going on in Russia. He was enthusiastic about American literature, Henry James in particular, and Joseph Conrad, and full of theories and views on anything.

On one particularly long walk in late autumn, but early on in their friendship, he confessed to Florence that he was a non-believer and that it was his belief that personality, rather than being pre-ordained, constantly evolved and changed during each person's lifetime.

'You see, Florence, the way I see it is that our personalities are the result of countless waves washing against us, shaping and moulding who we are. Sometimes, and especially if the environment remains constant, the changes may be almost imperceptible, but for some people, people like us, Florence, prepared to question our place in the order of things, the changes can make us almost unrecognisable from our past lives. Can you see, Florence,' he continued, speaking ever more enthusiastically, 'can you see, that we are all, every one of us, made up of thousands upon thousands of interactions, happening to us every minute of every day, each with its own pin-prick, defining and shaping us?'

Florence nodded and Alfred took her silence as acquiescence, continuing to talk at her, his stammer put on hold by the flow of ideas, his words and voice ever more urgent.

'We human beings are social creatures, Florence, and we develop our character in relation to each other. We're like stalactites, built up by the drip, drip of observation and approbation, word and gesture in some subtle ever-changing process. That is why the "me" you know now might not exist in ten years' time. Only if you grow with someone is there a chance you will stay connected and even then, who knows?'

Florence was intrigued, fascinated to have such an unlikely subject dressed up and placed before her. She wondered if this was an overt attempt to promote a claim upon her, by making him indispensable to her, but she decided not for that was not his way; but she was flattered, nevertheless, flattered that he would share his private thoughts with her, as if it was her intellect he was courting.

'But we manage it,' he would go on. 'The secret is adjusting the line between absorption and deflection. As I see it, we construct ourselves, our working selves, our day faces, wholly as others see us. We can't help it.'

'I don't see that,' Florence would answer slowly, 'this imaginary line. I don't even feel that I have any control about what happens to me. It just happens and I am the same person whoever I am with.'

But Alfred would just rush on, contradicting, challenging, stretching her, making her question her own being.

Florence shivered. She was not sure she wanted to be taken this far and the intensity of Alfred, his blazing eyes, both excited and frightened her.

And at that point, he would see that she was struggling and, like a fisherman, he would attempt to reel himself in so as not to lose her completely.

'Of course,' he said, redressing in his thoughts, 'the whole of life might be a fabrication and as Mr Freud has written in trying to interpret dreams …' and off he would go, expounding on Freud's ideas on the matter, or on Einstein's latest paper on the theory of relativity that was then in the news or such like.

And whatever he said usually made sense to her, she thought, if not always immediately, so well did he explain it.

Later, Florence looked back on their conversation and tried to pinpoint what had made her as she was, what cross words or smiles or grimaces or experiences in childhood had worked upon her until she became confused and just wished that Alfred would put his arms around her and say that he would see her right.

Alfred had been working hard over recent months to advance his own journalistic career. Latterly, he had persuaded Florence to try writing an article on her father's school, something she had taken up with considerable enthusiasm, but he was increasingly restless and unsettled living and working in Enfield. He was keen to share his own aspirations with Florence and eventually chose one of their long walks to broach the subject of his latest idea to her.

It was a warm May afternoon and after a cursory conversational preamble about the trials and tribulations of their respective workdays, Alfred stopped and steered Florence to a wrought iron bench beside a bed of begonias, opposite an ornate pond replete with a jubilee fountain, recently erected in memory of Queen Victoria. He took off his broad-rimmed hat and cloak, laid them on his knees and said quietly, 'I'm not to be satisfied just writing for a newspaper you know.'

He threw a pebble he had picked up into the water and watched the circular ripples expand and diminish. Thrusting his hands into his trouser pockets, he stood up suddenly and exclaimed, 'Damn it, Florence. I just want to do something worthwhile in my life, something I can leave behind. Don't we all want that?'

Florence looked up at him. 'Any writing you do is worthwhile, Alfred. People speak well of your column.'

Alfred sighed, ran his right hand through his thinning hair and sat down again.

'You're a kind woman, Florence, and clever for knowing the right thing to say, but I want to do more than write a column in a provincial newspaper and be sent to cover the meetings of the great and good of Enfield. I want to work with real writers.'

He paused. Getting to his feet again, he offered Florence his arm and after a few pensive steps, ventured, 'I wrote to Mr Hardy yesterday and asked him to allow me to publish a book of his poetry.'

Florence stopped walking and without letting go of his arm looked at him earnestly.

'But Thomas Hardy writes novels. I've not heard of his writing poetry.'

'Silly. Of course he writes poetry and fine it is too. It may not be what he will be remembered for, but he has a poet's touch.'

Florence blushed before rejoining, by way of mitigation, 'Then you should mix it up with some of his prose for there will be others like me who didn't know he did both.'

He smiled benignly at her. 'Perhaps then,' he said, 'I could pick some purple passages from his Wessex novels to garnish the book, to provide the frippery ...'

She interrupted him. 'Don't mock me Alfred, even gently. I don't take it well.'

'I'm sorry. I was only jesting. But I am sure of Hardy's genius in both genres and I know what an honour, what an opportunity it would be to publish such an eminent author. Don't you see what it could mean?'

'I do. But I confess I haven't read any of Mr Hardy's works. Father would not allow them in the house so I am hardly one to advise you.'

'Not read any of the novels? Then you must start now. And I will dutifully offer to manage the education of Miss Florence Dugdale into the modern novel with all its perils and entrapments. You shall start with one of my favourites. Tomorrow. I'll bring you a copy of ...' – he thought for a moment – '*The Well-Beloved*, and you must read it and tell me what you think.'

And she had done so and told Alfred a week or so later she thought it a queer story and odd that Pierston should in the end seek to love someone so much younger than himself, that such love was as unrealistic as it was unimaginable. Alfred merely laughed at her.

'You cannot measure affection in years, Flo. An older man might offer other things that are beguiling for many a woman. A wealthy man with the right connections and the promise of a prosperous widowhood to come has wooed many a lass I'm sure.'

'You are an old cynic, Alfred.'

He laughed at her. She was so serious.

'For sure I am and I know love is not like that. But Hardy is like that, he asks questions about what we think and the meaning of it all. He's not afraid to upset people by writing modern ideas that we all feel but seldom speak about. You must read more of him and some of his poetry too.'

He shivered momentarily as the sun moved behind a cloud before continuing, more serious, more intent than before.

'He would be a marvellous patron. Imagine if he agrees that I can produce this book of his writings, and when I get to know him I could introduce you too and speak of your literary aspirations. A friend of mine, Thomas Hesketh, who worked for Macmillan, says that Mr Hardy is very good at befriending young writers and especially pretty ones like you.'

'Hush!' Florence blushed at the thought. 'He wouldn't want to bother with me.' She paused and looked at Alfred mischievously. 'But then suppose he did and what if I got to know Mr Hardy, and what if, as you suggest, he has a roaming eye – wouldn't you be a little jealous?'

Alfred smiled at her. 'Envious yes, perhaps, but jealous, no.'

He took Florence by both hands and looked directly at her. 'I want the best for you, Florence, and for you to have the backing of Mr Hardy would be reward enough for me.'

He coughed, his face colouring as he did so.

'The truth is you may think well of me for doing this, but you shouldn't really. I'm much better as a harbinger of talent. You write well, you know. What I am doing is selfish, really, just relying on you.'

She smiled at him.

'Poor, generous Alfred. Thank you for your encouragement, but you know I wouldn't want to be introduced on the back of your coat-tails. I will read some more of Mr Hardy and make up my own mind about him.'

'And so you should. Maybe you could then be our go-between.'

'You presume so, Alfred, not on me, but on the future. You should not do that.'

The summer was long and dry with its abiding characteristic being a hot westerly wind that blew the dust and grain seeds about and seemed to make everyone irritable, although for Florence the time away from school and long evening walks shared with Alfred were a godsend.

They talked endlessly about their worlds, hers of boisterous and awkward children, his of editors, copywriters and deadlines. She read assiduously as many of Thomas Hardy's novels as she could find and even tried his poetry, although she found it unsatisfactory. She would talk with Alfred about what she had read and he to her of his letters to the writer and how he was ever more hopeful that Mr Hardy would agree to a collection. He was, nevertheless, surprised when Florence told him one day that she had written directly to the author and praised his writing and said how much she admired him.

'You should have waited for me to introduce you properly, Florence, when I got to meet him. What made you think it was appropriate to write so directly?'

'I had the idea from reading *Tess of the d'Urbervilles*.'

'And how was that?'

'From the dangers of not doing so, of just letting things happen to you. It was your idea to introduce me, remember. I just decided that I would do so myself. There. Now I can provide you with an introduction.'

Alfred smiled at her. 'You are a strange one. Is your meaning that you have actually heard from him?'

'I have. I've an invitation to visit him at his home near Dorchester. And I will do so when I am next at Weymouth.'

'I am impressed. Then you must go.'

'I shall,' she said. 'I shall go for both of us.'

She smiled and Alfred gripped her hand tightly. 'I can see I have underestimated you, my dear Florence,' and he laughed a gentle laugh that she responded to in kind.

Her visit to Max Gate was arranged for the last week in October at a time that she had been told would be convenient for her to call. She travelled by train first and then walked from the station at Dorchester to the house which lay on the eastern outskirts of town. Walking up the drive into Max Gate, as she later told Alfred, she was met by a servant, a young raw-boned girl who seemed to be of an unusually nervous disposition, her face all red and pock-marked, who showed her to the porch, curtsied to the master and promptly disappeared. After introducing herself to Mr Hardy, she was invited into the drawing-room to take tea with the author. Again the same servant appeared, even more ill at ease than before, and proceeded to spill the jug of milk upon the cloth beside her and down onto the carpet. Florence smiled sympathetically as she recalled the girl's horror, for which she was roundly scolded by the master. Whether she was just unnaturally clumsy or scared of Mr Hardy, she wasn't sure. All the time, Emma was nowhere to be seen although she was sure there was someone else in the house who could have been her, but nothing was said. Thomas Hardy was quite plain she felt, wondering whether it was fair that an author should be ordinary, but he was charming also and when she drew his attention to the flowering privet that bordered his driveway on their departure, his eyes twinkled as he picked a stem, bowed and presented it to her.

Alfred was intrigued. 'And what was the house like?' he asked her. 'Dark' was all she replied, surrounded as it was by hundreds of brooding Austrian pines, and not at all beautiful. He refused to have them trimmed, she was told by the gardener, for he believed plants and trees should not be unnaturally damaged. Beyond that there were just fields of turnips rotting in the ground. 'And the rooms?' She only saw one properly and that was gloomy and austere, with dark walls and drab furnishings and a few paintings and lithographs of Dorset scenes, but she promised to pay better attention next time. Oh, and the clock, the large grandfather clock she remembered.

'And Mr Hardy again, Mr Hardy?'

On that subject, Florence was less direct. He was a perfect host, she said, but there were no flashes of brilliance, no clever asides, nothing to mark him out as the genius he felt him to be. But there was more, surely, he pushed.

'Oh yes. He was dapper,' Florence acknowledged, but smaller than she had imagined. And you could see when you were close to him that his skin was dry and crusty, yet his eyes were luminous and alert and followed you about like those of a sparrow; and his moustache was heavy upon his lip and drooped at the ends. Was this like what he wanted to know?

And Alfred thanked her and desisted from asking her any more without ever having learnt anything at all that provided an insight into the great man, but with a feeling that she had shared all she knew or at least all she wished to share with him.

The next week she had decided she would write to Mr Hardy once again, this time to thank him for the honour he had bestowed by inviting her to tea and, what's more, send him flowers.

Alfred was intrigued. 'Flowers? Why flowers?'

'Because I want him to invite me back,' she answered before adding, 'for both our sakes. I want him to notice me.'

Chapter 9

DO NOT THINK YOU STAYED TOO LONG

Winter, when it came, for it was late, seemed more severe than usual. London was full of noise and clamour and the snow, which fell in substantial amounts on three separate occasions before Christmas, had shifted their companionable time indoors. When Florence and Alfred managed to get into the city, it was to the British Museum, one or two of their favourite art galleries or to a small tea shop in Holborn where they would ask for a pot of tea and scones with raspberry jam.

Teaching remained as much a challenge as ever, and with its deleterious effects on her health Florence was determined that the next year would be her last working in a school. She had been drawn in to a new, exciting world through her friendship with Alfred and had decided she wanted to throw herself wholeheartedly into her writing. Generous as ever, Alfred had arranged for her to share the newspaper column he wrote for children while she found her feet and she was grateful to him without properly telling him so. She still lived at home, yet her life had transcended it and she was increasingly removed from its daily goings-on and its familial functions. Her sisters were getting older and Ethel had already married and flown the nest. Consequently she was accorded more freedom, partly she suspected because her father trusted her with Alfred. She felt sure he saw him for the semi-invalid that he was and therefore an intellectual companion rather than a potential suitor, and as a consequence did not worry about her. Likewise, Florence had begun to think that other than their obvious fondness for each other and their common desire to write, there had grown a tacit understanding between them that logged their relationship as a deep and special friendship, but in her mind, no more than that. She felt she could depend on Alfred, utterly and wholly and yet her father was right. He did not arouse in her any feelings beyond that of closest friend and companion. When he touched her gently, held her hands, pecked at her cheek, he acted with the utmost propriety and seemed to have no desire or inclination to disturb the equanimity of what they had together.

Aware, no doubt, of his own frailty, Alfred had decided to love Florence in the most unselfish way he knew, to be her advocate and support in all things, for fear otherwise of frightening her away. Nevertheless, even he was surprised at the contents of the letter that Florence received from the great author early in the New Year. In it, Hardy profusely rebuffed the concern she had voiced that, perhaps, she had overstayed her welcome and insisted she call again. In its overture it was frank and direct, 'Just what one would suspect from someone capable of writing *Jude*,' said Alfred. Florence read the letter twice slowly and having digested its words and intent, gravely handed it to Alfred, for he might value it 'for the signature' as she said.

By March, the first glimmers of spring were appearing in the form of daffodils and hyacinths which had appeared in sporadic clumps in the small park across the road from Florence's family home. She had waited until the weather was a little more settled before deciding to follow up the invitation to visit the author once again. Eventually the cool damp weather abated and when her school holidays began she boarded a train to Dorchester. Dressed in a frilly muslin blouse and a long dark skirt, she looked every inch the school teacher she most reluctantly still was. Arriving in the town at dusk, she had booked a room at a boarding house from whence she planned to visit Max Gate the next morning.

Her visit, as she recounted to Alfred later (although he rightly suspected what he received was but an expurgated version with all the interesting bits left out), was a resounding success. Once again, she did not get to meet Emma who was away in Cornwall with Lilian, although another visitor, introduced as Mr Edward Clodd, was staying at the house. Apart from two servants who seemed both surly and ungracious, she saw no one apart from a succession of cats that seemed to have free licence to roam the house and grounds.

Mr Hardy, standing in the leaf-fringed doorway of the house, had met her. He was dressed in the clothes of a countryman with a coarsely-woven, long tweed jacket, a high-fastening waistcoat with a winged collar and black tie. Florence was amused to see that he was wearing striped knee britches, plus fours, sturdy socks and spats buttoned over his brown leather brogues. His chest was puffed out extravagantly, his head still and erect with his sharp eyes lively and alert. He ushered her into the sitting-room where she was warmly greeted by Edward Clodd.

'Hello, Miss Dugdale. Thomas had mentioned he had a charming young lady coming to visit. He did not exaggerate.'

He gave Thomas a playful wink which brought a sudden blush to Florence's cheeks.

After a few niceties, tea was taken in the drawing-room which was filled with a Victorian jumble of ill-assorted furniture. They sat, the three of them, on chairs with rumpled, poorly fitting covers and surrounded by potted palms, Florence placed between the two older men.

It must have made a strange scene, she thought. The darkly painted walls were lightened only by a few paintings and prints, although even these were nondescript. There was little afternoon light and what there was, was smothered by the velvet curtains that were partially drawn. Three ornate plates perched above the mantelpiece on which there were some porcelain jars – ginger jars, perhaps – while a fireplace framed in blue delft tiles smouldered and occasionally sizzled, but gave out scant heat. There was a tall candelabra standing by a chair with two candles in each of its arms and a worn rug thrown over bare floorboards. Alongside, there was a little table which held a chipped floral plate containing a rather overdone cake, crumbling along the edges where it had been sliced into eight uneven segments.

Florence was aware of the eyes of both Mr Clodd, whose weathered face and white beard and moustache she thought a resplendent evocation of the new monarch, and those of Mr Hardy which she remembered as being bluish-grey (she was trying to memorise such details for Alfred), resting upon her. She felt drawn in by the camaraderie of the two men who for a while forgot she was there in their conversation although their physical presence was strong and earthy as they leant across her. For a while, they engaged each other in earnest discussion about Thomas's new first floor study which overlooked the garden. Florence surveyed the room, until eventually her eyes fell upon a baby grand piano covered by embroidered cloths in one corner, leading her to ask impetuously, 'Who plays the piano?'

Her interjection, unexpected as it was, stilled the conversation of both men in mid-flight. They both turned to look at her.

'It belongs to Emma,' answered Mr Hardy blandly, before adding, 'not that it is ever played much.'

'Then perhaps I could play a little piece.'

At which, before getting any response, she stood up and crossed the room, removed the cover and proceeded to play a sweet minuet which ended to a polite round of applause from the two gentlemen.

By now, having been made very aware that they had not drawn Florence into their conversation, they set out to make amends.

'Our apologies, Miss Dugdale, for our rudeness. I was saying to Edward before you arrived how very kind it is of you to make the journey to see me again.' He looked across at Edward and she blushed with the thought that they had been talking about her before she had arrived.

'I promised last time that we would talk about your writing and I would see if there was anything I could do to help you. Tell me what you've been up to?'

And Florence, unabashed, proceeded to tell him of an article she had begun that she had entitled 'The Apotheosis of the Minx: A Study from the Life of the Many', which she had planned to submit to the publishers Cornhill. She had only started on its premiss, however, when Thomas brushed her earnest words to one side.

'Leave it with me, if you don't mind abandoning it, Miss Dugdale, and I'll cast my eye over it for you. It is best to read manuscripts without explanation, I always say, just as the reader will be expected to do in time.'

'That is very kind of you, Mr Hardy,' she flustered, removing an envelope containing the manuscript from her satchel where it had clearly been placed in the hope of just such an opportunity.

'The pleasure will be mine, my dear. I am delighted to be able to offer some assistance if I can. And that man of yours, Mr Hyatt. I owe him a letter also. Perhaps when you see him next you could apprise him of your thoughts and cast an eye over his selections. I'd feel a lot happier if it had a woman's touch.'

Florence folded her hands in her lap, smiled beatifically and lowered her eyes appreciatively.

'Thank you, Mr Hardy, you are most kind. Mr Hyatt is not my man as you put it, although he is a very good friend and I am pleased for him. I am sure that he will present your work splendidly.'

The tea was cleared away and after spending a few silent minutes gazing out the restricted opening afforded by the tall sash windows, she heard the dray to take her back to Dorchester draw up at the front of the house. It was already dusk and Florence was conscious of the impropriety of having stayed so long. Again, she tried to apologise.

'Miss Dugdale, please. You will always be most welcome here.'

Having half risen to wish her farewell, Mr Clodd settled back into his seat, took up his pipe and began attacking it with a penknife. Mr Hardy rose from his seat, and walked her towards the door.

On the porch, he turned to her and said in a quieter voice than usual, probably, she surmised, to ensure that he was not overheard by any of the servants, 'I wonder, Miss Dugdale, if you would consider assisting me with a little project I am working on while you are in London?'

'Of course.' Florence looked at the author enquiringly.

'It is the matter of an epic poem I am writing based on the Napoleonic wars. I haven't time to do all of the necessary research and would value having an assistant who can go to the reading room at the British Museum for me. People get very fussy about the details being right you know.'

'I would be honoured to assist, Mr Hardy. I have a half-day each week I could give over, and then more of course in my holidays. Will you let me know what you want?'

'That I will, Miss Dugdale. We take a place in London each summer so I will be able to be on hand should needs be. And one other thing.' He paused. 'Since we are now to be working together, I think we can do away with the "Mr Hardy", don't you? Do address me as "Thomas" please, or even simply "Tom" if you so wish.'

'I will if you so wish,' she answered, shaking his hand as she did so, 'although considering our ages it would seem rude for me to do so unless you were to call me "Florence".'

'Then "Florence" it shall be.'

There was a momentary pause, harmless enough, but there, nonetheless, for both of them to consider its significance as they wished.

And with that Florence climbed into the waiting dray and returned to her hostel in Dorchester where she spent a restless night before catching the morning train to Waterloo.

Florence's mind was racing during her trip back to London. She could not get over how quickly she had gained access to the inner sanctum of Thomas's life and the discreet thrill it had given her. Thomas was fascinating and an excellent raconteur and she kept revisiting the conversation they had had, blushing when she thought of the way he had looked at her. She had been intrigued by the absent Emma, the convivial Mr Clodd and the household at Max Gate. She tried to make sense of what she felt, but could not do so. She just knew that her future was alive with possibility.

Alfred was intrigued by Florence's account of her journey and especially Mr Hardy's apparent endorsement of his own project. When a letter arrived from the publishers Chatto and Windus in May saying that they had received the author's go-ahead for the publication of a pocket miscellany, Alfred's excitement was unbounded. He was hugely appreciative of Florence's efforts and lavished thanks on her for her success in "capturing" the attention of Mr Hardy.

'You are a dark horse, Florence. Who would have thought that you could have ingratiated yourself so? You must appear like a breath of fresh air to the old man.'

'Hush, Alfred. He's not so old, you know.' She paused. 'He's offered me some work.'

She half expected – hoped even – that Alfred would be a little jealous of this morsel although she had no need to make him jealous and knew the emotion was foreign to him.

'You should work at this, Florence, if you feel so inclined. I have no doubt how alluring you could be from what I hear of his roving eye.'

'And you. Do you find me so?'

'Of course. But you know it is different for me. My pleasure – and it is my pleasure – is to see you fulfilled. I could manage your life, you know, but I sense you have already run ahead of me. Helpmate to Thomas Hardy. Well, well!'

Florence blushed deeply and held out a hand to him.

'Dear Alfred. You are the sweetest man. I could not have done any of this without your suggestion.'

'Then I will keep suggesting.'

Within the fortnight, Florence had received another letter, thanking her for her recent visit and informing her that Thomas and Mrs Hardy were moving to London for the summer season and would be staying, as usual, at the Hyde Park Mansions. The letter added that it would be helpful if they could meet to discuss the work, to which he gave the title *The Dynasts* while he was in London. She replied to the address on the envelope which was his publisher's office and arranged to meet in the British Museum reading room the following Thursday.

She decided not to tell Alfred of the development. He had been unwell of late, partly, she suspected, from the extra pressures of producing the pocketbook. He had still not met the author and Florence felt disloyal knowing she had not pushed the suggestion forward. First, she felt, she needed to know Thomas better before presuming further upon him. That it was necessary for their dialogue to be conducted with a good deal of subterfuge made Florence feel uncomfortable, not for the unspoken deception implied to Mrs Hardy, but more from the fear of it ending. She found herself looking forward to their meetings, both for the association and for the company. Thomas – and this she could not tell Alfred – was not always discreet in his admiration for her and this fuelled an occasional tremor of desire that disturbed her. He was, she had found, amusing, sharp-witted and charming. And he liked her, that much was clear. She wondered whether he had spoken of her to Mrs Hardy, but concluded not, for his conversation strayed often now into a no-man's land beyond confidences.

Their early meetings were punctuated by the launch of *The Pocket Thomas Hardy* in August which took place at the offices of Chatto and Windus and which, for the first time, brought Thomas and Alfred together. Emma, meanwhile, had returned to Dorset which appeared not to be unusual. Of late, as Thomas had confided to Florence, she had wanted to remove herself from the fuss that accompanied him on such occasions. She had been displeased by some of the reaction to the publication of *Jude the Obscure* and he felt had lurched back towards the Church as a consequence.

'And you, Florence,' he had asked of her, 'what of your Christian faith? Are you a regular churchgoer?'

She had demurred as if to measure what her response should be. She started by talking about her reservations about the Anglican Church in which she had been raised, but when she found Thomas receptive to her agnosticism she was encouraged to be more forthright.

'In my view, Mr Hardy – Thomas – the Church,' she pronounced, 'is a hypocrite,' a remark that made Thomas chuckle.

'And your father – what does he think of his rebellious daughter?'

Florence didn't respond to his smile directly and took a moment before she replied.

'My father knows better than to try and interfere in matters of personal faith.'

Thomas smiled. 'Who would have thought it of you, Miss Dugdale, that you had this spirit? It is no easy thing to stand up to one's father in matters of religion.'

'It is not,' she agreed, 'but I am not as people see me, some will-of-the-wisp who has no mind of her own. My father at least respects that of me.'

The launch was a small affair. Thomas's heart was not in the project and all the misgivings he had about gathering up a few poems and extracts from a few of his novels were realised in the rather uneven collection that resulted. Alfred seemed both in awe of the author and exceedingly nervous as to how well the book would be received. While Florence had displayed a quiet, intimate rapport with Thomas, Alfred appeared not to know what to say. He was, Florence thought, so good at talking when just there were the two of them, but here his stammer seemed worse than ever and she felt both embarrassed and sorry for him.

Later, Alfred reflected on the day's events with Florence over afternoon tea in a little teashop off the Strand.

'I'm pleased to have met the great man at last,' he said. 'But I fear he wasn't particularly taken by the book.'

'Nonsense, Alfred. I am sure he was happy with what you had done. And I am pleased you have met him at last.'

He looked at her closely. 'You seem to enjoy his confidence, Florence.'

'I do – I think. And he is very nice to me. Do you mind?'

'Not at all.'

Alfred leaned forward and dropped his voice. 'On the contrary, I am excited for you. You make a wonderful siren, you know.'

'Alfred!' Florence blushed and glared at him and then broke into laughter.

'All I ask,' said Alfred, 'is that you tell me all, that you hold no secrets from me.'

'There are no secrets, silly, not real ones. But I'll share it all with you if you wish. Perhaps I'll write a book. Perhaps one that the Bishop of Wakefield would want to burn. That would be fun.'

And they both laughed at the thought that she could be capable of such a thing.

The summer weeks of school holiday were spent mostly in London.

Florence kept busy helping Alfred with his column while working away at the revisions he had made to her own piece. He had returned it to her with fulsome praise but with a number of pointed suggestions for ways of improving the clarity of her text. She was grateful and encouraged.

One afternoon Alfred called unexpectedly upon Florence not long after she had arrived home from school.

'Can you come for a walk?' he asked. 'I want to share some exciting news about someone I've met today.'

He led her by the hand and as they walked the two streets to his own home he started to tell her that he had discovered that the Irish writer, Katharine Tynan, who was a distant relative of his mother's, had apparently been living in Kensal Green for some years, where her husband, Henry Hinkson, was practising as a barrister. Although his mother had often talked about her, he had only found out that she was here, living in London, by accident when he was asked to interview her for yet another novel to be added to the many she had recently written.

Florence was excited by the news, not only because she had read her collection of poems *Louise de la Valliere*, but because she, Miss Tynan, was a close friend of William Yeats whom she greatly admired.

'That is as well,' said Alfred, 'for we have been invited to tea tomorrow.'

Eager to make a good impression, Florence and Alfred arrived at her home the next afternoon carrying a large bouquet which Alfred nervously thrust towards their hostess as she met them on the doorstep. Having settled to their refreshments, Alfred soon fell silent, having struggled with his stammer for a few awkward sentences, leaving Florence to pick up the threads of conversation. Undeterred, the two women conversed with such ease that before taking leave of each other they arranged to meet the following morning in Regent's Park, this time without Alfred.

They had chosen the Clarence Gate entrance as their rendezvous and duly found each other without any difficulty, before proceeding across the bridge of the same name to Queen Mary's garden. There, in the inner circle, they found a bench, wrought iron and wood, where they sat down side by side. It was a warm spring day and they were content to sit and talk, each uncovering the other, gossamer layer by gossamer layer.

As they did so, they found they had much in common. Florence was much taken with Katharine's soft accent and found her entrancing. She smiled when Katharine, who professed an antipathy to England, founded and fuelled by having been to school in that devil's armpit, Drogheda, said in the following breath that it was just part of the Irish cloak she wore when in London. Florence liked her wit and her irreverence, her observations on William Yeats and Maude Gonne. She enchanted Florence with her Celtic lore and her tragic anecdotes of whole families being wiped out by the famine which she wound into her stories and poems. She talked of her own family, many of whom now lived in England or further abroad in Australia and on the eastern seaboard of America. Florence, in turn, spoke of Hardy, daringly so, and of her own literary aspirations, of the claustrophobia that was Enfield and her school.

It was the best of starts, thought Florence, to the forging of a true friendship, as they said their good-byes and planned to meet again in two days' time. What fun she had had and how different from the conversation of the teachers back at St Andrew's.

On the last of their three meetings, after they had visited the National Gallery together, where they spent some short time looking at the few Anglo-Irish portraits of the 16th and 17th centuries that resided there, Katharine made a proposition to Florence.

'I have a dear friend in Dublin,' she told her, 'who I know is looking for a companion for his wife over the Christmas holiday. She is of unsound mind, dear thing, and a constant worry to her doting husband. She has a nurse, but the woman has her own family and wants a little time off herself over Christmas and so has asked for some extra help. It would involve little work – you would be a companion rather – but I would see you often and you would get to meet the literati of Dublin, that I can promise.'

The family Katharine spoke of were known as the Stokers. Sir Thornley Stoker, she explained, was an eminent surgeon, but also a proponent of the arts who held wonderful soirées and would include her, for sure, in any assembled company – 'for the Irish are like that,' Katharine would say.

'What a wonderful thing this would be,' thought Florence, seeing it as an opportunity to escape the drabness of a family Christmas in Enfield, and answered her without hesitation, 'Yes, Katharine, yes, do please ask them.'

Katharine smiled at her and pledged that she would write to Sir Thornley that very evening, thrilled that she had so pleased her new friend by doing such a small thing for her.

When she told Alfred, he was even more excited for her. 'More doors, Florence, more doors to walk through.' He looked at her and smiled knowingly. 'And for sure, Sir Thornley is a charming man and very popular – and well-read. If you can forget about Max Gate for a few days, you'll find the household lively, especially if the whole family are there.'

Thomas, however, was less pleased when she wrote to him and set out to dissuade her – 'Dublin in winter is not a pleasant place to be, believe me. I may well need you to help me with research at the British Museum. What am I to do then?'

Florence replied, explaining that it was only for two and a half weeks and still three months away, but that she would not jeopardise her friendship with Thomas 'for the world'. Nevertheless, she resolved that whatever he might say to her by way of persuasion, she would go.

Early into September, Florence was surprised to receive a note sent to her at her school. It was from Thomas, asking her to meet him at the entrance to the reading room at the British Museum on the following Saturday. She felt a little twinge of irritation at his expectation of her giving up her Saturday when she had planned a long country walk with Alfred and did not send a reply until the next day, although eventually acceding to the meeting. She spent the next three days wondering as to what it was he wanted.

He arrived at the due time, his cheeks pink from exertion, his small eyes sharp and penetrating. He was wrapped in a greatcoat and scarf to ward off the damp mist that was swirling in the streets outside. Cold and uncomfortable, he shook off the excess moisture before leading her through the reading room to a small alcove, away from the main court. There he ushered her into a comfortable chair of buttoned leather, so large and deep that she felt herself cast. From his breast pocket he took a reading room pass.

'Here.' He held it out to Florence.

'What is it?' she asked.

'For your work. A pass for the reading room. I've arranged it for you.'

Florence looked blankly at Thomas and took the pass from him. 'Thank you. I will make sure I look after it carefully.'

She placed it into her clasp-bag, exchanging it for a handkerchief which she took out to wipe her nose that had started to run.

Thomas looked at her kindly, placing a hand lightly on her shoulder.

'You must be careful, Florence. There is a new strain of influenza about. You mustn't allow yourself to get so damp. Promise me you'll change as soon as you get home.'

'I will, Tom. It was a rush and didn't look like rain when I left.'

'Always expect rain, Florence, and you'll seldom be disappointed.'

'How glum, Tom. It doesn't always rain here.'

'Perhaps not always. But I've spent much more time here than you. I'm almost a Londoner you know, for all the months I'm here each year.'

They sat there in silence before Thomas, after a furtive glance about him, placed a hand on Florence's arm.

'Florence, you have not met Emma yet,' he said, 'but I think it is time that you did. First, you need to know something about her – about us.' He paused, and cleared his throat before continuing.

'You need to know, my dear, that we are man and wife in name only. We don't have the same' – he paused as if considering his words – 'relationship that is normal for married couples.'

He looked directly at her. 'It has been this way for years. We may share a house, but we keep to our own space. We haven't shared the same bedroom …'

'Stop.' She held up her hands. 'I don't want to hear this. This is not for my ears, not now.'

'But it is. It is. I have grown inordinately fond of you, Florence. More than fond. Why should you mind?'

'Because I do. I mind you telling me. Can you not just think it! It is not right to put such comprising thought into words. It just spoils it.'

'Are you telling me you didn't suspect? I never sensed any discouragement on your part.'

She turned aside so her answer was muffled and fell away from him.

'I suspected that you might be estranged to some degree. Perhaps. But that is not the same as encouragement.'

'You still met with me. You were compliant in encouraging the feelings I had for you. You were receptive to what I was feeling.'

'That is unfair.' She felt flattered, awkward, defensive. Was this the Thomas she had been warned against, part writer, part terrier?

'Perhaps. But you know now. You have to deal with it one way or another, Florence. We all will. Here, take this with you. A small gift.'

At this he held out an envelope which she took from him.

He looked at her gravely. 'Good-bye, Florence. I think you should try to visit again before you leave.' And with this he put on his hat that he had placed beside him and led the way out through the Great Court, under its ornate segmented ceiling, onto the street outside.

When she was back in her room she opened the envelope. There was no note or message, no personal inscription, simply two signed photographs of Thomas Hardy, his face, as always, in profile. She laid them on a chair with a sense of irritation.

'How like him to give me photographs of himself,' she thought, before sweeping them up and placing them in the book of Tennyson's poems she had been reading. But they would not be wasted, she told herself. She had already decided what she would do with them. She would give them to Alfred. And she smiled as she thought how he would appreciate and treasure them.

Chapter 10

WRITE, AND WITH MINE EYES I'LL
DRINK THE WORDS

The Christmas of 1906 was the happiest in Florence's memory despite her being away from her family, from Alfred and paradoxically, she thought, from Thomas.

She had often returned to the words that Thomas had spoken to her at their last meeting and which she now saw as a test of some sort, a possible hurdle that she had avoided. She had no idea, even now, how seriously to take them, but seriously enough, she had decided, to dissuade her from going to Max Gate. She had, however, written to him and had received in return letters that were both measured and ambiguous. She mulled over some of his phrases, trying to read into the words some order, some sentiment, but in the end chided herself for doing so. Sometimes she thought he was laughing at her, that she was an amusement rather than, as she wished herself to be, amusing. Yet the overriding feeling she felt was one of exaltation. Theirs was an intimacy, albeit a fledgling one, and that thought sent a shiver of shock through her. She realised how much she was thrilled by the clandestine nature of their correspondence, the sense of some sort of impropriety, and that excited her. What's more, she was determined to hold onto the ground she had made and make use of the opportunity Alfred had unwittingly given her.

Arriving in Dublin in mid-December, having navigated the rolling walls of dense mist that had moved in off the Irish Sea, Florence found the city similarly grey and decidedly damp, as if a wet teacloth had been placed over it. The feeling soon evaporated, however, as she was collected by a smart young driver in green and gold regalia and was taken by elegant hansom cab with its extravagant livery and fittings through empty streets, lit by pale, faintly glowing oil lamps into the heart of Dublin. Eventually, after a distance Florence thought to be some two miles or more – she was no better at judging distances than she was Thomas's sincerity, she thought to herself – they turned into the top of Ely Place.

The eminent surgeon lived with his family in Ely House, close to the centre of the city in a delightful Georgian mansion, once occupied by the Countess of Ely. The brick building was four storeys high with tall rectangular windows and elaborate plaster ceilings and was, Florence thought, by far the grandest house she had ever entered.

The welcome she received was as warm and effusive as the day outside was dank and grey and the contrast was not lost on Florence. While she had come in order to assist the nurse who she only knew as Betty in looking after Lady Stoker, she almost felt from the warmth of the welcome that she could have been invited as a Christmas guest, simply for her own sake.

Florence soon came to appreciate the extraordinary household she had arrived at. She was placed in front of a roaring fire while a servant fussed about her, bringing her a cup of tea, a plate of cakes and a newspaper, the latter a gesture she found somewhat odd for the late afternoon. All around her, the energy and warmth of the house was complemented by a babble and noise that was both liberating and enervating, and when Sir Thornley came into the room she was pleased that he, also, epitomised the person who she had imagined should head such a bustling and jolly household.

'Miss Florence Dugdale. Welcome. Katharine has spoken so warmly of you.'

Thornley Stoker was, as her new friend had described him, calm and gracious and his kind and considerate face immediately put Florence at her ease. He explained that her duties as helpmeet were light as Lady Stoker's condition had somewhat eased of late, although her thought and speech remained erratic.

'She still prefers to remain in bed for much of each day,' he told her. 'It is often her way not to get up until after the family lunch has concluded.'

'And what should I look out for?' she asked. 'Are there any warning signs I need to be aware of with her condition?'

'The signs when they come will be evident enough,' he answered kindly. 'The truth is, none of us knows quite what to expect, day to day, so we just try to be ready for all eventualities.'

What Florence had not been prepared for, however, were the bouts of melancholy that overwhelmed the old lady at times, leading to embarrassing outbursts (except, she told herself, no one actually seemed embarrassed) and occasionally the need for her to be restrained and sedated in order to regain her equilibrium, as the doctor delicately put it.

For the first few days, Florence spent much of her time gliding about the house as if in a trance, admiring the extensive collection of books and fine china, the Chippendale and Louis XVI furniture, the artefacts and treasures that Sir Thornley had spent much of his life collecting from all around the world.

'This,' she found herself thinking as she delicately examined a beautiful ornate French carriage clock, 'this is simply exquisite', before finding herself, almost against her will, comparing the splendour and opulence of Ely House with the dull and functional furnishings and objects that filled the walls and surfaces at Max Gate.

For the rest of the time, she was overwhelmed by the kindness of Sir Thornley and fascinated by the comings and goings at the house. Visitors were frequent and while Florence had been employed ostensibly to help with the patient, her association with Thomas Hardy and with Alfred's maternal family, with whom the Stokers had a long-standing connection, meant that she was quickly drawn into the family circle. The arrival of Sir Thornley's brother and his wife (another Florence, she noted approvingly) for Christmas and New Year saw in a period of boisterous revelry in which her presence was both expected and therefore taken for granted.

The realisation that Bram Stoker, whose novel *Dracula* had caused such a literary sensation only a few years earlier, was Sir Thornley's brother only came to her days before she had left England. Alfred had not told her initially and even when she had asked him directly a few days previously if there was a link between the author and the family she was to attend on, having deduced the possibility, he seemed to pass it off with a shrug.

During the sixteen days spent at Ely House, Florence felt the whole world of Irish literature had opened up to her. She found herself talking to Florence Stoker about Oscar Wilde, to whom she had been betrothed before marrying Bram after the latter had swept her off her feet. Oscar had been such a dear friend, she told Florence, a dear, dear friend, but he really didn't have any idea – about what, Florence was not sure. A tragedy, was all she said, what had happened to him in the end. She and Bram had made their peace with him soon after their own wedding, but the trial and subsequent disgrace had put an end to any social contact, and now, of course, it was all too late to do anything.

On Boxing Day, she was invited to join Sir Thornley in visiting No. 3 Ely Place Upper which was the residence of Frederick and Annie Dick, but more significantly the meeting place of the Theosophical Society to which W. B. Yeats and Maud Gonne were frequent visitors. To find herself in the middle of such an august group that included the poet and his erstwhile mistress as well as George Russell and the writer George Moore, who happened to live next door, suddenly made Florence nervous and self-conscious. Before long, she found herself in the centre of the group and was aghast at first when they started to ask *her* about her own writing and her knowledge of Thomas Hardy, who they seemed to greatly revere. Though she was overwhelmed and confused, being asked to see Thomas, "her Thomas" as she had started to very occasionally think of him, through other writers' eyes, and eminent literary eyes at that, she felt she acquitted herself well, saying just the right amount to satisfy.

Thornley, as always, was kind and solicitous, leading her by the arm to the casement window where he reassured her.

'You mustn't feel at all awed by these people,' he said with a smile. 'They are just wordsmiths, spinners of tales. They cannot boast a decent profession amongst the lot of them.'

'But that is what I want to be too. A writer.'

'For you, Florence, it is the right thing to aspire to. You look like an author should look, dark and mysterious, no doubt supported by a wealthy patron, writing away to your heart's content. This lot' – and he waved his arm back to the group gathered around the hearth – 'drink and talk far too much to ever be so interesting.' He laughed gently. 'I am sorry. I should not be making fun of you.'

'I don't mind at all,' she answered earnestly, 'if that is what you are doing. I am just grateful that you are taking the trouble with me.'

Other luminaries called at the house – some she knew of by name. Most lived in the concentration of houses and streets which appeared to radiate out from Ely House. One such visitor was Oliver St John Gogarty, like Sir Thornley a surgeon as well as a writer and social observer and who was effusive in his greeting and conversation. But it was Sir Thornley who made the greatest impact on her. A few years younger than Thomas, he had all the graces and charm that Thomas did not and she enjoyed her time with him above all. She had taken care to be as considerate and intelligent as she could in his presence, and was surprised and gratified that he seemed to find her opinions and her company both interesting and desirable. How much she had grown up over these two weeks, she thought, and how much bigger her world had grown.

Leaving Dublin was not easy and she was quick to agree to an invitation to return the following Easter. She had never been made such a fuss of before and could not believe that she had been propelled into this fairytale literary milieu through Alfred's selfless consideration. She wanted to write; she wanted to belong. She was ready to serve an apprenticeship and, what is more, was happy to serve others along the way if that was what was required.

Florence could now count amongst her acquaintances, alongside Katharine of course, Bram and Florence Stoker. That they lived in London and had done for many years was another opportunity that she saw had fallen to her. Bram was Henry Irving's business manager and amongst his other responsibilities was that of managing the actor's own theatre, the Lyceum, to which he promised to send Florence tickets for some future performance. It was all too exciting.

She was soon brought down to earth on her return to England. A brusque letter had arrived from Thomas, each word forcibly in its place. While she was glad of it, for she knew her relationship with him needed to be fed and nurtured, it paled beside the spark and wit of the conversation she had known daily over the previous weeks. He asked her if they could meet at the South Kensington Museum on the following Saturday for he had something to give her.

That their meeting was again to be clandestine (his instruction to her was to meet in the architectural gallery – by the Trajan column – around 4.00 p.m.), both excited and worried Florence. She was discreet but nervous also, not for her sake but for theirs, for the necessity of there continuing to be a "theirs". For once, Thomas seemed ready to talk about her, and importantly her writing. His own work *The Dynasts*, the subject of which she had helped him research, was largely finished and sat now with the publisher. Her own article, meanwhile, re-written after his earlier suggestions, in his view needed further tidying, for which he gave precise directions, before she was to submit it to a Mr Edward Datchell at the

Cornhill Magazine, who was already predisposed to receive it. Florence was grateful to him and allowed his hand to hold hers longer than usual, longer in truth than would have been seen as appropriate should anyone have been watching.

'And Ireland,' he asked, 'was Dublin as dreary as ever? And Sir Thornley? Was he as I had suggested he might be, a little too gregarious and familiar?'

'He was not. He was decorous and polite and treated me very well,' Florence had answered.

'Treating you well is what I would expect of him.'

'Then you would not have been disappointed. Have you anything else you wanted to say?'

Defeated, Thomas retreated into the mundane. 'And your job, what were you expected to do, apart from looking after Lady Thornley?'

'I was part helpmate, part companion to them all. They were very kind to me, Tom, and I do long to tell you all about them and all the people I met.'

But Thomas didn't want to hear everything, Florence thought, as she proceeded to answer his questions one by one. Nor, she realised, did she want to tell him every detail of her time there, for she was inclined to keep a little to herself. He seemed satisfied, although he kept returning to what she thought of Sir Thornley, which was the one subject on which she was most reluctant to answer.

On returning home she picked up the package he had given her. Mindful of the earlier signed photographs, Florence was less than expectant, so was especially pleased when she found inside a copy of *Wessex Poems*, lovingly inscribed to his 'Dearest Florence'. His heart, she reflected, may be well-guarded, but it was alive, nonetheless. He was a dear friend, she thought, as she re-read the deeply personal inscription he had written, but she did not love him as he appeared to love her. It was not for want of trying, but simply – and sadly – because she believed she was incapable of doing so.

The publication of 'The Apotheosis of the Minx: A Study from the Life of the Many' in the prestigious *Cornhill Magazine* amongst such well-known writers as Virginia Woolf and G. M. Trevelyan was a personal triumph for Florence. She sent off a copy to her father, which she inscribed, 'To dearest Papa from your aspiring writer and daughter with love F.' She sent another copy of the magazine to Thomas and read and re-read what she had written to ensure it still felt like hers alone. Perhaps, she confided to herself, just perhaps she could be taken as one of the chosen, as a writer, as an equal. Perhaps now she belonged. But while she wanted to believe this, and was willing others to believe this, she could not entirely convince herself.

She was grateful to Thomas for helping her so and for his advice, compromising though it often was, and for his opinion. When he berated her for even considering to accept less than a guinea for each thousand words she had written for the children's story she was preparing for *Country Life*, she felt like saying, indeed shouting at him, 'But it is not the money, Tom, don't you see, it is not the money. I just want to be accepted as a writer.'

Alfred, meanwhile, was intrigued at the change in Florence on her return and was also eager to hear all her news from Dublin. She had positively glowed when she met him at the Lyons tea shop in Holborn early in the New Year and spoke well of Sir Thornley, the family and their close circle, and the wonderful company they kept. 'And they have asked me back,' she ventured and Alfred said how delighted he was that his introduction to Katharine had reaped such a prize for her.

'They are so interesting, Alfred. They talk with such passion and self-belief and like writers, even when discussing Home Rule or the bogs of Connemara. I have never been in the company of so many interesting people. And I have made some new friends too. Sir Thornley's brother Bram – whom you almost forgot to mention to me – and his wife, Florence, have invited me to visit them too, for they live near here and themselves have many interesting visitors. Did you know that?'

'I did, Florence, but the truth is you are rather more decorative than me and therefore a little more useful.'

'Don't be so silly, Alfred. Without you, I wouldn't have known any of them. Without your encouragement, I would never have had the confidence to approach Mr Hardy. It is you who are special, Alfred, for you love me by looking after me. You may have a queer way of showing what you feel, Alfred, but I know where my debt lies.'

Alfred looked at her. How tired he looked, she suddenly thought. How unwell. How long had it been since she had asked how he was feeling?

He deliberated for a few brief seconds before answering her earnestly.

'Florence, I don't want you to feel indebted to me, I want you to feel liberated by me – do you understand?'

She smiled back at him, a brief, shallow smile. Dear, dear, Alfred, she thought, who knew no joy beyond this vicarious loving of her. How sad, how pitifully sad he seemed. She wondered what would make him happy, truly happy. Should she write a proper book, would his name on the dedication page be enough? If she were, one day, to have a son and call him Alfred and ask him to be the boy's godfather? Perhaps. She simply didn't know.

The return visit to Dublin next Easter was one she looked forward to with great anticipation. As the time neared, she was anxious that something would yet prevent her from going, that the weather would be too fierce, that there would be strife in Ireland as occasionally threatened, that the family would change their minds. She should not have concerned herself so. With Miss Webb, the family nurse, having left to have time with her family in Donegal, the family were relying on her and were as anxious as she for her arrival.

She was met at the harbour, this time by Sir Thornley himself, who kissed her slowly on each cheek. As he did so he said, 'We've missed you my dear,' in a voice so resonant with emotion that she felt a small tremor in her own answer that was so soft and grateful in its appreciation that she hardly recognised it as hers.

They sat in silence for much of the way back to the house. It was only after they had crossed the Liffey that Sir Thornley said anything more than the normal courtesy of asking how her crossing had been.

'My dear girl,' he started, looking straight at her, 'you need to know that my wife has had several severe turns of late. At this moment she is sedated, but the result has been that she has become more unbalanced, more fitful than you will remember from your previous visit. You will witness a state of mind that manifests itself in a form of paranoia. She will be abusive. She will say and do things that could be unsettling to you. She may even want to throw things at you, but you must remember she has little self-control. She is ill, Florence.'

'I am so sorry.'

Florence looked at him, her eyes transfixed.

'Don't be. I just wanted you to be prepared.'

He laid his hand on hers in a soothing gesture, but one that exceeded the few seconds that was strictly necessary.

At the house, the atmosphere, as expected, was somewhat subdued. Part of this change in ambience she put down to the change in season. Winter had been uncompromising yet invited fires and jollity. March being more ambiguous and representing the cusp of change with its grey brooding sky would not allow for such equilibrium. There was less noise, less conversation, fewer people about.

Lady Stoker was asleep when she arrived. Sir Thorley introduced Florence to her daily routines, erratic as they were, and the medication which it would be her responsibility to administer. She was shown to her room, not the same one in which she had felt so at home three months previously, but on the same floor on which the Thornleys had their rooms. For Florence, her expectations of the fortnight ahead were dimmed a little, yet as she sat on her bed that night she smiled inwardly at the thought of being in this house and in the company of the family she so adored.

Lady Stoker was indeed much changed since Christmas and had become, as Sir Thornley had intimated, difficult and unpredictable. She did not take kindly to nurse Betty Webb's absence and, at first, was sullen and rude to Florence. Her comments more than often were coarse and scathing, particularly about her husband, at one time calling Florence another of Thornley's "parlour girls". But Florence demurred, ministered to the old lady as best she could and within a week was effective in achieving a truce of sorts. Before long the family saw she had somehow managed to ingratiate herself with the patient, that she was better able to ride the mood swings than anyone else and felt her calm and soothing nature was admirable, simply admirable.

There were few visitors. Mr Gogarty called twice, but his conversation with Sir Thornley was surgical rather than literary. Florence had several hours alone when Lady Stoker slept and endeavoured to spend these writing. At one such time, she glanced up to see Sir Thornley had entered the sitting-room where she was busy with her notebooks and was looking at her intently. She blushed, lowered her eyes to her writing, half expecting a word or comment, but when she looked up again he had gone, as noiselessly as he had come.

The following evening, her last night in Dublin before returning home,

Florence retired early to pack her suitcase. She was walking along the hallway towards the bathroom when she was accosted by Sir Thornley heading towards his study carrying the evening newspaper.

'Would you like a dram, my dear,' he asked, 'before you turn in? I can recommend it for last thing at night.'

Florence was not sure what to say. A dram? What is a dram?

'A whiskey, my dear, a whiskey, Bushmills, good Irish water to help you sleep.'

He was so full of merriment and she so confused and embarrassed by her ignorance that she felt it implicit on her to accept. He led her to the end of the hall and into his study, where he opened a mahogany cabinet and removed a bottle of whiskey and two etched glasses and poured what she imagined was a so-called dram into each. Handing her one, he sat down in his armchair and motioned that she do likewise on the smaller chair opposite.

Having had her first sip, Florence looked up and was aware he was looking at her intently.

'So how have you found my wife, Florence?'

She stumbled, the whiskey burning her throat before answering a little awkwardly, 'I am managing. She is, as you say, unwell and not of sound mind and in that light, everything is comprehensible.'

'She has not been easy,' Sir Thornley said, 'not now, not for some years.'

'I can see that.'

She watched as he slowly turned his glass in his hand before holding it up to the light to study the diffused amber.

'Nor has it been easy for me.'

Florence shifted uneasily in her chair and regretted that by sitting centrally there was not an arm on which to balance herself properly. She stared at her glass and at the liquid which had scoured her throat when she had swallowed her first mouthful rather too enthusiastically. She looked at Sir Thornley, and thought once again how distinguished he looked with his olive green eyes and arched brow, how his aquiline nose gave his face form, how regular his teeth were and his mouth, how neat and even, in fact, was the whole ensemble.

'Company. Companionship, call it what you will.' He paused. 'I brought you – invited you,' he corrected, 'back here as a companion not just for Lady Thornley, but as you possibly suspect, for me also.'

He looked up at Florence, who had averted her gaze, but would not talk again until their eyes settled on each other.

'A companion. Nothing more. For me also. I've suffered too from her affliction, perhaps even more than she has. You know, she has no idea what she does or says or how her illness affects any of us.'

Florence looked down at the floor. She did know what to say, how to respond. She wanted to excuse herself, but did not know how to.

As if sensing her unease, Thornley gave her the opportunity she desired.

'I will have another dram, my dear. You need not do so. When I ask you back to Dublin, I hope you will not feel compromised by our conversation, for all that I mean is to say how fond of you I have become. It is time to make sure my wife is in bed, for her ladyship' – on which word he placed a certain ironic stress – 'will no doubt perform again tonight with her perpetual craving for attention.'

Florence rose and moved towards the door, then paused and stopped. She turned, took two steps back towards the chair where Sir Thornley sat, recumbent and still, leaned down and kissed him on the cheek.

'Thank you.' She stood up and looked at him.

He raised his glass, smiled and extended a hand towards her. She turned away without acknowledging its presence.

'Good-night, Sir Thornley. If I can be as good a friend and companion to you in the future as you have been to me, I would be very honoured to do so.'

Florence returned to England in time for the summer term, always the most tolerable of school terms in her view for it was shorter than the others and there was time for her in the evenings after classes finished. Her return to the classroom served to remind her how necessary she felt it was to finish with that phase of her life. She had strengthened her resolve in Dublin to tell her father, and when she got back to Enfield tendered her resignation.

'You're a headstrong and foolish girl, Florence, wanting to give up the teaching,' he had said to her, but she was not to be deterred.

'You are wrong, father,' she had countered, 'wrong about that and wrong about me. Writing is the thing I care about most. It is what I am best at and it is how I want to earn my living.'

And that was that, for he knew her mind, once set, was not likely to change.

Often now, when school had finished, she would catch a bus into central London where she would meet up with Alfred. Thomas was also in London quite regularly and she had met with him several times at the reading room, and once at Hyde Park Mansions when he was staying there. On that occasion, he took great pains to tell her to bring her notebooks and to look as would befit a secretary, a request which she understood, but which hurt her nonetheless.

It was apparent to Florence that Thomas was starting to become emotionally dependent on her, at least in his imagination, which she had concluded was more active than he was capable of being. It excited her to think that she was now his muse, that at that very moment she may be providing him with the inspiration to write. She liked this sort of relationship, one that was uncompromising, unthreatening, but she knew also that there would inevitably be demands placed on her. She sensed it. She felt it, this desire of his; she read it in the margins of his letters to her. Often she did not know how to respond to his words and increasingly doubted her ability to rebut his more persistent entreaties.

And then occasionally, as she would admit to herself, she thought of Thornley, of his remarkable disclosures to her and how they stirred her and, yes, how willingly she would go back to Dublin. At such times she wished that her life could be less complicated, that someone else could manage it for her. 'Thomas, oh Thomas,' she would find herself thinking in such moments, 'if only you were not so old and had the courage to make an effort for us before it is too late, before I grow tired of waiting for you to do something.'

Later that year, she accepted an invitation to visit Max Gate. She told her family and Alfred that she was travelling down to see a dramatization of *Far from the Madding Crowd*, although she did not hide the fact that she had been invited to tea at Max Gate. Emma was absent, once again, abroad in the north of France with her niece, although, as was the pattern, there was another person standing alongside Thomas in the drive waiting to greet her.

Hermann Lea, who lived nearby, was busy researching a book about Hardy's Wessex, a project of which Hardy thoroughly approved. In recent months, so Florence gathered, he had become a regular visitor to Max Gate. Again their time together was brief; words were left hanging, nods and glances made to suffice. Florence was sure Thomas had confided to some degree in the young man about their friendship, if even just to warn Mr Lea from saying anything to Emma at a later date 'for fear it may distress her.'

The afternoon tea was remarkably similar to those she had enjoyed previously, even down to the choice of cakes, and passed off well. Mr Lea was a jolly conversationalist and his project entertained and amused them, as he pushed Hardy on several place names which the author tried to recall.

'It could have been Bulbarrow, I don't remember. Does it really matter?'

'It most certainly does, Thomas, if we are going to be accurate. If you are not sure if you had any particular hill in mind, choose one now that would be likely.' And both men laughed at the thought of constructing the ancient kingdom around a group of novels whose whole world was a fiction and setting it in the hills and heath that lay all about them.

Once again, on leaving Thomas slipped Florence a gift, clumsily wrapped in brown paper. A book. Which one this time, she thought? It was not until she was back in London and in her room that she opened it to find not one of his volumes as she had expected, but the *Rubaiyat* of Omar Khayyam, a book, as she reflected, that lovers give to each other.

Chapter 11

O MEMORY, WHERE IS NOW MY JOY?

Before leaving London again to spend her next holiday in Ireland, Florence had had an urgent message to meet with Thomas. He had travelled to London, ostensibly for a meeting with his new publishers, and was staying at his usual address in Maida Vale.

Unusually, she was irritated by the request. She thought it quite unreasonable of him to ask her to take time from her last term of teaching and felt guilty that she had feigned a sickness in order to do so. It was, she decided, his presumption that she would do so that rankled, along with deceiving her own father when she had already had considerable time off through one malady or another.

They met this time, at Thomas's request, not at Hyde Park Mansions, but at the London house of Edward Clodd whom she had not seen since they had first met two years earlier at Max Gate. Edward met her at the door, was duly solicitous over a simple lunch, and then excused himself to return to his office at the London Joint Stock Bank where he was a director. Florence was unsure as to whether this was connivance on the part of Edward and Thomas, but was dutifully polite and appreciative when he excused himself, leaving her and Thomas on their own.

Florence had felt that Thomas was agitated throughout lunch. Whatever it was that had caused him to arrange their meeting was weighing heavy on his mind and she determined to ask him directly as to its cause as soon as Edward departed.

'What's wrong, Tom?' she asked when the door closed shut. 'Why have you asked to see me so urgently when you know it has meant me having to lie to my father?'

'Why? Why lie?' he asked. 'Why did you not tell your father that you were meeting with me?'

'Because he would not condone leaving my classroom for a luncheon. Also', she added, 'because he doesn't know of you, other than that we've met once or twice. He doesn't read very much fiction, so you would have little advantage with him. He doesn't know any of this.'

'This. And what, pray, is "this" that you speak of?'

'This subterfuge. This unspoken arrangement you have with me. These expectations you have.'

He looked at her, reached forward and lightly touched her cheek.

'And what are they?'

'Tom, don't patronise me. What is so urgent?'

He paused and looked at her.

'I don't like this going to Ireland, Florence.'

'But why? Why, Thomas? It is a job, to be a companion; it is a means of livelihood.'

'I fear it could become more than that to you, Florence.'

'What do you mean?'

'It's your good nature that makes it more, that's all. You think you are always under an obligation to make people find you agreeable. It is that which makes you vulnerable to such as Thornley.'

'How dare you talk to me like this, Tom, as if I'm some naïve shop girl.'

He raised his finger to his mouth.

'Hush, Florence. It is not meant as a criticism of you. It is praise, praise for your good nature, your generosity of spirit always wanting to look after others, stray dogs like me and Thornley. But keep it for me, Florence, for me.'

There was a brief lull as she picked up her tea cup and stirred it slowly.

'And besides, you have a perfectly respectable job.'

'Yes, and you know how I detest it. What's more, I will have finished with teaching in a few weeks. After that, I will do whatever little work the newspaper can find me, but without being a companion as well, Tom, how would I live? My writing doesn't pay for me to live.'

'Then I will help you to write and be published.'

Florence fell silent, then said quietly, 'You have already helped me a good deal in this respect. You cannot help much more, I think, without wielding the pen for me.'

'But I can. If you don't want to go back to Dublin, then don't go. I will help you.'

'How? Do you propose I come and live at Max Gate as your companion? Or Emma's even? Perhaps I could look after her cats.'

'Now it is your turn to be sarcastic, Florence. Don't be so. It doesn't become you. I can help you.' He reached across the table and took her hand. 'I can help you, Florence, with your writing and in getting published, but it will be you, your talent and ideas that will earn you a living. I will merely open a few doors for you.' He paused a moment. 'And the cats are ours, not just Emma's. I am fond of them too.'

'I am sorry for saying that. But what you propose is not enough to live on.'

'Then I will employ you as my secretary,' he said; then added, as if he had somehow overreached himself, 'It would be unofficial of course, just between us.'

He paused again, hesitating, retreating further, choosing his words more carefully as he did so.

'It would be doing research, mainly. I have been invited to produce an anthology of William Barnes's poetry. Perhaps it could be in assisting with that?'

'And you would pay me?'

'Well, yes,' he answered, 'but it could not be a lot.'

'Then what? How do I make it up to what I need?'

'By your writing, given time.'

'And until then, Tom, I need to find my own way. By going to Dublin. By being a companion. Until I don't need to anymore. You are wrong in supposing I might not want to go back. Quite wrong, for the work and company is most agreeable.'

He looked uneasy, leading her to respond, 'Now what is wrong with that?'

'Dublin is not England. It is not home. The Irish …'

He stopped, and she continued for him '… are charming and hospitable.'

'You see,' he said emphatically, 'that is exactly what the Irish are. They are charming and hospitable to the point of persuasion. They can turn heads with their loose words. But they are not trustworthy.'

She stared at him. 'Tom, you cannot truly believe this.'

'Florence, I assure you, I know Dublin and the Dubliners. I went there once and stayed with the Lord Lieutenant of Ireland who confirmed what

I have told you. Mrs Henniker lived there for some years and she has told me of their disarming nature and their dalliances. I think you are making a mistake going.'

'Tom, I am going to be the companion for a sick, deranged woman. I am staying with the kindest family who treat me as one of their own. I am not open to dupery or being taken advantage of.'

Thomas shuffled awkwardly.

'And you must go, of course. I am sorry to talk so and worry you, although I do so for your sake.' He reached for her hand. 'For your sake, Florence.'

She remained motionless, her hands tightly knotted in her lap. She was sitting upright now, her limbs tense and restrained, her whole demeanour seemingly ill at ease. Her brown eyes stared impassively at Thomas and her lips were tightly drawn. Who was this man who made demands on her? Why should he threaten her happiness? Why could he not understand her as Alfred did?

As she posed herself the question, so she found herself answering it.

'Because he is Thomas Hardy. That is why,' she thought. That was what she needed to remember. Thomas Hardy. And this was just another indication of how much he adored and needed her. That was the reason. She felt happier in the answer she had provided for herself.

'Tom, I must go. Here.' She handed him a small parcel. 'For Christmas. A new collection of poems – but written by that Irish poet, Mr Yeats, I am afraid.'

He muttered an embarrassed 'thank you' as he took the book from her.

'And I have nothing for you,' he said.

'Nonsense,' she replied. He seemed all his sixty-seven years. 'You have given me the promise of security and so much help. And unless I am mistaken, you have given me a little of your heart.'

She stooped and kissed him on the cheek. He pulled himself up from the chair and she allowed him to put his arms about her and hold her perfectly still for many seconds before disentangling herself and slipping out of the doorway, leaving him stretching a plaintive hand out for her.

The boat trip from Holyhead to Dun Laoghaire was wild and stormy as a brisk north-westerly swept down the Irish Sea. A flurry of irregular white tops and a heavy swell accompanied the boat for the whole duration and

Florence sat perched on the aft deck willing the journey to be over. Because her passage had been booked this time to Dun Laoghaire, some eight miles south of Dublin, she had offered to take the train into the city, an offer she now regretted. She looked about the harbour as she struggled with her rain-splattered suitcase towards the railway station on the off-chance that her precipitous words of independence had been ignored because of the inclement weather, but she was disappointed and quietly lamented the inauspicious start she had made to her stay.

The train journey into the central station was mercifully brief, but again there was no sign of anyone waiting for her. She tried to remember what had been arranged, but could not do so, and feeling decidedly less enamoured of the whole escapade hailed a hansom cab to Ely Place.

Despite her travails, however, and her gathering doubts, the welcome at Ely House was warm and effusive. Sir Thornley had been busy operating all day which had the effect of excusing him in Florence's mind for a slight she had surely only imagined. When he came in he was as hearty as ever, kissing her warmly on the cheek and offering her a sherry to accompany his brandy.

Lady Stoker had rallied a little over recent weeks, yet even so Florence was glad that she was to be a companion rather than her nurse as previously. She had not forgotten her earlier conversation with Sir Thornley that had both shocked and enthralled her at the time, but decided that she should just get on with her job and help with the preparations for Christmas. Bram and his wife and their two children were having Christmas in Galway with her family, so it was to be rather more restrained than the previous year, but nonetheless there was a constant stream of friends and well-wishers at the door, keen to partake of Sir Thornley's malt whiskey, share his roaring fire and enjoy his good-hearted bonhomie.

Florence again found herself on the floor of the house with Sir Thornley and Lady Stoker, whose adjoining rooms were separated by a changing-room of considerable dimensions. She was spared much of the day duties in order to be about should her ladyship have need of her in the night time, a vigil Miss Webb was glad was being fulfilled by someone else.

On her third night she was indeed disturbed, and quickly made her way to Lady Stoker who was making a strange howling noise, part sob, part scream. As Florence administered a draught to the old lady as she had been shown how to do, she was aware of Sir Thornley standing in the doorway, just out of his wife's range of vision. As the effect of the draught was felt by Lady Thornley and she fell into a fitful sleep, Sir Thornley motioned to her. Picking up her lamp she followed him through the dressing-room into his own room where she suddenly started, as if the impropriety of being there had just struck her.

'I should not be in your room, Sir Thornley,' she said quietly. 'It is not right. And with her ladyship only next door.'

Thornley took both her hands and looked at her.

'Florence. Dear, dear Florence. There is nothing wrong with you being here for a few brief minutes. I am not asking anything of you other than your company.' He looked at her plaintively. 'Believe me, I would never jeopardise our friendship, Florence.' He squeezed her hands. 'But I cannot, will not, apologize for feeling as I do and wanting to spend this little time with you.'

He let her hands go and gestured slowly towards the door. 'Florence, if I have offended you by speaking too frankly, please leave and I promise I will not think any the less of you for doing so.'

When she was back in her room some short time later, Florence was aware that she was shaking, not from shame but from the lack of it. He had not offended her; indeed, she realised, was unable to do so. He wanted so little from her, and to share a few short minutes with him, given all he had to endure, was a joy to her. Thank God, she thought, to be wanted. It was not a dishonourable thing to offer comfort; indeed, her instinct told her to the contrary. Whatever else she may be, Florence knew she was eminently well-suited to the role of companion.

Christmas was a strange time as the number of visitors dried up the closer the day approached. Florence found herself thinking of her own family, though she did not let herself dwell on the distance between them.

After church they returned to the house where tea had been prepared. Lady Stoker was quite lucid and joined in the festive conversation, conducting herself without blemish for the remainder of the day.

As always, Florence handled her with a patience and gentleness that the others admired. Even her irrationality could be made sense of, thought Florence, if one was patient and observant. Although the family had been rather nonplussed when she instructed Florence to call her Emily, a freedom she had not even accorded her own nurse, they were now grateful that Florence appeared able to manage the erratic behaviour of the old woman.

Thornley (for she had dropped the "Sir" at his instruction) was as hospitable as ever. Florence had marvelled at his unflappable manner, how after a long day in surgery he would return home sometimes to uninvited guests, and slip easily into the role of munificent host, as cordial and generous in time and attentiveness as anyone could be. The fact that she knew that he had his own demons, that he was not always so light-hearted and gregarious, and that she, she was his confidante, warmed her. It was her place to help him keep these moments of loneliness and self-doubt at bay and to hide him from the world, and she was thankful for her little duty.

At the same time, she intuitively knew that what they shared in private, even in the spirit of their accord, was not immutable, that it was to have no public face. And that while Thornley was as attentive and well-meaning as ever, he was a man whose persona straddled and subsumed hers until she was no more than a shadow. Strangely, she did not mind.

Her return to England was more forgiving than it had been a year earlier. The thought of no longer having to endure the stress of standing in front of a class liberated her, and somehow gave her strength and a sense of well-being she had not previously experienced. Although she was aware of the financial gamble she had taken, she felt remarkably indifferent to the prospect. Thomas's words before Christmas had given her the impetus and the justification for seeking life as a writer.

In February, the third and final part of *The Dynasts* was published to muted acclaim, though Thomas was of no doubt as to the value of what he had written.

He had recently spoken to Florence about joining him and Emma to watch the production of scenes from *The Trumpet Major* in Dorchester Town Hall. For Florence, the thought of meeting Emma for the first time unnerved her. She wondered how Thomas had talked of her to Emma, whether she should behave like a secretary or a friend – or both. She was aware of the older woman's formidable reputation and her strong religious convictions that clashed so directly with those of her husband. She wondered if Thomas told her that she, like he, was an agnostic. Or that she dabbled in writing? What else had he told her, if anything? She feared a difficult visit. She feared being asked questions.

In the event, the visit proved anything but trying. Emma was in a very good mood and continued to be so for the whole of Florence's visit. She did not appear to mind her husband monopolising the poor girl for his work. Nor did she seem at all perturbed when Thomas walked Florence slowly around the grounds of Max Gate, though Florence did notice her at one point looking out at them from an attic window, a sight that made her flush and tremble ever so slightly. Thomas seized the few private moments they had on their walk to tell her how much it meant to him that she was there "as his" although Florence felt unable to answer him coherently, conscious of maintaining her reserve with Emma's eyes imagined set on her, suspicious and malevolent. It was not like Dublin, she thought. Nor, indeed, was Max Gate like Ely House, which was light and civilized and welcoming. The dark pines, the malignant foliage, the pastiche of dark greens and black crowded in on her, as did Thomas who was by now breathing too closely and who, she decided, was most definitely not Thornley either.

Florence was accommodated for the two nights she was there in the servants' quarters along the corridor from the three local girls that the family employed and who were like three peas in a pod, all sullen and uncommunicative. They watched her with tight, suspicious eyes.

Florence and Thomas had little time together and she could sense a mounting frustration on his part as he started to snap at the housemaids and gardener. Introducing her to Emma had been a risk and while he felt pleased with how the meeting had gone, he saw that he had begun a deception which would take some effort to sustain. It would require energy and care, she realised, as extra layers would need to be laid gently, one upon another, until some natural construct emerged that they could move easily in.

Thomas was a frequent visitor to London that summer, although he did not take up rooms at Hyde Park Mansions. This was in part due to the fact that Emma, whether through choice or persuasion, decided not to accompany him. Florence, meanwhile, did what she could to avoid the daily trip into central London by arranging to stay with her aunt so that they could meet up, which they did regularly during the weeks he was in the city. She was soon made aware that if Thomas was going to employ her, he was also going to ensure she earned her salary, petty though it was. As a result, she found less time than she had imagined for her own writing as he engaged her on his not inconsiderable correspondence and on preparing the anthology of William Barnes' poetry.

They met usually at Edward's house in Kensington where they were often left alone. Sometimes he spoke of helping her with her writing and made recommendations as to how she could edit her work to advantage and pointing her towards various periodicals and newspapers. While journalism was not what she had intended, she had several articles accepted by *The Globe* and *The Daily Mail* and felt a sense of achievement in earning money even if from writing for the popular press. Many writers had trodden the same path, she told herself, and there was no disgrace in it. Nevertheless, she was most pleased with the publication of two of her stories, 'Cousin Christine' and 'Old Time Tales', though she was disappointed afterwards to reflect on how few comments she received, how transitory they seemed and how little she was paid for what had been many hours of painstaking work.

Thomas had grilled her endlessly about her time in Ireland and received a cheerful and reassuring report. She was not returning at Christmas she told him, for she needed to be with her family, but would spend some weeks there in the autumn to assist the nurse, for Lady Stoker was beginning to prove more troublesome. But she would be in London otherwise and was happy to travel to visit Max Gate as required for the performance of her duties.

'You do sound rather formal, Miss Dugdale,' Thomas teased her. 'I want you to think of Max Gate as a home of sorts for you too.' And he would bemoan the lack of time and space they had, and though he would cradle and kiss her when she occasionally allowed him, she felt the need to keep him at arm's length in this city where he was well-known, apologising to him, 'I am sorry, Tom, but this is not the time or place for being so familiar.'

Her life had changed enormously and at times she would stop and ponder its trajectory. She had given herself over to forces outside her control. Alfred, her one constant, appeared to be working as hard as ever producing his various anthologies, as if counting down the clock. He enjoyed hearing of her meetings and urged her to 'live, my dear, live, for that way you will have lots to write about', although he showed little inclination to include himself in anything. She thought of Thornley, wise and gentle, such an esteemed and cultured man, and of Thomas, less so, and the access he had provided her to another world. Was it wise to dally so upon her future, making light of her various predicaments? And what was her future now, as everything seemed to be becoming more complicated and less transparent? In the end she resolved she would do nothing, but trust the world would sort itself out, as it had always appeared to do in the past. As was her wont, she expected life to resolve whatever riddles it set itself.

In August, Florence went to stay at Max Gate for almost a week. Thomas was busy assembling another collection of his poems and she was pressed into service, perched beside him in his study, work she found exhausting. They settled well together, she thought, and she was conscious always of Thomas's fervour, of his small intimacies, and wondered if they were meant. He would reach across her, touch her unconsciously and stand so close behind her so that she would feel his dry breath on the nape of her neck. Only once, when Emma had gone into Dorchester to do some shopping with one of the servants, did he dare to take hold of her. His frustration was so urgent, so compelling, that Florence let him press against her, watching carefully over his shoulder as he did so lest either of the two remaining servants should appear.

On the last day of her visit he whispered to her that Emma had suddenly announced she was going to Calais for several weeks with her sister and niece. She had booked a room at the Hotel Famille, where she had stayed before and intended "to write". Aware that Florence was due to leave for Dublin the following week, he pleaded with her to revise her plans, for this was an unexpected opportunity for them.

'An opportunity – for what?' she asked quizzically.

He did not appreciate the levity in her response. 'For us, Florence, dear God, for us to be together. Why do you pretend?'

She looked at him. She did not feel what he felt, she thought. That part of life was not important to her and the subterfuge simply made her weary. She would need to respond to his feelings, she knew, and to meet them in some way, but it was not desire that drove her. She worried at times that she was not capable of love although she knew she could care as much as any woman, but that would not do for Thomas or Thornley. And if it was not love, what right had she to expect anything?

'I don't pretend, Tom, it's just unfortunate timing, that's all. I have made a commitment to the Stokers and must go. Can you not understand that? They rely on me.'

'As do I, Florence, as do I.'

'I know you do, Tom. But you know me well enough to know I am not one to shirk my obligations. I cannot be expected to drop everything because of some change in plans that Emma has made. Don't you see? I need to be back before Christmas also, for I've even promised my family that.'

'Besides,' she said looking sympathetically at him, for his brow was creased and shoulders drooping, 'the time alone will do you well.'

'At my age, such sentiments are hardly reassuring,' he murmured, before kissing her on the top of her head.

So he was to be left alone. He smiled ruefully as he reflected on the irony of it, and wondered briefly if the President of the Immortals had indeed decided to make sport with him as well.

Chapter 12

THE AMANUENSIS

Florence had recently become aware how far she had grown apart from her family. She scarcely saw her sisters now, primarily because she so seldom went home. Her mother's bouts of depression had somehow unnerved her and the time to be spent together over Christmas promised to be joyless and grim. She could not help thinking how much she had enjoyed the two previous years with the Stokers, how much the family had made of Christmas, while here, in Enfield, she reflected, what a sombre, sober – and even worse – provincial lot they all were.

On Christmas Day, Florence expressed a reluctance to attend church with the rest of the family, and although she eventually relented, her attitude shocked her mother and sent her spiralling into a cloud of depression for the remainder of the day. Christmas dinner was a trial with her father's evangelising rhetoric arousing in her the urge to challenge him about the Church, about education, about woman's suffrage, about anything, until he asked her to behave like a daughter ought to behave at her parents' table.

Florence's sisters had grown up during the past three years. They looked upon her with dismay as she dismantled their festive spirit with her sharp words and patronising comments. Afterwards, she remonstrated with herself on being so selfish, so stupid as to spoil the day when she knew how good her parents had been to her, but the damage had been done.

She saw, at the same time, and not just through her own eyes, that the family was already in the act of fraying, as conversations began that only related to pockets of interest, accessible just to some, but never all, of those gathered. It was inevitable, she told herself. She thought of them all, sitting around this table, as the seed-head of a zinnia which, when all the seeds were ripe, had suddenly exploded. That was like us, she thought, the way that we are, the way that nature made us. We are ready to explode. In fact, she corrected herself – we have already started to explode. What was once as familiar as breathing was now no more. Here we are, broken into little fragments, all part of the whole, but in reality dispersing into new and separate worlds as strangers. Never again, she thought, would the parts fit snugly together, for after the diaspora there were always going to be loose bits and jagged edges and gaps where daylight had got in. And Thornley, he was part of the daylight, she thought. And Thomas. They don't belong here at all, but they are part of me. How insular we are, she pondered, how alone; the only certainties are within us; all else is guesswork.

Once, she thought, she had known everything about her sisters – their secrets, their best friends, the colour of every dress they wore, the truth behind every smile and sulk, every posture and subtle nuance. But no more. Ethel was thirty-two years old and married to Edmund, who worked in a bank and was on a separate trajectory. When they talked now Florence felt that she hardly comprehended anything about her. Her sister had no interest in books, in literature, in the sensory world, but looked forward to starting a family, to going to music hall, to making plans with Edmund that would be exclusive, not a part of the Dugdale table. And yet, as children, they were so close, like shadows.

Constance she calculated was now twenty-five and had followed her into teaching, proving as enthusiastic and capable as Florence was not. Eva was twenty-two, and like her mother before her had taken work as a private governess. She was, thought Florence, so quiet and refined, the mimic of her mother, and enjoyed playing the piano and singing in the St Andrew's Church choir. But what more? What made her sing? She confessed to herself, sadly, she had no idea.

And Margaret, Florence thought, Margaret was a child still, although at fifteen years old she knew that was no longer true, for at that same age she had already started her training. What did she know of Margaret? And she thought also, terrifyingly, what do they know of me? What would they think of me if they knew me better?

Sitting in her room with her book – she had started a regimen of reading Trollope on Hardy's advice – she thought of her childhood when the family had lived in Sydney Road, nearer to the town park where they often played, and of how life changed when they moved to Southbury Road after Eva was born. Margaret had arrived in 1893, the year before

Florence began her teacher training, and she thought to herself that she had hardly been aware of the late arrival. Perhaps if it had been a brother it would have been more newsworthy. She had shied away from looking after her while she was a baby as her sisters cooed and smothered her with affection, and now it was too late to be much more than an accomplice after the event. She knew few of her interests, none of her friends and little of her heart. So much had gone.

For the rest of Christmas, she made more of an effort. She sat with her father and talked about whether the Old Age Pensions Act that was coming into law would really break the cycle of penury and misery for the elderly. They read *The Times* together and followed Ernest Shackleton's expedition to the South Pole. She helped her mother cook, asked her sisters about their work and outlined the plot of a new story she was writing with Margaret and Eva, who were closest in age to the audience she was writing for. But she did not feel encumbered to share anything more than they already knew, as she felt they would neither understand nor condone the life that had unfolded for her.

Writing for the newspapers was exacting work and Florence was aware how much more robust and assertive she needed to be to succeed in the job, qualities she knew she lacked. At least she was working, she kept telling herself, albeit temporarily, for *The Standard*, either writing articles for children or essays of local interest. She had persuaded the editor to allow her to write one or two literary reviews, particularly of the new wave of Irish writers, which provided a little more of the stimulation she craved. But it was not really what she aspired to.

In February she was somewhat surprised to receive a note telling her that Sir Thornley was in London and enquiring if she would agree to accompany him to a dinner party at his brother's house. At first, she found it hard to visualize Thornley in London, away from his own hearth, but replied without forethought or compunction that she would be delighted to do so. Secretly she was thrilled at being taken further into his circle of family and friends and that he had wanted to see her in this different setting, not as a wardress but as someone he esteemed as worthy to accompany him.

The trip through the London streets by hansom cab, thoughtfully arranged by Thornley, was a treat in itself. Florence watched the light dust of snow silhouetted against the glow of the street lamps, and in a sudden spasm of acknowledgement thought of Alfred who had given all this to her and was never able to enjoy it. She resolved to contact him the very next morning.

Bram and Florence Stoker lived at 27 Cheyne Walk, the most desirable address in Chelsea, in an impressive white Georgian house with elaborate black railings. It was so imposing that Florence shivered at the effrontery of her even being there. As she had been on first entering Ely House in Dublin, Florence was struck by the grandeur of the hallway and the size and extravagance of the room into which she was ushered with its intricate plastered ceilings and William Morris wallpapers. Sir Thornley came out to meet her, apologised that the doorman had not immediately fetched him as requested, and led her gently by the arm into a room full of people. Taking a glass of champagne for her from a tray being passed about the room by a manservant, he guided her towards an elegant diamond-tufted settee that sat beside the enormous fireplace where Bram and Florence were in earnest conversation.

Rather than sitting down, they stood there obliquely, glasses cupped, until Bram noticed her. He started as he did so.

'Florence, my dear lady, welcome.' He was as effusive as she remembered him from two years back, as warm, as eloquent. 'How clever of my brother to have chosen such a lovely consort to grace us this evening.'

He turned to the woman he had been talking to before Florence had arrived. 'Miss Florence Dugdale,' he said by way of general introduction to the group, before steering her to face the woman, whom she instantly recognised.

'Ellen, may I introduce Miss Florence Dugdale who is Thornley's guest this evening. Florence, Miss Ellen Terry.'

Miss Terry nodded, but had clearly been caught mid-story and after the briefest acceptable interval turned back to the group she had been entertaining, resuming her conversation to the delight and amusement of her growing coterie of admirers. Florence looked for Thornley, who had remained a pace behind her, took his arm again and this time steered him to a quiet part of the room.

'Why didn't you warn me?'

'Warn you, my dear? Of what?'

'The people. All these grand people.'

He drew her to one side and whispered conspiratorially, 'If you are thinking of Ellen, she is hardly grand. Her life is pure burlesque. She was married at sixteen, onto her second husband before she had dispatched the first, took a third, and had more lovers than was decent, even in the world of theatre.' He chuckled at the picture he had so spontaneously drawn of her.

'Then why is she here?'

'Why? Because she is Ellen Terry. Because she was Henry's lover and now that Henry's gone, Bram makes sure he includes her in their social life. Although,' he added with a smile, 'she's turned more than one dinner party on its head.'

Before she could ask further questions about who else had been invited, a loud gong sounded and was accompanied by the announcement that dinner was about to be served, precipitating a move towards two glass doors which opened, leading to a wood-lined dining-room, dominated by a long bog oak table set with twenty-four places.

Moving towards the table and finding her place name, Florence was pleased to note that Thornley was seated opposite her although, as she reflected, she would not be able to engage him without those on either side of her being included in their conversation.

At the table she was introduced by Thornley to his nephew Noel, the son of Bram and Florence Stoker, who was sitting beside him. Noel's fiancée Nellie had been placed some distance down the table, much to the young man's annoyance, although he greeted Florence cordially and quickly warmed to her presence. On her right, she was introduced to Hall Caine, whose name she immediately recognised from a play that had been in London the previous year, based on a novel he had written. Of the full extent of his writing Florence started the meal wholly ignorant, but by the end he had ensured that she was much better informed.

The meal was sumptuous and often Florence would look across at Thornley, who would smile at her while making conversation to all around him. The proceedings were interrupted only once, before the dessert, when Bram stood up and proposed a toast to Henry Irving, who had died four years ago that very day.

'To the memory of our greatest actor,' he said looking down the table and waving his glass several times like a band leader's baton, demurring at the same time to Ellen who sat beside him, 'and, of course, to our special guest – Henry's special guest – our greatest ever actress.'

Florence could not help but notice that Florence Stoker appeared unmoved by the gesture, as if the whole ceremony embarrassed her. More evident, though, was the reaction of Noel Stoker, who neither got out of his seat nor raised his glass in the actor's memory.

Leaning across the table, he hissed at Florence, 'Did you know, that was – is – my first name, Irving. Irving Stoker. That is what father called me.'

'Why do you not use it?' Florence asked, sensing even as the words spilled out the inappropriateness of her question.

'Because my father gave his life to that man. It was Henry Irving this and Henry Irving that and not a thought for mother and me. He was a tyrant.'

'But, Mr Stoker, your father is charming.'

'Correction, Miss Dugdale. My father appears charming. And that is as it may be. But he is weak and obsequious and this is the result.'

Looking up, Florence noticed Thornley looking at her and she coloured. He gave her a discreet shake of his head to say "Leave him be, Florence" – a course of action she had already decided on of her own volition.

The rest of the evening passed off without any other discomfort. She had noticed everything: the antique rugs, from Kashmir she guessed, the wrought iron lamps, the ornate sideboards with their inlays of white wood and ivory, the Rochester brass chandeliers. And it was all perfect, simply perfect.

At the conclusion of dinner, the guests stood and mingled while awaiting the arrival of carriages. Thornley had offered to accompany her to her aunt's where she was staying, but Florence had declined, although in doing so she had agreed to see him two days later.

'Such a grand evening,' was all she could think to say in parting. 'And such interesting people.'

'And did you meet Sir Arthur Conan-Doyle?' Thornley asked.

'Is he here? He cannot be,' she replied, before seeing the man himself standing beside the fireplace lighting up his pipe.

'Thornley, I do wish I'd been introduced to him,' she said as they headed towards the door. 'You were unkind not to do so.'

'There will be another time. He's like family. Always here.'

Having thanked her host and hostess, Florence was taken to the hansom cab that was waiting for her. Her journey back across London passed in a trance as she tried to make sense of the world she had just exited.

As she had told herself she must do, the next day she called on Alfred at the office of the *Enfield Gazette*, only to be told he had not been at work for some weeks, but that she could try his lodgings if she cared.

Florence was perturbed to hear the news and walked the half-mile to where Alfred lived with a growing sense of unease. She knocked on the door and was surprised when Alfred opened it dressed as if for work.

'Florence. What brings you here?' He was cordial but not warmly so, as if the surprise of her visit had disarmed him.

'I've come to see how you are. Will you invite me in?'

He collected himself before replying with mock nonchalance.

'You, a single lady, coming into a bachelor's home?' He smiled a weak smile. 'Rather, an invalid's home. They'll' – and he pointed down the road – 'those that see you will probably take you for another nurse although you are far too pretty for that.'

'Alfred, what's wrong with you?'

'Wrong? My tuberculosis is being troublesome again.'

'Tuberculosis?'

'Yes. Surely you knew what was wrong with me?'

'How could I have known?' she asked.

'Because I have had it for years. Could you not guess?' He paused. 'I am surprised I never told you.'

'Well you didn't.'

'Then I must have had a reason. I must have thought, "Alfred, tell Florence and she'll be gone." It is why I have made it my duty to do what I could for you, although I suspected you must have forgotten me with your new life.'

'Alfred! That is not so.'

She tried to sound indignant, but could hear that her rebuttal lacked conviction.

'I am indebted to you. You have given me every opportunity that has fallen to me. You have been my best, my only dear true friend.'

She looked at him as he leant against the wall, his concavity more pronounced than ever, his skin red and lined, his eyes bloodshot.

'Hush, my dear. I know. Tomorrow I am going to Wales. I have been haemorrhaging – just a little – but I am advised to go to the Brecons to a spa to rest the lungs.'

She stared at him. 'Alfred, you will be alright, won't you? I mean, you will get better?' She stopped herself, then said, 'Tell me, is there anything I can do for you?'

'Florence, there was only ever one thing I asked of you. To make the most of yourself; to write; to be happy and fulfilled. It is what I want most for you.'

He started coughing, gently at first, but was soon doubled up in paroxysms so violent that his whole body shook. She stepped forward to put an arm around him, but he waved her away.

'No, Florence. Leave me be now. You shouldn't be about me like this. Please go.'

With the imperative ringing in her ears and with tears welling in her eyes, she quietly let herself out and, haunted by the visitation, slowly walked the short distance to her home.

She had had several letters from Thomas of late, and could not help but reflect on a correspondence that had started as 'Dear Miss Dugdale' two years previously and was now 'Dearest Florence'. She thought of how she had been neglecting him also and knew how angry he had been when she wrote in glowing terms of her dinner party at the Stokers'. What she did not, would not, tell him about was her meeting with Thornley two days after the party and twice further in the week he was in London. Thornley, she knew, was discreet, as she was too, and Thomas, Thomas was in Dorset. She refused to allow herself to feel guilty that she was being in any way disloyal to Thomas by spending such little time befriending a man whose needs and feelings were understandably not extinguished simply because his wife was a lunatic.

Thomas's response was to say that he was coming to London and would be doing so throughout the summer, without Emma, who had told him categorically that she preferred to stay put in Dorchester. Because of this, he urged Florence to take lodgings in London that he would pay for, as he needed to see her, often.

They met first at Edward's. 'Edward must know everything,' Florence thought. 'I can be Thomas's secretary in some company, but he knows how deep we are, even if Thomas has not told him so.'

When she called, Edward was, once again, out and Thomas wasted little time pleading with her to help them find somewhere private, for he could not risk being seen regularly about the city in her company "for her sake".

He was more demanding, more amorous than she had known him and when he clumsily tried to embrace her, she had demurred and gently pushed him away. Exasperated, he sat down in his chair and looked ruefully across the room. She saw he had been hurt by her response to him.

'I am sorry, Tom. I just wanted you to give pause and not always rush things so.' Whereupon she knelt down beside him, and rested her head upon his knees while he stroked her hair.

Thomas was staying at the West Central Hotel in Southampton Row for several weeks and Florence saw him most days. She had borrowed a flat near Baker Street which is where he preferred to come, although they often met together in the reading room at the British Museum.

In early July, he asked if she would accompany him to a new dramatization of *Tess of the d'Urbervilles*, an invitation he then rescinded only a few days later. Emma, it transpired, had decided to make the trip to London and it would be impolitic for them all to go together.

'Do you let that woman determine everything you do?' she demanded.

'You must be sensible, my dear.' He was clearly upset by her reaction which even she knew to be unreasonable. 'I have arranged for Edward to take you.' He held her hand as he said this, a habit she had noticed he adopted when engaging in earnest conversation.

'And we will meet with you there? Surely if I am with Edward there would be no harm in that? Emma would expect it now we are acquainted.'

'I would rather not.' His face hardened a little. 'It would serve no purpose other than to assuage your pride. She is my wife.'

With his stinging rejoinder Florence desisted, before changing tack.

'And what am I to you then, Thomas? A keepsake? A companion? A handmaid? Perhaps I should tell her myself what you ask of me.'

He looked at her pleadingly and she suddenly felt sorry for him. Pity, she thought to herself, pity – that's what I feel: pity for this poor old man, pity for his mad wife and pity for me.

He stood completely motionless, his grey eyes beseeching her. 'You are my dear friend, Florence. You are my love.' He said it so sweetly, so sincerely, in such a pleading voice that she softened and allowed him to come to her.

They met several more times while Thomas was in London although he seemed little inclined to write, spending most of his time preparing a new anthology of his poetry. By contrast, Florence had been writing a good deal, but apart from a few bland articles had not managed to get anything published. Thornley had bought her a typewriter, a gesture at which Thomas bristled when she told him, though when he did so she was curt in her reply: 'You could have bought me one, Tom. You are meant to be my mentor, after all. What point is there being your protégé if you do nothing to encourage me?'

And standing up, she turned on him again, leaving him with one final reprimand: 'It was sweet of Thornley to buy me one and churlish and mean-spirited of you to think otherwise.'

The production of the operatic *Tess* passed without either couple seeing the other. Florence resented leaving the performance as the final curtain fell, but felt it wrong to show her anger to Edward, especially since earlier that evening he had extended an invitation to her to join him and Thomas and several other friends at his house at Aldeburgh. It would be for a week in August, he had told her, when the weather was always its most settled. There would be several people staying and Hermann Lea had agreed to accompany her so she would not have to travel alone.

Florence was surprised that the invitation had come from Edward and not Thomas himself, but as he explained to her later, it was a question of propriety.

And Emma, she had asked, would Emma be there? Or would she know that *she* would be there?

Thomas was measured in his reply.

'I have no intention either of telling her or hiding the fact. You know full well she has never been to Aldeburgh and does not approve of Edward.' He stood up. 'You will be there as my secretary. I will be working. London is no place to be, let alone to work, in the middle of August.'

He paused before looking towards her again.

'And it will do you well to have some sea air which is a great restorative.'

'And you want me to come?' she asked again, wanting to hear him proffer the invitation given in his stead.

'Very much,' he answered. 'Very much indeed.'

The week at Strafford House turned out to be the happiest time that Florence had spent with Thomas. Several of Edward's friends and family were staying, including his daughter Edith Graham, and William Archer whom she knew of in London as the drama critic for *The Times*. Others called in at odd times and the whole household appeared to Florence to be somewhat bohemian and shambolic. The servants, notwithstanding the lack of routine, seemed well used to meals being asked for at different times of the day and all the comings and goings.

On the second day they were there, Herbert Wells arrived with his pregnant lover, Amber Reeves. There had been considerable public speculation about the author's new relationship and Wells was keen to lie low until the furore passed. Their presence caused a certain consternation in the household and, allied with the fear that the press could soon find them, they departed after a few days to Le Touquet-Paris-Plage where they would spend the next few months. All of this was to the chagrin of Thomas who was concerned lest the newspapers found out he was there also and in Florence's company. The great joy of Aldeburgh, as he told Florence, was its anonymity. It was somewhere he could be himself and Wells had no right jeopardising that because of his careless meanderings.

Hermann Lea who had come ostensibly as her companion for the journey to Aldeburgh only stayed for two days, but his departure appeared to have been already arranged and while there were other people staying at the house, Florence was not inclined to seek out a woman companion. As a result and for almost the first time she could remember, she and Thomas had some considerable time alone. It appeared to be an unwritten rule of the house that what happened in Aldeburgh stayed in Aldeburgh, and with that in mind Thomas appeared keen that they spend as much time together as possible.

Over the next few days he and Florence explored the town, walking the length of the shingle beach to Fort Green Mill at the southern end of the parade. With his interest in the Napoleonic era, Thomas was keen to walk to Martello Tower, a coastal defence built during the war with France. They set out mid-morning and on reaching their destination he spent a happy hour looking over the fortification until he was satisfied he had absorbed all he required of it.

On the way back they stopped and sat together on the pebbled beach, he in his tie and jacket, she with her straw hat clasped in her hand, and talked for the very first time of what the future could hold for them. As usual it ended with Thomas declaiming, 'I will not let things stand in our way, Florence, I will not. I will find a way that we can be together' – to which Florence, weary and angry by now, replied, 'But how, Tom? You never say how.'

Then they made their way back to the house, their private moment over without any resolution.

Edward was, as ever, the gracious host. He and Thomas spent a little time after breakfast each day talking about old acquaintances and the morning paper, where the recent flight of Louis Bleriot had led to a series of leading articles.

'It will change our lives, mark you,' said Clodd, reading the full account that had appeared in *The Times*. 'Mind you, maybe not in our lifetimes. Flying across the Channel may not seem much, but it is prophetic. Wells may be right after all, damn him.'

And he chuckled out loud.

Quite often, however, the talk turned in on Hardy, Max Gate and Emma.

'She's become simply unreasonable, Edward,' Thomas started. 'She now believes she is a gifted writer and asks why I should presume to have the monopoly on having such a talent in our marriage. She has become insufferably pious and sees herself as the pillar of the local church, especially since the uproar over *Jude*.'

He looked into his cup of tea, around which he had wrapped both his hands.

'In the house, she has taken to hiding herself away in her room and just scribbles in her notebooks, so the servants tell me. I fear she is growing more irrational. Nor is she discreet and doesn't care how rude people think her.'

'Have you ever thought of leaving her?' asked Edward.

Thomas's grip on his cup tightened.

'Never. I could never countenance that.'

'What if she is ill, Tom? She sounds quite strange from your account. I remember you saying there was a strain of mental weakness in the Gifford bloodline.'

'Perhaps. And yet …'

He stopped and looked up. He was guarded and suspicious by nature, yet instinctively he trusted Edward. He could not confide in any other person in quite the same way, but he wanted to draw their talk to a close. Enough had been said at this moment. Looking across at Edward, he appreciated how accommodating he had been with him and Florence and resolved to send his old friend a crate of wine on his return to London.

Edward, however, was enjoying himself and was disinclined to stop the gentle teasing.

'I wonder what Emma thinks of Florence?'

'Should she think anything?'

Edward looked at Thomas, a smirk drawing upon his face.

'Perhaps. Perhaps the first question should be whether Emma knows the young lady is here in your company and, if so, what she thinks the old man is up to, taking his attractive young secretary away with him.'

Seeing Thomas squirm, he laughed out loud. 'Don't worry, man. Of course she would not care a tinker's, for she thinks that no one else would put up with one such as you.' He paused and lowered his voice. 'And because she thinks that, any fault is not yours, but hers.'

Again he chuckled at his friend's apparent discomfort, drawing a forced smile from Thomas.

'It is not a subject to jest about, Edward,' he answered. 'And whatever Emma might think, she would be wrong, for even I don't know the answer you are digging for.'

The two men looked at each other, complicit in their understanding. The wind rattled the windows.

Where was she now? On the beach? In the library? Resting up in her bedroom?

He leant forward and said softly across the table, 'When asked I say she is my amanuensis. And so she is.'

'Then you sell her short,' exclaimed Edward. 'If you were describing her to one of your coterie of admirers, you might get away with such an anodyne label, but not to me, Tom. You're no old fool and I know you. All I can say is that you are a lucky man having her ready to look after you like a devoted daughter.'

Thomas chuckled.

'I think you underestimate the both of us. I would not get from a daughter the comfort I seek from her.'

He half closed his eyes and smiled across at his bemused host.

'And to think I never believed half of what they say of you. You undo me, Tom, you really do.'

And both men laughed in a way that, had Florence heard them, would have made her pause and wonder at what two old men could find so funny.

Chapter 13

THE MAX GATE MÉNAGE

Dear Florence, he thought. She had been so quiet and retiring when they first met; now she seemed a changed person, earnest still, but more confident in the company of others and altogether more prepossessing. This he attributed solely to his own influence, for it was he who had drawn her out and encouraged her to write, albeit a little hesitantly, while providing her with the company and milieu in which to do so. What's more, his friends were approving of her, that much was evident, and this added to his own vicarious pleasure. She was charming, discreet and beguilingly sanguine and he knew that, if he was to hold on to her, it was incumbent on him to find a way to inveigle her into his household.

The time they had spent together at Stafford House had, in Thomas's eyes, been very successful. Florence had appeared happy to be seen in his company, and maybe, he thought, was not finding him as old and peculiar as he sometimes feared he must appear to her. Nor had their interest one in the other gone unnoticed. Edward had written to one of their mutual friends that 'Hardy and the lady are enjoying themselves' and so they were. They had ventured, at last he thought, a little beneath the surface of their daily lives and with few demands placed upon them other than the daily ritual of dinner, they could spend their days and evenings as they saw fit without fear of anything too much being made of it.

Despite the calm, Thomas was anxious to discuss their future in relation to that of Emma: a subject he knew was certain to make Florence uncomfortable. He had been frank with her about the state of his marriage, she would agree, but he was intransigent still, unwilling or unable to change anything.

'But I need you near me,' he kept saying to her, to which she would answer by asking, 'Then tell me how, Tom, tell me how you expect to manage this thing you want?'

He would sigh, look away and say nothing.

Florence had given in to most of his demands of her, but not wholly so. She could not, for instance, countenance his insistence that she lease a flat in London, especially as she now had the Lyceum Club to stay at when in London. She had even made her own plans to take a place in Baker Street, but felt no inclination to tell him. If Thomas wants a private place in London, she thought to herself, then let him arrange it. Nor would she give up her position in Dublin, though she was well aware how much it upset him.

The week in August had, nonetheless, been a turning point in their relationship. The place had given them what they wanted – time and a degree of solitude. When they returned to Aldeburgh for another week in late October, they found it easier to fall again into the same somniferous rhythm, although this time it was, as she reflected, a little like the weather, less settled and without the sun's ardour. She put this down in part to the company staying in the house which included Ford Maddox Ford and Gilbert Murray, who were not prone to sobriety or reserve and were apt to turn mealtimes into conversational romps from which nothing and no one was spared.

The fortnight following their return, and in the company of Thomas's brother Henry, they set out for a tour of the northern cathedrals of York, Durham and Edinburgh. Florence was happy to be with Thomas and in his keep, yet all the time she was aware that her own life was being put on hold. Such times, however enjoyable, were compromised and did not represent the role she wanted to play in his life.

As usual, her imminent return to Dublin troubled him.

'Why do you feel so beholden to these people?' he asked, to which she replied as she invariably had, 'Because it is a job, Tom. It is all very well for me to follow you about, but you do not pay me to do so. Do you see me publishing enough to feed myself otherwise?'

Having escaped the tedium of Thomas's incessant badgering, Florence found her time in Dublin over the Christmas of 1909 more fraught than usual. Lady Stoker's condition had deteriorated and, unlike on her previous visits when she felt she had the measure of the old lady, this time there was a distance between them. At times Lady Stoker would flay her with her sharp tongue and sounded, thought Florence, the embodiment of evil, so malevolent, so spiteful was she towards her. At other times Florence wondered if she knew or sensed what had passed, what still might pass, between herself and Sir Thornley.

Christmas was a muted affair. Lady Stoker's condition dulled the atmosphere in the house and the conversation, consequently, was hushed and respectful. The weeks after Christmas were even more fraught as her mental health continued to deteriorate, and two days before Florence was due to leave Ely House the decision was taken for her ladyship to be committed to an asylum.

Her illness had also affected Thornley whose own health had begun to suffer, much to Florence's consternation. Over the New Year he had made the decision to retire from his surgical post and other positions he held including that dearest to him, his directorship of the National Gallery. It was, Florence thought, a gloomy old time.

Lady Stoker's deterioration, Florence was aware, would also have implications for her own future as it was probable that she would no longer be required when Lady Stoker was confined. Consequently, she feared the possibility of losing the regular contact she had with Thornley, more than she had thought likely. She was his companion by default only, but she had grown inordinately fond of him and knew that he too cared for her in some small way, as he had frequently shown her.

Before she left Dublin, Thornley tried to offer Florence some words of gratitude for looking after his wife so compassionately. It was evident as he did so that she was becoming upset and so he offered words of consolation.

'Don't be sad for her, Florence. Whatever happens now will be for the best,' he said before he realized with a start that it was not his wife for whom Florence was sad, but herself.

The shock was momentary.

'Your leaving now does not mean the end of you and me, Florence,' he whispered. 'It will not.'

He extended his arms towards her and cradled her head in his hands, an action she found reassuring.

'And I will be in London sometimes.'

He reached into his pocket and carefully took out an antique ring that he clearly intended to give to her as a parting gift. He passed it to her slowly and deliberately.

'Here,' he said. 'This belonged to my mother. Wear it sometimes, won't you?' He kissed her then, not as a companion, but affectionately, in a way she had not known before but had often imagined him doing.

Florence returned to England in early February 1910 to darkening clouds. In her absence, she had received an invitation to join Thomas to travel to Swinburne's grave at Bonchurch on the Isle of Wight on their own, a suggestion which she quickly agreed to although the day was long and tiring. Hardy was much moved by Swinburne, despite the hypocrisy of his lying beneath a cross, at which sight he commented sardonically, 'He'll not sleep well under that.'

Not long after, she and Thomas travelled further east, to Chichester, to look at the cathedral's architecture, again in the company of his brother Henry. It proved to be a novel experience for Florence, travelling with the two brothers and sharing their conversation. Henry she liked very much, finding his earthy humour and West Country dialect at odds with Thomas and yet she thought both men similar in their mannerisms and in their old-fashioned courtesies towards her. But once again she felt the same frustrations, the same irritations as before, that because of Thomas's sense of propriety they could go nowhere without his asking someone from the family to accompany them.

When Tom was busy looking at the carvings in the nave and chancel, Henry and Florence sat on a wooden bench in the close, waiting patiently for him to finish making his notes and talking quietly to each other. Henry's banter as always was nonchalant yet gently probing. Invariably he returned to the subject which fascinated him – why Florence, who he felt was so young and attractive, was drawn to his brother.

'Why do you spend so much time with Tom?' he asked. 'He's old enough to be your father.'

Florence smiled at him.

'That may be Henry, but he's good company,' she answered. 'Young men are all show and spittle and little else while Tom is wise. And amusing,' she added after a pause.

But Henry was not satisfied and pressed her further.

'You're a fine-looking woman, Florence, too fine to spend so much time at that gloomy house with a mad woman. And Tom cannot be easy. When he's writing, I know he's the devil's own company.'

But she would defend her position, and that of Tom, resolutely.

'He might be a trifle curmudgeonly at times,' she acknowledged, 'but he's a good man, Henry.' She rested a hand on his forearm. 'I'm not there against my will, you know. I like him too.'

Henry shook his head in disbelief, and patted her hand, smiling quizzically at her as he did so.

Soon after, they were back at Aldeburgh, again in Henry's company. Florence was growing used to the lifestyle of a writer's consort and her gradual acceptance by the Hardys. The few days they managed together at Edward's meant a good deal to her, though occasionally she wondered where it would all end, this artifice. Regardless, she had resolved to enjoy the time she had and began to feel at ease with Edward's hospitality. She even started to look forward to each new set of his friends descending upon the house, who would see she was more than Thomas's secretary and treat her accordingly. It was a strange world she had come to inhabit and she knew she had been fortunate in finding it; yet there were times when she would feel intensely sad and pensive recalling the kindness and decency of Alfred and the well-meaning devotion of her parents, all tucked safely away in Enfield.

Before long, Florence was meeting with Thomas in London on a regular basis. Thomas had, however, decided that their luck would not hold out for ever. He was mindful that his name had appeared in the local paper once before, on their first visit to Strafford House when they were caught on the mudflats. On their most recent visit, he had been disconcerted when one of the maids at Aldeburgh brazenly presented him with a hairclip she said she had found upon his bed, as if such a thing was part of the normal goings-on in the household. And while he was indignant at the very suggestion and scolded her roundly, he knew that he would need to take more care in future.

As a consequence, he thought it would be helpful if Florence became better acquainted with Emma before anything precipitous happened which might render such a benign acquaintance impossible. Once they had established a relationship of sorts, he reasoned, he could mention her name openly and invite her to visit without feeling the need to find reasons for doing so for she would belong to them both. It would not be easy blending the two. They were so different, yet he was determined that Florence should try to ingratiate herself with his wife, earn her trust, even become a confidante if that's what it took. He knew it was asking a lot of her, to maintain such a ruse, but she had already instigated that on her own, he thought, not acknowledging that it was he who had planted the seed and first grown the deception.

The initial step in bringing the two women closer together was an invitation that Thomas engineered for Florence to attend a lecture that Emma was to give at a literary meeting at the Lyceum in early May. After being postponed for a fortnight due to the death of Edward VII and the royal funeral which transfixed all of London, it seemed, the lecture was more successful than Thomas could have hoped. Florence not only agreed to attend, but was subsequently effusive in her praise of Emma's talk. Emma, in turn, was delighted by Florence's flattering words and her apparent interest in the subject, and as on their previous meeting both women fell into an easy conversation, somewhat to Thomas's bewilderment. Soon after, it was Emma who extended an invitation to her to visit Max Gate in the summer. Florence smiled to herself, wondering what Thomas made of it all and strangely stirred by the indelicacy of the situation that was unfolding.

Thomas continued to assist Florence with her writing and spent considerable time proofreading an article she had penned on W. B. Yeats based on the poet's interest in mysticism, tinkering with both her style and content. A little reluctantly, he had done his best to promote her journalistic ability with one or two editors he knew, but was aware that what was needed was to provide them with copy they would want to print. It did not seem unreasonable, therefore, when his own seventieth birthday loomed in early June, that he suggested to Florence that she might write a piece on himself for the national press.

'I am sure they will be looking to run something,' he stated, without any hint of modesty.

'But what should I write? I know very little of your life apart from the last few years and what is already known. You have told me barely anything at all about before we met and the things that I have learnt since about you, Tom Hardy, I don't think are proper to print.'

Somewhat abashed by what she had said, she smiled at him and he responded with a quiet chuckle of his own.

'Then I will prepare it for you,' he answered.

While appreciative of his offer, the gesture unsettled her. She didn't want his help in this way. She just wanted him to support *her* writing, not offer to draft stories and articles for her. After all, if he didn't feel she could write well enough, he should tell her so. What's more, and this she had not told him, her interest in journalism was waning and it was no longer what she most sought to do. She wanted to write books, she kept telling him, and she wondered, not for the first time, whether the encouragement he had shown in her writing previously had dissipated somewhat, whether he had started to see her as less capable than he had once believed she was.

In late April, he wrote to her to say he had taken a flat in Bloomfield Terrace in Maida Vale for the next three months, announcing that, contrary to what he had thought previously, at least for the initial period, Emma would be accompanying him. The letter both surprised and perplexed her as did the fact that he did not explain his change in circumstance, though she wondered whether her own meeting with Emma was not behind it.

Her fears were allayed the following day when an invitation arrived for her to attend an afternoon gathering at Maida Vale hosted by Mrs Hardy. She had heard tell of Emma's afternoon gatherings from Thomas, who invariably dismissed them as a babble of women with literary pretensions, trying to talk themselves a book, a label she thought quietly he would no doubt apply to her also. She was curious, and mindful to be sympathetic too, in the light of his misogyny.

When Florence arrived at No. 4 Bloomfield Terrace, she was greeted at the door by one of the servants from Max Gate, dressed in her customary navy blue frock with its starched white collar, whose Dorset accent seemed strangely at odds in its London setting.

Entering the sitting room she was intrigued to see a number of other women there, mostly writers, a few of whom she had heard of. Emma took her by the arm and introduced her to Lady Grove and May Sinclair, both regular attendees, and within a short time she had been passed around all the assembled company like a new lapdog. At this point, the women were all asked to find a chair and, once seated, Emma began to speak to her audience about the new book of poetry that she was planning to have published 'at some time in the future': an announcement that met with murmurs of approval, even tacit admiration. This was followed by a discussion about two young writers who had published nothing more than the occasional short story, but of whom much was expected. Florence noted the names of Virginia Woolf and Katherine Mansfield and wondered whether she could persuade her editor to allow her to interview either of the young ladies for the literary section that appeared on Fridays and often seemed, as she saw it, bereft of anything remotely female or modern.

The afternoon concluded with a Dorset cream tea that was accompanied by general conversation of a decidedly more informal nature, and not, as Florence noted, much about literature at all.

Before leaving, she went over to Emma and offered to help read her new poems 'as a friend, not as a journalist' – an offer that clearly flattered the older woman, who asked again if she would not come and visit her at Max Gate soon.

Before she had the chance to do so, there was another event that pushed her forward into a more public role with Thomas. The announcement of the first birthday honours list of the new king, George V, included the name of Thomas Hardy as a recipient of the Order of Merit. Florence was a little surprised at the announcement, knowing as she did that he had previously turned down a knighthood, much to the chagrin of Emma. When he came next to her flat (for she had relented to his pleading and allowed him to do so very occasionally), she could see that he was, in fact, delighted by the award and had already made plans to travel to the investiture in mid-July. And once again, fate conspired to take a hand in the proceedings, "in true Hardyian fashion" as Thomas thought, for not only could Emma not (or would not) attend the investiture ceremony, but she had suggested Florence do so in her stead, as his secretary and protégé. And as Florence accompanied Thomas, so delighted was he by her unexpected presence that she wondered what it meant, whether their being together like this in the public eye was a precursor for the future. Any further she would not go. It was too much for her to imagine what this future might be. She knew that her life, her opportunity to be somebody more than she would otherwise be, was dependent upon her being patient, learning to serve and to be companionable in all its fine nuances, if that was what was to be required of her. This was to be her way of retaining her life with Tom, she reasoned, giving him what Emma could or would not. And then, just as she was feeling settled and comfortable in her persuasion, Thornley or Alfred would enter her head and she would lapse into confusion.

Florence's visit to Max Gate was conducted on a quite different footing from previous visits. This time she was there as Emma's guest and while the servants were no doubt a little nonplussed, they were also, Florence noted, more attentive and respectful. Thomas, meanwhile, fussed about them for a period of time as they talked harmlessly about very little of moment, before retreating to his own study, clearly frustrated by his irrelevance.

Emma, it transpired, was busy preparing the small collection of prose and poems for some future publication and was keen to involve her new friend who had so generously offered her services. Florence took the poems in turn and read them carefully, offering some careful thoughts on each. One in particular, 'Acceptors or Non-Acceptors', she felt a fine piece of writing and Emma was delighted when she told her so, though not completely convinced by the sincerity of the younger woman's endorsement, so ringing was it.

Thomas, meanwhile, could not fathom what was happening as the two women conspired to largely ignore him, and when the opportunity presented itself accused Florence of being manipulative.

'You cannot think Emma to be a good writer,' he said to her while walking about the garden, a situation he had taken some pains to engineer.

'She is competent enough, Tom,' Florence answered thoughtfully. 'I don't care much for her subject matter, but she is proficient.'

To which Thomas, unable to judge the humour of her answer, responded with an exasperated wave of his hand, dismissing any such thought in an angry gesture.

Florence remained at Max Gate for the remainder of September. Thomas continued to appear both pleased and irritated in turn by her wooing of Emma as he saw it and bemoaned how much time the old lady took up. Instead of assisting him, as he thought she would naturally do, Florence, now she had some freedom in the matter, chose to spend most of her time writing for herself and assisting Emma. She had gone as far as to type out Emma's story 'The Maid on the Shore' and had even written to publishers on her behalf.

They had little time alone together, though it appeared to Thomas that Florence was disinclined to mind overmuch. At one stage he did manage to persuade her to walk with him into the nearby woodland where they ended up arguing about Emma and returning to the house separately, though discreetly so to ensure there was no talk from the servants.

135

Otherwise, they remained house-bound, largely through Florence's own disinclination to wish it otherwise.

He was more successful in late September, however, in persuading her to accompany him to Maiden Castle, the prehistoric earth fort to the south of Dorchester. He was desperate to talk to her alone, to try and dismantle the seeming alliance, the tangle that was developing between Florence and Emma, almost, he felt, to his exclusion.

'Is it how it appears,' he asked her, 'that you like Emma?'

'Does it appear that way? If so, then perhaps I do. For sure, Tom, I don't *dislike* her. The truth is I would never bother to think about it that much,' she replied. 'Emma is complicated and earnest and doesn't always speak well of you, but she is not without her redeeming qualities.'

He was clearly uncomfortable with her answer.

'You know it complicates matters unnecessarily. It doesn't help being so close to the woman.'

Florence turned, her face angry and her words sharp and pointed.

'Then what do you suggest I do? She likes that I am here. I feel more like a companion to her than a secretary to you. I feel I'm of use to her and that's what matters. It is a role I do well, I think. The arrangement suits both of us. And I am here, at your beck and call, which is what you wanted of me. Is that not enough for you?'

'Of course.' He looked back from the top of the mound in the direction of Dorchester. 'It is just that it could make it more difficult.'

'And how can it be more difficult, Thomas? You bring me here, make demands of me and offer not one idea or resolution for my future, nor any comfort or security. What am I to think?'

'That I love you.'

'Love? Love? What does "love" mean to Thomas Hardy? The love that did for Tess?' She looked at him, her eyes bulbous and demanding. 'Your love, if that's what you call it, is a flighty thing. It is just a word to you, Thomas, just a word.'

She paused, drew herself in and lowered her head, breathing deeply. Several seconds more passed in complete silence, broken only by the sound of a crow passing overhead. Her face when she lifted her head again was more gentle, more understanding. She held out a hand.

'I am sorry, Tom. I know you do. It is just difficult.'

They continued on, not speaking, across the grass expanse that marked the top of the castle, alone apart from a number of grazing sheep. Reaching the northern ramparts again, they had started on down a path that cut through the concentric mounds of earth when he took hold of her hand and urged her to stop.

'I know it's a strain. For both of us. But be patient, Florence. We'll have some time together next week at Aldeburgh and I'll try to find a way to make you feel more secure.' He leant over and kissed her slowly on the cheek, his blue eyes rheumy and damp with an old man's emotion.

The next day Florence found on her pillow a small posy and a card attached with the date and the words "Maiden Castle" upon it, and resolved to be more attentive to Thomas also, for she knew she was fond of him and that, despite the uncertainties, they served each other well.

That very weekend there was another visitor to Max Gate. William Strang had written some months before to ask if he could paint the great author's portrait, something to which Hardy had readily acceded. Strang was accommodated at the house while he had sittings with Thomas, during which time he was persuaded by Thomas also to undertake a sketch of Florence. About his own portrait, Thomas was indifferent. But about the sketch of Florence, he was ecstatic, and while exclaiming that it was so much more than he had asked (or hoped) for, he was delighted that it represented her in all her beauty. The artist had captured her large, intense eyes, her face so perfectly cast looking out in that serious and steadfast expression he so adored. And her gaze, while seemingly fixed on the artist's palette, he imagined as extending further until resting on him, lovingly watching her transfiguration. While so absorbed, he suddenly realised he had not considered arranging a sitting for Emma before asking his favour of Strang that had turned out so spectacularly well. Now that it belatedly occurred to him, he felt it neither prudent to show Florence's sketch to her nor even mention its existence.

The few brief days that Thomas and Florence enjoyed at Aldeburgh were a welcome respite from Max Gate. Despite Florence's protestations that she had enjoyed her time in Dorset, there was an underlying tension that Thomas fuelled and then had to endure. He was pleased to get away, and once again Emma was indifferent to his doing so.

As always, Edward was a charming host and owing to the inclement weather they spent more time than usual with the other guests, including James Frazer, whose work *The Golden Bough* Florence had not long finished reading, and the historian James Bury and his wife Anne, a meek and sallow woman who remembered having met Florence on a previous visit, although Florence had no memory of her at all. It was a quiet time, quieter than usual, and Thomas was glad of it.

'And so, tell me, what have you come up with?' she asked. It was the first time they had been onto the beach, muzzled as they were in scarves, hats and coats. The winds had scarcely abated, the sea was thumping against the shore and the spray could be felt from where they walked, the salt stinging their eyes.

Her question hung in the air for a good few seconds before he answered.

'I'm not sure yet. I know I need to provide you with something. I know that living like we are at Max Gate is no answer. But I don't know what to do. The truth is, Florence, I am unsure of Emma and her mental health and what she is capable of doing.'

'Why not leave her then?'

'Leave her?' Thomas stared at her. 'For God's sake, Florence, I thought you had befriended the woman. Can you think of the scandal that would cause?'

'What scandal would that be?' she asked him, her voice rising in inflexion against the noise of the sea. 'People might say, thank goodness he's rid of that gloomy, unsociable creature. Scandal!' She said the word again, trampling heavily on the first syllable. 'I would have thought, Tom, that you were not afraid of scandal after all you have caused with your pen.'

'But you like her, you like Emma. You told me so.'

'Like? What is like? Everybody has some part that's likeable even if the whole person is not. I could like anyone for a purpose. Look at you, Tom. You're just afraid of what the world would say. They might disapprove but they would not abandon you. It is I that would be cast as the scarlet woman and I am not afraid.'

Thomas, unable to answer, fell silent, so that by the time they had found their way back to the house again, their thoughts had retreated, each into each, and they both knew that the subject would not be aired again this holiday.

October saw a sudden cooling in the weather and Florence was caused to wonder how long she should stay away from Enfield. She had had a letter from her father saying that her mother was poorly, and resolved that she should go home. Before doing so, Thomas was keen to take her to meet his sisters Mary and Kate, who still lived in the family home in Bockhampton.

Once again, Florence wondered whether Emma knew where they were going when they left Max Gate. With Thomas, she was never sure what had been said, what the old lady knew or understood. She thought how unconcerned Emma had seemed about her accompanying Thomas to Aldeburgh or if she even knew, and wondered if she thought that no one as young and solemn as she was would ever entertain her husband's eye, despite his proclivity for younger women.

She found Mary and Kate warm and effusive and, once sure of their ground, critical to her of Emma.

'We've not been to Tom's house for years,' Mary proffered. 'She has made it a haven for the Giffords with their peculiar ways, but not us. Thomas might ask us as he does, but that's no good if the lady of the house objects.'

Florence they took to without being fully conversant with why Thomas had brought her to tea or what she did at Max Gate. And she decidedly liked them.

'How sad,' she said to him on their return to Max Gate.

'You see how it is for me now, Florence,' and he touched her hand briefly, then raised it in his own and kissed it softly before letting it go.

Florence continued to encourage Emma, though having initially felt that the older lady could in fact write quite well, found most of what she did produce dull and sententious. When Emma invited her to accompany her on holiday to Boulogne, just the two of them, it was the excuse of her own mother's health that Florence fell back on, for she knew she would have found such a trip as claustrophobic as it would have been compromising. Emma was not pleased. And when a few days later Emma looked at her strangely and asked whether she had noticed how much Thomas looked like Dr Crippen, who that day had been sentenced to be executed, she felt it was time to leave.

On her arrival at the family home in Enfield, Florence was met by her mother, who was struggling with depression although otherwise in good physical health. She found her mother's dark moods exhausting, and yet she recognised in herself the same mixture of depression and self-pity. As one who prided herself on being an excellent companion, she felt guilty that she couldn't naturally extend the same sentiment, the same sense of duty to her own mother. But she could not.

Of Alfred, little had been heard other than that he was still absent and hadn't been back to Enfield, although her father had heard from him some days back that he would be home at Christmas, health permitting. Florence left a card for him, and thought briefly of visiting his family, but time did not allow for it before she was expected back at Max Gate.

She had written to Edward Clodd following their recent stay at Aldeburgh and was pleased and surprised to have had a letter in reply asking how things were between her and Emma. Evidently, she thought, Thomas had confided in him for he was plainly curious about what he somewhat crudely wrote of as the 'Max Gate ménage'. She was cautious in her response, though not impolite, expressing as she did her intense sympathy for Emma and then for Thomas also, unwittingly giving credence to the comedy Edward had imagined of them all, gathered like prize boxers in a ring, constantly sizing the other up.

Despite the unease she had experienced with Emma on her last visit, Florence was persuaded to return to Max Gate before the month was out. Both Thomas and Emma met her, and after tea Emma took her through a detailed account of how Thomas had been given the freedom of the town of Dorchester, an event both she and Thomas had previously agreed it was best that she avoided. The weather, meanwhile, had turned and a succession of grey, overcast but nevertheless mild days gave way to biting north-easterlies which kept them inside. Florence used the time to continue with a children's book she was engaged on, describing unusual animals, but yearned to be writing some much more substantial work. About her, about them all, the household seemed to co-exist with no hint of disharmony and she started to grow more comfortable in her role as an accepted member of the family.

Her composure, however, was disrupted the following week by a letter that arrived from Ireland notifying her of the death of Lady Stoker. Florence's distress, the extent of which surprised her, was not such as she could readily share, although when Thomas's favourite cat chose to die a day later, she was angry beyond words that he could make such a fuss and display over some creature without her being able to tell him that she was grieving for Thornley, and through him, for herself. Not for the first time, she saw into the man, self-pitying, self-absorbed and a little pathetic.

As Christmas approached, Florence was caught between the expectations of her family that she would come home and those of Thomas that she would remain at Max Gate. The fact that Alfred had returned to Enfield was a consideration for her, but not enough to counter the persuasion that Thomas exercised in wanting her to stay in Dorset.

It was a mistake. Christmas morning had been quiet enough, with Emma going to the service at Stinsford alone, but Thomas's proposal to take Florence with him to meet his sisters after Christmas dinner aroused in her a fury of indignation. The argument that ensued was protracted and savage, driving Florence to her room. Through the walls, she could hear Emma accusing Thomas of giving his sisters the opportunity to turn Florence against her, while in another outburst she heard mention of the sketch of Florence that she had found, and although she didn't know the context in which it was said, the revelation made her uncomfortable. Not knowing what to do as the argument moved on unabated, room to room, she covered her ears with a pillow and vowed to herself that she would leave the next day and make sure that she never returned to Max Gate again when husband and wife were there together.

Chapter 14

YE HAVE BEEN CALLED UNTO LIBERTY

Florence's departure from Max Gate caused considerable consternation. Thomas was angry with Emma for making such a scene by casting aspersions upon his siblings, and indirectly on Florence, and even, heaven forbid, on himself. Having worked so hard to arrange the accommodation of Florence within the inner sanctum of his family, his irritation was exacerbated by the fact that all efforts had seemingly been undone. And not, so Emma led him to believe, because of Florence at all, but because of his family, and Emma's inability to get on with them.

Mary and Kate were openly hostile towards Emma and had thought her mad ever since an acrimonious exchange almost a decade earlier. Henry had less to say on the matter and as a rule kept his counsel, yet his dislike of the woman was palpable. Thomas, in turn, was frustrated, unable as he was to tell Emma that Florence had already met the family members, for to do so would betray his earlier subterfuge when they had previously visited Bockhampton.

For her part, Florence was also angered and embarrassed by the hostility that erupted between Emma and Thomas and that she had unwittingly been the subject of the argument. It was, as she had once dreaded it might be, some penance exacted on her for living in such close proximity to the one – or was it two people now, she wondered – who she was deceiving.

While Emma, later, took great pains to exonerate Florence from being in any way the subject of the dispute, she was inevitably singed by it, largely through her own guilt, and could not wait to get away.

Florence left the next morning for Enfield despite the entreaties of Thomas and Emma for her to stay. Max Gate had become an embittered, gloomy place and had started to close in, squeezing the life and breath out of her. She longed to see her family again and Alfred too, and to resume her life in London, away from provincial ears and eyes and the claustrophobia of Max Gate. London, she felt, offered her the greatest chance of happiness. But she knew it was not a matter of place only. Despite their occasional moments of repose, Thomas had done nothing to make her feel secure, had promised nothing and given nothing, and his self-interest and timidity sat in sharp contrast to the generosity of Thornley. While she might pine for Thornley, he in turn was still in mourning for his wife and appeared to be in no hurry to see her again. She had recently had a letter telling her that he would not, after all, be coming to London in January, news that unexpectedly depressed her.

She found her own family all rather dull and subdued. Christmas had been quiet and her mother's recent illness had dampened the festive mood, although they all professed themselves pleased to see her. She was determined not to repeat her previous year's outburst and endeavoured to be as solicitous and helpful as possible. Her patience was short, however, and without giving away openly to her frustration, she felt the pettiness of life; Enfield, too, could be rather provincial, she reflected wistfully, every bit as much as Dorchester. She determined that she would not stay long.

She had heard that Alfred had been quite ill again and had gone back to his sanatorium in Wales on Boxing Day. She was disappointed to have missed him and resolved to write to him soon. She wanted to be able to offer him a little comfort in his exile, to let him know all her news, for she knew how much he enjoyed hearing about the Hardys and Stokers and their ilk; she wanted to tell him how much she cared about him, how she looked forward to meeting up before too long and just talking, talking about anything and everything. She wanted to write all of this and wondered why she had not done so over the past months, but knowing, whatever reason she gave, he would understand and forgive her.

Florence's departure did at least galvanise Thomas into action and a promise to help. He wrote to her within hours of her leaving, pleading with her to return and pledging to make a much greater effort to support her, now that Emma's behaviour had forced them into a clandestine friendship which would inevitably make their life more difficult.

Part of the help he suggested came about unintentionally, the result of an introduction he had made for her the previous month with an old friend of his, Florence Henniker.

They first met over tea where Thomas, as was his wont, dominated the initial conversation.

Having helped both women into their chairs and poured the tea, he directed his conversation at Mrs Henniker.

'It is – what – nearly eighteen years since we first met; such a long time, my dear. I remember we even wrote a short story together in those early days – 'Spectre of the Real', wasn't that what it was called, Florence?'

Turning to Florence Dugdale, and without waiting for an answer, he continued to sing the other woman's praises. 'She is such an excellent writer, Florence, and a good friend, as well as being kind and intuitive and generous to a fault. There,' he said, turning to Mrs Henniker, 'I believe I've made you blush.'

Florence Henniker smiled at him. 'You exaggerate, Tom,' she said, placing her hand on the other Florence's, 'but I am delighted to meet you, my dear, and to know all about you.'

After which she turned her attention from Thomas to Florence, and the two women talked so eagerly that by the end of the tea they had established a rapport which, given the right encouragement, Florence sensed could burgeon into an incipient friendship.

On her return to London, only a few days later, Mrs Henniker called upon Florence at the Lyceum where they immediately resumed their conversation; during the course of meandering across a range of subjects, so keen was one to know more of the other, Florence Henniker offered the information that she lived with her husband, Major General Henniker, at their home in Southwold, Sussex. So well did the two of them get on that by the end of the afternoon she had felt encouraged enough to invite Florence to stay.

The visit which took place a fortnight later proved wholly successful. The two ladies talked of their families, of Thomas about whom Mrs Henniker had considerable knowledge, and of their writing. Despite their social differences, Mrs Henniker having had a very grand upbringing, as she discovered, Florence felt she conducted herself well enough to win her hostess's approbation as well as her support and was delighted when she was invited to assist with Mrs Henniker's writing as her personal secretary.

They were an odd match, Florence appreciated. Mrs Henniker was as elegant and poised as she was not, and yet Florence felt she was genuinely interested in her. She would not have been disappointed had she known the content of a letter sent to Thomas in which her new friend described her as a 'most interesting type of femininity – a modern emancipated young woman' though she may not have recognised herself as such. Nor did she then suspect that the other Florence once entertained a place in Thomas Hardy's thoughts that she now occupied herself.

As well as providing this conduit between the two women, the immediate consequences of which he could hardly claim credit for, Thomas resolved to encourage Florence's writing more directly by interceding for her.

In January 1911, he travelled to London to try and appease her and by way of affirmative action to visit the editor of the *Cornhill Magazine* to encourage him to publish a story, largely it transpired his own work, called 'Blue Jimmy: The Horse Stealer', under Florence's name. Florence was both touched and embarrassed by this gesture, at his willingness to share his own writing with her and, by so doing, became complicit in some small deception exercised on the unwitting editor.

Later they met at her flat in Baker Street where he was duly penitent, both for the embarrassment at Christmas and for not being of more assistance to her. Under the weight of his words (for he wielded them well, she thought, as he properly should), Florence felt her reserve waver as they stood locked in the doorway before she capitulated and led him into the sitting-room.

'Tom,' she said, when he had told her of the meeting and the decision of the *Cornhill* to proceed with publication immediately, 'do not think I am not grateful, but that story is more you than me.'

He brushed away the comment. 'Nonsense. The idea was yours, the drafts were yours, and I merely did what an editor would do.'

She looked at him earnestly before replying. 'Then I am most grateful.'

They looked at each other awkwardly, neither speaking for the moment.

'I want to do more for you, Florence. I'm afraid Emma is quite irrational and is accusing me now of having disturbed the great friendship that was between you and her.' He waited for her to respond. 'I understand that you don't want to rush back to Max Gate, although I hope you may feel differently someday. In the meantime, I am to be in London a good deal. I hope you will entertain me being here.'

She found that she could not readily answer. Yes, she would be there for now, even for the foreseeable future perhaps, but could not say more than that. What if Thornley was to ask for her? What if she could somehow find the means to make her own way and didn't need his patronage anymore? But in the end she acquiesced, thinking that perhaps it was not just the utilitarian value of Thomas Hardy she required, but occasionally the company of Tom himself.

He had told her that he was to spend much of the year preparing a new and definitive edition of verse and novels – *The Wessex Edition* – for his publishers, Macmillan. It was a task that would involve endless hours of reading proofs and writing a general preface to each of the twenty volumes of novels and poems, as well as considerable time away from Dorset. Perhaps, now, they could agree something more formal, some arrangement, or at least arrive at some understanding.

He started to read her a poem he had written for a series of stories provisionally called *Satires of Circumstance* that he was intending to publish in the *Fortnightly Review*, titled 'Over the Coffin'.

He read the last verse without looking up at her once:

> *Well, there was a word to be said by me!*
> *I divorced that man because of you –*
> *It seemed I must do it, boundenly;*
> *But now I am older, and tell you true,*
> *For life is little, and dead lies he;*
> *I would I had let alone you two!*
> *And both of us, scorning parochial ways,*
> *Had lived like the wives in the patriarch's days.*

When he finished and glanced across at her, rather than smiling at him knowingly as he had hoped, she was visibly embarrassed and angry.

'Why do you write something so provocative, so transparent?' she asked, clearly irritated by his verse. 'For a man to seek of his wife to blindly accept other attachments is tantamount to sanctifying bigamy.'

'It is not,' replied Thomas – but he was taken aback by her response and having hinted that the poem was about them and Emma spent the next ten minutes disassociating the subject from their own, too parallel, situation.

'Why write about what will never happen?' goaded Florence. 'In your own situation, Emma would never entertain such a thought. Heavens! And you would never leave her, as you have so frequently told me.'

'I don't know that. Circumstances change.'

'What do you mean you "don't know" that? What has changed? What is ever likely to change?'

Thomas looked at her, his face tight and intense. She could see the veins in his forehead throbbing.

'Emma. Emma has changed. She is a nightmare and seems determined to embarrass or provoke me at any opportunity. She is impossible with guests and openly criticizes me and my work. I fear she has the curse of the Giffords.'

'What curse?'

'Mental instability. It is in their blood.'

'Then leave her, Thomas, as I have said before. Leave her.'

'I cannot,' he said, before adding after a respectable pause – 'not yet.'

He looked at her and said conspiratorially, 'Edward has said the same, you know, that I should leave her. Of course, he did as much to his own wife, so has no qualms about such matters.' And he reached out for Florence fearing he had said more than he should have, both trusting and fearing her in turn. She reluctantly took his hand, acknowledging by doing so that she knew that nothing would change between them, at least in the immediate future.

In early February, Sir Thornley let Florence know that he was coming to London and would be staying at his club. She looked forward to seeing him again and to hearing news of the family. She was not, however, prepared for the change the last three months had wrought in him and the extent to which his health and appearance had deteriorated.

'My dear Florence,' he exclaimed on seeing her, his arms outstretched and welcoming. She responded to him with her old affection, kissing him on the cheek before allowing herself to be led by the hand to an alcove containing two leather buttoned chairs. A waiter came over to collect their order. Both eschewed the choice of alcohol and settled for tea and sandwiches.

Florence was disturbed and upset seeing Thornley so diminished. The warm and affable companion she had known had aged and the whole personality changed by dissimulation. His eyes were dull, his speech slow and imprecise and his hands which he tried to keep resting on his lap were trembling visibly as he spoke. At the end of his account of his wife's final days and the effect her illness had on everyone, he fell silent.

Florence leant over, took his hands in hers and said in a manner that, had not Thornley been patently ill, would have been considered brazen.

'I thought there was a chance that you and I would have some life together. Not before,' she added quickly, 'but after Lady Thornley had gone, and after, of course' – she added carefully – 'she had been decently mourned. Maybe then.'

Thornley looked at her closely. 'You are a dear thing to want to look after a sick man like me. Let me say the offer is a generous one and perhaps, perhaps when I get better,' – and here he smiled weakly at her, a grey wan smile – 'we should talk about it again. Meanwhile,' he added, 'do write. I like to hear from you about Thomas and Emma and what the old man is up to now. And, of course, you must tell me all about your own work. Are you writing now?'

Florence told him about the article she was having published and another children's book she was preparing and he seemed pleased for her.

After a few extraneous meanderings, they parted as old friends do, he kissing her on the cheek while simultaneously gripping her hand, before she made her way back to the Lyceum where she gathered herself up and wept at the waste of it all.

Encouraging Florence in her writing, Thomas knew, was very important to her, but in the spring and summer he had also taken the liberty of planning several trips for them both, on which they could travel without the spectre of Emma. It involved making members of both their families complicit in their intrigue, but Thomas seemed not to mind.

In April, they set off to visit the cathedrals at Lichfield, Worcester and Hereford accompanied by Florence's sister Constance. It was a strain for Florence having her sister along with them, quite different from the effect of Henry on their previous tours. Thomas, though, was much taken by her, to the point of trying to match her with his younger brother, 'who,' he commented despairingly, 'needs the hand of a wife to guide him.'

It was a subdued group that headed north, for travelling was not easy and the weather was unkind. Reaching Hereford, however, their mood brightened when Henry joined them for the last leg of the journey, much to Thomas's pleasure.

While their privacy was inevitably compromised with the two younger siblings in tow, the talk of the group still invariably returned to Emma.

'Do you think she is safe at the house by herself?'

It was Henry who first asked the question as they were sitting in the close of Hereford Cathedral.

'She's safe as long as I am not there to provoke her,' retorted Thomas.

'I don't know how you've put up with her. I'd have shown her the door before now, that's for sure.'

'Maybe, Henry. Maybe that's why you've never married.'

'Nor would I be tempted to if it meant taming such as her.'

Thomas said nothing and the conversation showed every sign of dying out before Florence interjected angrily, 'Why have you allowed her to behave this way, Thomas?' Immediately, she regretted her outburst.

Both men looked at her.

'Don't ask such things, Florence, for they are part of the conundrum of marriage,' replied Thomas softly, an answer that satisfied her not one whit and only left her feeling angry and frustrated.

While Thomas and Emma were, to all intents and purposes, estranged from each other, Florence, at least publicly, was estranged from neither. Emma had been writing an account of her childhood in Cornwall before she had met Thomas and had asked Florence to read it for her, and by this process the two women renewed their acquaintance. Thomas, meanwhile, published twelve of his fifteen short stories in verse in April 1911 in the *Fortnightly Review* which he had labelled *Satires of Circumstance* to a generally good reception.

Florence, having already chided Thomas for one of his offerings, was similarly critical on seeing the whole body of work.

'Why write these poems that are pitted against marriage? People will read into them your other desires, your restlessness, your own dissatisfactions and they will cast aspersions on the both of us. Why be so oblique, Tom? Why not act on your heart for once instead of more words?'

He looked offended, reddening as he spoke.

'Because poetry is meant to be oblique. Because I can say what I feel without being categorical, without being pinned down by each word or syllable. Because poetry allows for ambiguity while telling truths.'

And Florence just looked at him and nodded slowly. 'Then beware the truths they tell, Tom,' she said by way of conclusion, 'for they say much about you.'

She had kept busy with her own writing. When Hodder and Stoughton published *The Book of Baby Beasts*, in which her contribution was to provide a commentary in prose and verse to accompany a sequence of animal pictures in colour drawn by the young artist E. J. Detmold, she took considerable pride in the result.

'It is not so easy writing an accompaniment for paintings, Tom,' she would say. 'But I can't feel that I am accomplishing much. It's not important work, is it?' And he would reply without any enthusiasm, and though he would spend time trying to convince her otherwise she could sense he didn't believe in it either.

In June, they were again at Aldeburgh with Edward and a group of his friends, some of whom Florence had become better acquainted with over the course of several visits. She and Tom talked little of Max Gate, or of the future, but of writing and writers, and of religion and belief. Most discussions were enjoyable banter, the sharing of thoughts about other guests, but occasionally they would argue about some point or other, each realising how stubborn and intractable the other could be.

One such discussion began while on a walk along the beach front and was prompted by the criticism he had read that morning of his new *Wessex Edition*.

'They are always looking for fault, wanting to dismantle my work because it doesn't please them. As for calling me a pessimist,' he said forcefully, 'that is so much piffle. If anything – and I distrust any such labels, my dear – I would describe myself as a meliorist.'

He paused as if waiting for a response, for her to ask for an explanation. When she sought neither, he continued, oblivious to her indifference.

'I have always, always believed that we can, through our own efforts and initiatives, improve society. We are not passive beings. In my novels you can read how my characters engineer improvement and change and better themselves. That is surely evident.'

She considered his words for a minute before responding.

'But it is more often not so with you, Tom. Many of your characters just seem to make matters worse even when they are trying to do otherwise.'

Florence would rarely question Thomas on his writing, but felt compelled to push him on the point. 'In my reading, fate always seems ready to conspire against your characters. Where is the hope in your novels?'

He reacted sharply. 'There is hope. There is hope, sometimes even if cloaked in despair, but you just cannot see it, Florence, for sometimes you are blind to it.'

She responded as if stung.

'Blind? Yes, I'm blind, Thomas Hardy, for why else would I be here with you? Blind to hope, that I am. And you are too old or too foolish to see it.'

She turned on her heels and walked off in the opposite direction, leaving him where he was, stranded on the beach.

The early summer was cool and wet and remained so until after Midsummer's Day when there was a spell of settled weather. When not out riding on the Rover Cobb, his bicycle of which he had grown immensely fond, Thomas was as keen as ever to continue his excursions further afield. First, he organised that he and Florence, accompanied by Mr Dugdale, went north to Carlisle and the Lake District. While the trip was successful, it was a strange thing, thought Florence, she and Tom travelling with her father acting as chaperon. When she listened to the two men talking, she was struck by how their interests were not dissimilar, how being of the same generation drew conversation from people that others could not partake of. Looking at them sitting together on the stone wall outside Dove Cottage, Florence speculated on what her father thought, now he was complicit in their arrangement. Had it not been a famous man she was with, would he have been so unquestioning? Or did this outwardly moral and stentorian person just not think the unthinkable, that there could ever be more than friendship between his headstrong daughter and this old man?

The following month, Thomas took Mary and Kate on a rare family holiday, leaving both Florence and Emma behind. Emma took the opportunity to write to Florence inviting her to join her for a holiday at Worthing, an invitation which Florence accepted with no little trepidation. She need not have worried, she thought later; Emma was as warm and generous towards her as she had previously been. They were soon discussing their writing and Florence felt bold enough to share an article she was writing on Rudyard Kipling, asking for Emma's critical comments. In turn, Emma invited her to peruse a collection of fifteen poems entitled *Alleys* that she had painstakingly gathered since 1900 and had already arranged with Longmans to be published later in the year.

However, as she confided to Florence, Thomas was not happy with her poetry.

'He thinks I cannot write as he does,' she said. 'Maybe I cannot. Maybe I don't want to write as he writes. But does that mean I cannot write? What nonsense. We can all write in some form or other. It is being a woman that damns us, Florence, as in all things.'

As autumn fell, Thomas returned to his own writing. He had recently had a letter from the director of the Fitzwilliam Museum in Cambridge, Sydney Cockerell, who asked if he could visit. When he did so the two men established an immediate rapport. Sydney was solicitous and persuasive as well as strong on flattery, and after some discussion Thomas agreed to hand over the responsibility for a number of his manuscripts, charging Sydney with writing to curators and archivists at a number of universities as well as the British Museum. It was the start of a friendship that was to mean a great deal to Thomas whose own doubts about his literary legacy were compounded by the misery of Emma's increasingly erratic and accusatory behaviour at home. But for Sydney, it was a coup, finding Thomas so naïve, so ready to part with his manuscripts without appreciating their value.

In between her various trips away and her writing, Florence determined to spend some time with her sisters, something she had not done for several years. She particularly enjoyed seeing Constance who had kept her in touch with the school and her former colleagues and who, in return, quizzed her endlessly about Thomas. Alfred was a frequent topic of conversation and on one visit home she and Constance went to visit him, only to be turned away by his mother as he was too unwell to have any visitors.

Florence's friendship with Mrs Henniker, also, had entered a new phase as she became a regular visitor to the family's house in Stratford Place. The original purpose of her visits, which was to type Mrs Henniker's manuscripts and occasionally help walk the family's two French bulldogs in nearby Hyde Park, had been superseded by an altogether different role. More often than not, she would now find herself there just as a friend and companion, an accepted member of the family, partaking of the company and conversation of the many interesting and influential people who frequented the house, as well as enjoying the largesse and hospitality of her generous hostess. When she found out that the Hennikers knew the Stokers from their time in Dublin, her delight knew no bounds and she talked openly to Florence about her affection for the family, even sharing some of her confidences with Thornley, without ever knowing if she was saying more than she ought.

She saw Thomas most weeks, usually in London, but increasingly in Weymouth, where he had arranged rooms for her at Grosvenor House on the Esplanade. He would visit her regularly there, coming in by the rear door to ensure he was not seen and run the risk of becoming the subject of gossip.

In late October, she accompanied Thomas to Aldeburgh once again and found the time spent together as enjoyable as any she had known in his company. On this occasion he seemed especially attentive and keen that she could see good in him.

'Do I not show you affection, my dear?' he asked her. 'Have I not learned to look after you better?'

And she would concede that he had done so and was altogether more caring and sympathetic.

Since the debacle the previous Christmas, as she acknowledged to him when pressed to do so, he had endeavoured to help ease her financial situation. He had promoted her writing, as he often reminded her, and had introduced her to Florence Henniker who, in turn, had offered her friendship and paid employment. What's more, he had paid her an allowance, ostensibly for the secretarial assistance she gave him, although he knew it was not altogether accurate to describe it so. He had helped prepare her articles for publication and to show her how to become better recognised as a writer, for he had learnt that was the way to her heart.

He was also encouraged by the fading presence of the Stoker family. Since the death of Lady Stoker, Florence rarely spoke of Thornley, although Thomas didn't realise that she had decided not to do so, as she knew it would upset him. Consequently, she did not tell him of Thornley's ill-health or of seeing him in London; nor did she react to his tirades against the Irish which she were sure were rooted in his dislike of what he saw as her relationship with Thornley.

In early December, and in the company of his sister Kate, Thomas and Florence undertook another tour to Gloucester, Bath and Bristol. It was cold, bitterly so, and Florence was more susceptible than the others to the vagaries of temperature, succumbing to a chest infection. But worse was to follow on her return, blighting her Christmas and turning her world askew.

Arriving back at her rooms in Grovesnor House, Florence found a telegram waiting for her from her father. The message was curt and bald: Alfred Hyatt had died that day after suffering a haemorrhage in his lungs. She looked at the date and saw it had been sent three days previously and collapsed on her bed, distraught. Alfred. Her dear, dear Alfred who had always acted so selflessly towards her. Alfred, who had shown her the purity of love. She started to sob violently, frustrated to be in Dorset when she wanted only to be home, in Enfield. He was only aged forty, she remonstrated with the God who shared her room at that moment, and did not deserve to die, not now, not like this, not without her being there. It was only the solitude that stopped her becoming hysterical, for true hysteria needs an audience, but she sobbed long into the night, nevertheless.

The next morning she left Grosvenor House and caught a train back to London. She wrote a note to Thomas, telling him the news, without letting on the extent of her grief. It was only later when she wrote to both Edward and Florence that she gave voice to the depth of her feelings, telling them that Alfred had meant more to her than anyone in the world and that she would gladly have died for him. In a brief moment, her world had turned on its axis and she was consumed by the despair of losing the one in her life who was, by her own belated admission, irreplaceable.

Thomas's response to Florence was brief and his condolences, written on a visiting card for her to communicate in person to the family, seemed oblivious to the extent of the grief that was visited upon her. Did he not know, she thought, of Alfred's part in her life? Did he not know anything?

Back in Enfield, Florence remained inconsolable, wracked with grief and guilt. She could not bring herself to attend the funeral service and was overcome with sadness and self-reproach. She regretted bitterly that she had been touring the West Country when Alfred fell critically ill and that the news had come too late. Yet between the paroxysms of grief for Alfred came the gradual realisation that this was of her making. It was always likely to end this way for her and Alfred, at some future time, for she had chosen another trajectory. Only now, now that it was too late, had she been forced to measure the cost of what she had chosen and what she had given up. It was this balancing of accounts for decisions made, of a world subsequently lost to her, and a true heart parted, which hurt her most of all.

Two days after she arrived home, she received a Christmas card from Thomas. She was hardly aware of Christmas being only two days away when she opened it and read the inscription: 'With best wishes for Christmas and the New Year. Ye have been called unto liberty. – Galatians V 13.'

Florence stared at the words for a long time. Liberty? Liberty? What did he mean? There was no freedom in this. This was the worst thing that could happen. Alfred was forty, for God's sake, not some old man who had had his three score and ten. How could he? And as she fumed and festered, she was sure that Alfred's love was worth more than any old man could muster. He had not wanted her to look after him, and when he was sick would not allow her to even think of doing so. He believed in her; he had never questioned what she had done or the reasons wherefore; and he had given without charge. And she had taken it all greedily and now it was suddenly gone. His parting was, she realised, another door closed to her.

She screwed up his card and threw it onto the fire, retreated to her room and wept uncontrollably until Eva found her, poured her a stiff brandy and put her to bed.

Chapter 15

THE CONVERGENCE OF THE TWAIN

The grief that Florence felt propelled her to the edge of her senses. What had she done abandoning her home and family and those she had grown up with, those that were her lifeblood? What had she been thinking, allowing herself to be drawn by Thomas into his narrow, provincial world? Who had she thought she was, parading her petty ambitions and literary pretensions?

She could not summon the strength to attend church at Christmas and for days following Alfred's death she would unexpectedly break down and weep profusely, the tears of an unwitting survivor, full of guilt and self-pity. Having decided she must visit his family, when she eventually did so she was quite incoherent. Instead of offering words of comfort, she found herself weeping in front of them, leaving them perplexed as to how she could feel this much emotion for their Alfred, thereby confusing grief for remorse.

When, a week later, Alfred's brother returned the letters she had written to Alfred, carefully wrapped in a black bow, she broke down again, punishing herself for her other life, for not loving Alfred as she should have, for allowing him to pretend that they both had wanted a platonic friendship when she knew *he* felt otherwise. She knew, sensed at least, that he longed for her overtures, but they had never come, and now she must live with the consequences.

She had humoured him, appeased him, allowed him to float in and out of her life, but she would not allow him to settle. And now she felt a sickening mix of guilt and remorse. All too late. Always, always too late.

Despite the artificial hiatus provided by New Year, Florence remained distraught and wracked by grief and during the following days at home rarely got out of bed. Her parents and sisters worried about her as she

156

receded from them and her depression made them vigilant, fearful of her state of mind. Only Margaret, now just eighteen – what can you know at eighteen? Florence thought – was able to talk to her, and even then the words that Florence offered in return were perfunctory, shallow, devoid of emotion.

She had received a consoling letter from Mrs Henniker who realised from Florence's own letter to her just how monstrous was the loss that she felt.

'I am so sorry for you, my dear friend,' she wrote, 'I just didn't realise Alfred meant so much to you,' on reading which Florence turned on herself yet again, saying under her breath, 'No, because I felt he had no place in the world I had with you or Thomas; because perhaps, perhaps' – and even then the unspoken words failed her – 'I was just a little ashamed of him.'

The thaw in the frozen sea of her self-pity was slow in coming and it took another sadness to soften the sharp edges of her own grief. In early February she received a telegram from Thomas telling her that Major General Arthur Henniker had died of heart failure, the result of being kicked by a horse. The effect on Florence was to pull her back from the edge of her own tragedy and to shift some of her attention to the plight of her friend. It is often another's tragedy that buries one's own, she thought, and strengthened by the necessity for her now to be strong to console Mrs Henniker, she set out for Southwold immediately to provide comfort for her recently acquired, but already dear, friend.

The funeral of the major general passed off with due solemnity. Thomas had sent a note, but had decided against going which, given his proclivity for attending funerals, Florence thought unusual. There was sadness, of course, but the service itself was restrained and muted. The army took over much of the arrangements and organised the cortège and there seemed little for either of the Florences to do. A dignified reserve epitomised the public extent of the family's emotion. Mrs Henniker herself was steady and assured, typically unflappable, even in her mourning clothes, and Florence resolved to be more like her in the future.

The shadows, having been disturbed, started to fade again. Florence returned home and began to write again, slowly at first, but with more purpose as the month passed. By the end of March she had finished off the first draft of her manuscript for Hodder called 'In Lucy's Garden'.

A few weeks later, Florence and Mrs Henniker met in London to produce a memorial book for the "Major General", as he was always addressed even by his wife. Florence decided that Thomas should be prevailed upon to provide some verses, by way of consolation, which he agreed to do although the irony was not lost on him. Some nineteen years before, he had fallen in love with Mrs Henniker, writing her love letters and poetry and desperately trying to entice her into an amour, and here he was, now, writing to praise the husband he sought to cuckold.

The memorial service went ahead smoothly, although there was little emotion, that having been spent at the funeral several weeks before. Florence had an aversion to memorial services so soon after the event and thought it was like some ghastly afterthought, pumping up the dead before the corpse had properly stilled.

In the aftermath, Florence spent several days with Mrs Henniker at her home in Southwold. The friendship between the two women had grown and the hostess had become a confidante for Florence. Their personal grieving had merged in mutual empathy, their sympathies pooled to create an appreciation of the cycle of regeneration. They found they were able to talk more freely, that the death of others had liberated them in this way at least. Nevertheless, Florence's suggestion to Mrs Henniker that she was seriously considering entering the Catholic Church came as a surprise to her.

'Why, my dear, why? I always thought you a good agnostic, which is vastly preferable to being a bad Christian. We've enough of those.'

And Florence answered, not responding to the light-hearted jest of the other woman, 'Because I cannot stand being let down anymore by the promise of something better. I am thirty-two years old, Florence, and I do not want to grow old trusting people who either disappear from me or never keep their word. At the moment, at least the Church would offer me some certainty. They say they're good at that, even for unbelievers like me.' She sighed a long, deep sigh. 'I just want something else to look forward to, an escape from all this.'

'Do you?' asked Mrs Henniker. 'Do you really need such a thing? Don't you think you are being a little melodramatic? What is the "all this" you talk about? Believe me, Florence, there are worse lives than the one you've chosen.'

She lowered her voice and said slowly, 'Nor do you need to give anything more of yourself away – you do too much of that already. Learn to be a bit kinder to yourself, Florence. There isn't a Church that can do that for you.'

And she smiled at Florence, who in turn gave a weak smile back before answering, 'I am being silly, aren't I? Just thinking of Angel Clare should have told me that,' and they both laughed.

At Max Gate, Thomas and Emma were as far apart as they had ever been. They rarely ate supper together, but like cats kept to their own territory. Emma's recourse and defence in all things was the Church for she had become more pious, more judgemental than ever, and railed against his atheism whenever she had the opportunity. She continued to write her poetry as well as filling her diaries with poison against her estranged husband and, increasingly, the disparate company he kept, citing the godless Clodd as a devil in their midst.

Thomas, meanwhile, had been moved by the terrible tragedy of April 1912 – the sinking of the Titanic with the loss of over 1,500 lives – and before the end of the month had produced his great poem 'The Convergence of the Twain'. He sent a copy to Florence who read it and was stirred as if anew by his poetry, his mastery of language and the sentiments therein. She decided to write and tell him – only the second letter she had sent to him since leaving Max Gate the previous December.

He responded to her letter within days with an overture to meet again soon, the upshot being that she agreed to travel to Aldeburgh with him in May "as before". Except, as she knew, it would not be "as before" for the world had turned on its axis and she was apprehensive, more now from her numbed feelings and a mounting indifference than anything else.

Aldeburgh was a painful experience for both of them. Thomas had belatedly realised now the place that Alfred had had in Florence's affections and had made every effort to improve matters with her by being sensitive to his memory, praising the work Alfred had done for him in producing his earlier anthology. But it was not just that, Florence thought; that was just the tip of the iceberg. It was Emma, it was Thornley, it was her family and his. It was trying to eke out an existence with the scraps of work she received from Florence Henniker – but for how long? – and by her meagre writing. She was working on the second draft of her novel 'In Lucy's Garden', and was about to have her second collaboration with Edward Detmold published, *The Book of Baby Birds*, but she knew these alone would not sustain her, body or soul.

Thomas seemed unsure even of what to say to her. He was as affectionate, as needy as ever, and she responded companionably, but their worlds and wants were tangential. Of Emma, apart from bemoaning her further decline, Thomas wanted to say little. Divorce was not mentioned although he was persistent in reaffirming his devotion to Florence.

'So we are friends then?' she would say.

'More than friends,' he would reply.

'How? How more than friends? I have other friends who do practical things to help me. Mrs Henniker is a friend.'

'And I am the one who introduced you to her. Doesn't that count?'

'Not really. That was one moment on your part. It is I who have made it what it is.'

They walked often along the beach, he an old man of seventy-two years and she an uncertain thirty-three-year-old, both mindful of *anno domini*, the passing of years, treading parallel paths. How much more time might he rightly expect to have, thought Thomas. Not much. And Florence, feeling her days passing without any perceptible change to their rhythm, was conscious of the breath of youth ebbing from her.

There was no agreement, no discussion, no mention of the areas where their lives diverged. Nor of Emma or Thornley or anyone else for that matter. There lay unspoken between them a quiet acceptance, bordering on equanimity, and yet while Florence felt unruffled by the weekend away, there was no reassurance either. It was just time spent, with some little gain and pleasure, she agreed, but without promise, without expectation.

She wondered, as she often did when alone with Thomas, about Thornley from whom she had not heard since the early New Year. Thornley, always so gracious and considerate, who had responded to her when she had answered him. He was the counterweight of Thomas, each being all that the other wasn't. And so the news that reached her in early June from Bram, that Thornley had died the previous week and had been buried in Dublin even before she received the letter, saw her already flagging spirit crumple.

Her resolve to emulate Mrs Henniker, likewise, was forgotten as she again sank back into mourning. To have lost first Alfred and now Thornley in six months plunged her into a black spiral, and again she responded by retreating from the city out to Enfield. Her family knew nothing of Thornley, other than that he was the husband of the patient Florence had cared for on and off in Dublin, so any public grief was inappropriate and yet she grieved, nonetheless. It was, she lamented, as if her life was being stripped from her, layer by layer until she was laid bare. And when she was alone, later that night, she wept not just for Thornley but for herself, for her sorry life most of all, until it seemed all the liquid had been drained from her.

Later, after the emotion had receded, she wondered, in a brief spasm of concern, what Thornley had done with her letters to him, whether they had been destroyed or were lying there somewhere waiting to be discovered. Who was she to write to apart from Bram, she asked herself, for while she knew several other members of the family, she was not sure they would welcome a letter from her.

The first contact from Ireland came not from family, but in a missive from a notary informing her that she was a significant beneficiary of Thornley's will. When she read that she had been left the very considerable sum of two thousand pounds, she swallowed hard. This was enough, she realised, to make her an independent woman. What she could not understand was why she did not feel exhilarated by the information, tinged as it was, of course, with great sadness. What was it that made her feel so? Why should she feel so ambivalent when presented with this "gift"? Thornley had cared for her, had wanted to provide for her, had even loved her a little or a lot – surely that was enough.

Part of her worries soon became clear when, following the bequest, came the whispers and innuendo. These dark, guarded sentences and oblique criticisms manifested themselves in letters and conversation, to her and others, in effect accusing her of inveigling her way into Thornley's affections, even of being his mistress. At first, Florence was unmoved by such vitriol coming from members of the family she had never met, but when both Bram and then Katharine indirectly accused her of as much, she was deeply hurt. Money, she thought to herself, even when given for the right reasons, in gratitude and affection, too often could provoke an unjustified response, full of jealousy and spite. How awful people are to think such unkind things when money is about. It was only later that she became angry. Damn them all, she thought. I cared for him like no other. What's more, I cared for him as they were unable to do. And he cared for me too. But for all her internal bluster, she knew that her relationship with the Stoker family, which she had valued so much, had ended with

Thornley's own demise. Even this gift of independence that he had bestowed upon her, however well-meant, had exacted a price.

Florence heard nothing from Thomas about Thornley's passing. His next letter, instead, was full of the recent visit of W. B. Yeats and Henry Newbolt who had come to Max Gate to present him with the Gold Medal of the Royal Society of Literature. While pleased with the honour accorded him, he recounted the considerable embarrassment and annoyance caused by Emma during the visit and how he had banned her from the room for the actual ceremony and speech.

'She was awful, simply awful,' he wrote. 'She came in dressed like a frump and started talking the most dreadful rubbish to everyone. I swear she did it to embarrass me. I simply had no choice but to send her out.'

But if he expected any sympathy from Florence he was mistaken. Her reply was sharp and pointed.

'She is yours, Tom, for better, for worse, as you have told me. You must make of your marriage what you can. What you complain of is of no interest to me.'

Adding to her irritation was his failure to acknowledge Thornley's death in his letter. When he later protested that he hadn't heard the news, she simply did not believe him. Because of Thornley's considerable reputation, his death notice had been prominent in the national press and she knew how avidly Thomas read the obituaries. And yet, while she curtly mentioned it in her own reply, she omitted to mention the legacy, feeling it best not to raise an issue that he could easily misconstrue.

The matter was not to lie dormant for long. In early August, Thomas wrote to Florence asking if they could meet in London later the same week. She was surprised at the urgency implicit in the note for they had talked only sporadically of late, but acceded to his request. Over recent weeks, she had rarely been into the city, preferring to stay in Enfield and get on with her own writing or to be in the company of Mrs Henniker.

On this occasion, she met him at her sister's house in Clapham, something she had arranged for the purpose. Thomas, when he arrived, seemed more alert, more purposeful than she had seen him for some time.

'What is it?' she asked, sensing that the meeting did indeed have a greater significance than a desire for her company.

'It is this,' he said and held out a letter from Bram Stoker. 'Read it.'

She looked at him apprehensively, but took the letter from him, frowned, and read it carefully. When she finished, she handed it back.

'It is outrageous,' she said. 'Scurrilous. A libel. What he's written is a libel, Tom.'

'Is it?' he asked her. 'Is it? A man you have worked for sporadically, for no more than a matter of months, leaves you two thousand pounds, enough to buy two or three houses. Enough, I would guess, to set you free of me too.'

'That is not fair, Tom, I would never think like that and nor should you. It does you no credit. He was a generous man, that's all.'

'For sure he was generous. For sure, he had a lot to be grateful for too,' he answered, 'for he sent this too.' He held out another letter, this time in Florence's writing. 'It seems there was rather more going on than I knew.'

She started and stared at him.

'Tom. He had no right.'

'You had no right, Florence. It was you who had no right.'

She looked down at the floor and answered him slowly.

'I am sorry then. Sorry that this has come to light. Sorry for any hurt I might have caused you, although you have no reason to feel so aggrieved.'

He brushed her protestations aside.

'So Alfred first, Alfred I could understand, but this old goat, he was nearly as old as me.'

'He was not an old goat, Thomas. He was a dear friend and a good man.'

'Evidently.'

She paused, wondering if there was more to follow.

'So tell me the purpose of Bram Stoker's letter? Explain what he expected to achieve other than venting his anger at his brother's generosity?'

'Purpose? To warn me. To tell me what sort of companion you actually were to Thornley. To let me know how I had been deceived. No doubt he intended to exercise the family's anger at you by using me as a conduit. How do I know?'

She turned her eyes away from his gaze.

'And what do you expect me to do, Tom? Give the money back? Say sorry for bringing some joy to his life – God knows, he had much to endure. As have I – old men and mad wives!'

'That is enough.'

'Enough. It is enough, Tom. I am free now, as you say. Free. I have an income to do that I most wish to do.'

'That is nonsense, talking like that, as you well know.'

Florence glared at him defiantly.

'Why? I am published. I can write. I will write.'

He looked at her and shook his head.

'It will not be so easy without me, Florence, not without me behind you.'

He moved closer towards her and she felt herself reach for the arm of the chair.

'It is not just a matter of money,' he continued. 'Yes, you can go and live independently. You always could if you had been prepared to humble yourself and not had such pretensions. I would never have been published if I had expected others to pave my way as you do. I did it myself, Florence, not through always waiting for someone else to open doors for me.'

She looked up at his face, stern and harsh, hovering above her. She sighed, her head drooped dejectedly and when she next spoke, her voice was changed.

'So what do you want of me, Thomas? Tell me, what is the purpose of your rebuke?'

'I want your companionship. I want your love and affection, as I always have. I want you, Florence.'

'Like you have wanted so many others? Like you wanted Lady Grove?'

'Lady Grove?'

'Yes. Lady Grove. And Florence Henniker, I suspect, although she would never say so. You shouldn't write so much in your letters for you know not where they end up. And how many others?' She stared directly at him. 'You are habitually unfaithful, Thomas. You are the goat, I fear.'

'You're wrong, Florence.'

'Wrong? I'm not wrong. And besides, we both know you cannot find a place for me. That much you've always made clear.'

'You've made it so. Not me.'

'You have given me very little hope, Thomas. Is it any wonder that I should have sought some companionship elsewhere? But companionship, Thomas, companionship, not to just be some servant, some handmaiden.'

He rose from his chair and took up his hat.

'I tell you again. I am in love with you, Florence.'

She looked at him, unblinking, saying nothing, impelling him to continue.

'I will be writing to Mr Stoker reminding him that such disclosures as are in his letter should remain between us. No doubt he will want a favour too at some stage, but that is where it will lie. The money that has been left to you is soiled in my eyes and I would prefer you to get rid of it, although I know that is unlikely – probably impossible in fact for you, but that is how I feel. Between you and me, Florence, I am prepared to be the next chosen, even to a dead man.'

And without adding any further solecism, he kissed her on the cheek and left.

Life at Max Gate was strained to the point of fissure. There had been a steady stream of visitors throughout the summer. In July, Emma had felt well enough to host a garden party and later to lead an expedition of the Fordington St George Needlework Guild to the seaside. She gathered a small circle of friends about her and enjoyed the occasional trips into town. But between her and Thomas there was constant feuding and little social communion. Few visitors were invited and several desirous of visiting were dissuaded from doing so. The recent experience of the visit from the members of the Royal Society had made Thomas cringe and while Edmund Gosse still called occasionally, Edward rarely did so. Even when Lilian came for the summer, much to Thomas's irritation, finding her as he did meddlesome and wearying, she did not stay long. Indeed, there was to be a rare moment of unspoken consensus when Emma, weary also of her niece's endless prattle, sent the young lady away.

While her physical health seemed robust enough, it was clear that Emma was becoming more and more eccentric in her utterances, her dress and her behaviour. The servants grew increasingly wary of her and her erratic behaviour as prescient of worse to come.

In October she played through her regular repertoire of tunes on the piano and then closed the mahogany lid with a bang, declaring that she had finished with playing the instrument. Her words to Thomas, rare as they were, dripped with vitriol; she even turned on the absent Florence more than once, as if finally, crushingly, she had realised the duality of the younger woman's presence in their household.

Florence, chastened by Bram Stoker's actions, had meanwhile written to

Thomas to ask for his forgiveness and he had responded more generously than she could have hoped. She was fond of him, she knew, at times even inordinately so, and while not superstitious in such matters was scared now of losing a third close friend. Friend, she thought as she wrote to him, was that what he was to her, this old man? She had meant none of this, had neither courted it nor engineered it, but she had not controlled things to avoid it happening either, as she had come to realise, and that, ultimately, was her fault.

To Mrs Henniker she said nothing of the will and her ensuing conversation with Thomas. She hoped it would be forgotten, that it would pass. She hoped also that Thomas may have need of her again, as a secretary, even if just in London, that she might make herself of use once more. He had been right. She did not know how to use her good fortune to help herself and would be content just to be needed again, even on the same terms as before. And of Emma she thought very little, although an occasional flash of pity or irritation would sometimes cross her mind at the impediment she represented in their lives.

November started darkly with a prolonged spell of rain unprecedented in Thomas's memory. The lawns at Max Gate were sodden, the driveway awash, the nearby rivers gorged and swollen.

Not surprisingly, there were even fewer comings and goings at Max Gate. Emma had employed her own personal maid, Polly Gale, to wait upon her. She had even started to take her evening meal, previously the one contact she had with her husband, in her room as well.

Late in the month, Rebekah and Catherine Owen, who had been acquaintances and devotees of both Thomas and Emma for more than eighteen years, made another of their regular visits. Thankfully, they were not accompanied by any of their tedious literary acquaintances from New York, although their presence alone was enough to send Thomas scurrying to his study upstairs. His absence left Emma with the responsibility of looking after the pair, something that pained her, but which she did stoically. They had come down to Dorchester to see the production of *The Trumpet Major* being put on in the town that week. As they made clear to Emma, they were keen that Thomas accompany them that evening, but it so happened he had already made arrangements to attend on the following two evenings, first on his own and secondly, and surreptitiously, in the company of Florence. Some time before, he had persuaded Florence to come to Weymouth, ostensibly to see the performance in the nearby town, but had also made plans for the next day to meet at her rooms in Weymouth where he hoped they might have some time alone.

It was not to be, any of it. For either, as the fates conspired.

The next evening, November 26th, Thomas had gone off to see the production on his own, having been regaled by the Owen sisters on how, despite how hard they had tried, the cast had seemed unable to do justice to his wonderful story, before they headed north again. It was a long night for Thomas during which he was encouraged to join the cast on stage after the final curtain. Having done his public duty, he hoped that he would avoid any such public clamour the next evening when he was planning to attend with Florence.

Despite the lateness of his arrival back at Max Gate, he was already working at his desk early the next morning when Polly came down the stairs from her room that lay adjacent to Emma's to alert him that the mistress was unwell. She exhorted him to come quickly to look at her mistress. He was unperturbed at first, and then merely dilatory, resolving to finish the short paragraph he was working on, when Polly's voice, more urgent than before, pressed him to put down his pen and move up the stairs to Emma's attic room. He had not entered the room for over a year and struggled to climb the stairs that rose steeply from the corridor outside his study. He was too late. Emma, having lapsed out of consciousness, was already drifting away from him, morphing from a physical presence to an idealisation of something else, a hybrid creature who would not easily forgive him, nor allow him to forget the ill-will he had borne her.

Chapter 16

LIGHT WIND ON A STAIR

The war continued to go badly in Europe. The Battle of Jutland had proved inconclusive, while on the battlefields of Northern France the number of British casualties continued to mount. Conscription had been introduced and rationing tightened. The public mood, reflected in the newspapers and in the muffled conversations of towns and villages, was sombre, fuelled by the growing list of local casualties. What had once seemed remote had now become intensely personal.

The death of Emma four years previously seemed a distant memory, lost in the last flutter of Edwardian decadence and grandeur that had been well and truly extinguished by the war. Thomas and Florence seldom strayed from Max Gate now and saw few people, apart from the very occasional visitor or local tradesman. Aldeburgh was off-limits, Thomas had decided some time back, and travel outside of Dorset had little pull for him anymore.

The death of Mary, followed soon after by disagreements about her will, gave Florence further insight into the disparate relationships that existed amongst Tom's siblings and especially the avarice and jealousy of Kate. After Mary's funeral, Kate became increasingly contemptuous of her two brothers, accusing them of wanting to drive her to penury. Her invective upset them both and despite the bulk of Mary's estate being derived from Tom's own largesse, both he and Henry eventually decided to defer to their sister in the settlement, save for a few of Mary's paintings. Thomas was too weary to argue with her, while Henry had been unwell and therefore uninterested which made Kate's job easier in getting her own way, but at a cost. While Thomas had further acceded to her wishes in one respect and had included her alongside Florence as a future beneficiary of his own estate, he abandoned his weekly visits to Talbothays and was much colder

168

towards her, making himself scarce whenever she called at Max Gate. Even when she visited Tom and Florence on the occasion of their wedding anniversary, he made no effort to welcome her or draw her back into the fold. Kate may have been saddened and disturbed by the reaction, but could hardly have been surprised.

They were all, Tom, Henry and Kate, getting older and more inflexible, in body as well as in mind, as was particularly apparent in their sporadic conversations. The knowledge that all three of them, the remaining siblings of Thomas senior and Jemima Hardy, were childless also hung over them, leaving them to contemplate the extinction of their branch of the family. It was simply a matter of time now before that happened, when the hearts of all three, diminished and weary of the war and each other, would give out.

After the death of Mary, Florence had taken on a more significant role in family matters. She was wary of the family and wary also of the effect the past two years had had upon her. Even Henry, who she had seen as her friend and confidant within the family, had become more reserved, more distant with her, resorting to calling her Mrs Hardy on occasions for no apparent reason other than a harkening back to some previous time of deference. Just as her presence had made Tom younger, so it aged her in equal part, each seeming to trade years with the other. It was she that must be the lubricant for the family's turning, she thought to herself, for there was no one else, at least in her mind, capable of doing so.

Florence had been concerned that after Mary's death Tom might turn again to the Gifford side of the family for comfort, but he did not do so. She was aware, always, of the signs, sensitive to any allusion to Emma, conscious of Tom's desk calendar frozen on March 7th. She was irritated by the letters that still arrived from other writers praising his elegies and upset by the fact that he recently seemed obsessed with his early novel set in Cornwall, *A Pair of Blue Eyes*, which was linked inextricably with Emma and their courtship over forty years previously. For some months, he had been overseeing its revision for a new edition of his novels at the exclusion of his other better-known novels and drawing from it for his new work. She felt miserable, trapped, without friends and robbed of the promise of a writing career that she felt had once beckoned. Like Emma before her, she had learned that Tom was less than encouraging to anyone wielding a pen at Max Gate other than him.

Thomas, meanwhile, wracked as he was by dysentery brought on by stress and thoroughly depressed by the war, was perpetually gloomy and irritable. He had taken to his bed over Christmas in 1915 and did not lift himself out of the pallor and gloom until the middle of January.

It was a depressing time, as Florence wrote in her diary, when a period of reckoning beckoned, but she was fearful of writing down why she felt this was so. She wrote to Rebekah about her fears, the sense of censure she lived with, while remembering Emma's notebooks, so full of venom and hatred towards Tom and his family (and, in one harrowing reference, to herself), and vowed to leave no such record when she passed on. But it did not stop her thinking ill of her situation and often of Tom, and writing of it in her letters.

Throughout the first half of 1916, Florence and Thomas made little effort to pull themselves out of the slough into which they had been cast. Wessex helped keep them amused and entertained although few others saw any humour in the wire-haired terrier that held forth at every opportunity. Even here, their enjoyment of the dog was singular, each finding amusing behaviour that the other ignored. A further complication was that as Thomas's mood and health improved, so Florence declined. She felt increasingly hemmed in by him, imprisoned by the lengthening shadows of Max Gate and surrounded always by reminders of Emma's abiding presence. He had grown more intractable, seeming almost indifferent to her at times although he did not intend to be so, but the effect was the same, leaving her in a sorry and solitary state.

She often thought how she had sought refuge in this marriage when all else had been lost, how she had gone to Thomas with a proposal she knew he would accept. Yet it was the wrong time. It was the wrong time in her life to have done so. She had not come to terms with the waves of grief that had pummelled her, nor properly considered the implications of the legacy she had been left by Thornley. She should have paused, waited for a while. As for Thomas, she had once cared for him, had envied him, did care for him still, but she knew she did not love him. She wanted to, wanted to feel more than admiration, but she could not. Nor had he encouraged her to share any part of him, past or present. She could satisfy and please him, she knew, and look after him, for she had always done so, and could provide what he wanted from her, but she did not care for him as she cared for those she had lost. He was seventy-six years old now and though still relatively fit and alert, she found his demands upon her person less palatable than they had once been. It was true she had acknowledged, at least privately, the responsibility of her sex for the care of a husband, to do what she could to make him content if it was within her remit to do so. However distasteful, however demeaning, it was a duty, nothing more. She would not allow herself to feel compromised in any way. It was right to feel detached, right also not to involve the emotions, for that way she could function as a person, sexless and impartial.

Thomas had always been thus, she thought to herself; he had not aged in that respect at least and more was the pity, for she found his demands on her time and person increasingly exhausting.

While conversation at the house had become muted and contained, Florence sought solace by writing letters. She still wrote to her namesake, Florence Henniker, but it was in Rebekah Owen and Lady Hoare, an admirer of Tom's writing whom she had met two years earlier when they had visited the family's country house at Stourhead, that she confided most often. Each week, as she had done for most of the past two years, she penned a letter to each, sharing with them tales of the state of her marriage, complaining about Tom and about the servants who seemed determined not to like either of them. Her letters were too inclined to offer insights about the minutiae of life at Max Gate, mentioning the family row following the reading of Mary's will, how she was repelled by the habit of the country folk of kissing the corpse before a funeral (as told her by Kate), the lack of gentility and company at Max Gate and all manner of subjects and things she knew she shouldn't properly write of.

Her unhappiness was mirrored by Thomas's desire to eschew London in favour of Max Gate and by so doing avoiding all the company and stimulus she craved. Their replies, hungry for details about the Hardy's and their household, were both sympathetic and encouraging, teasing from her the occasional indiscretion amongst the many felicities that flowed from her pen. Increasingly isolated, Florence was less cautious, less deferential in her correspondence, closer to the ego of the writer she imagined herself to be.

By 1916 Europe had drifted into a remorseless war of attrition with heavy loss of life and extended lists of casualties affecting the whole country. There was a fresh roll of soldiers' names appearing in the local press each week, of those who had died from Dorchester and the surrounding villages. If the human losses and the shortages weren't enough, the Battle of the Somme was making it difficult for anyone to look forward with optimism, to see any progress being made, any purpose being achieved. Frank's death had tempered Tom's patriotism and he seemed ill-inclined to do very much at all to help with the war effort or on the home front. When his poem 'Quid Hic Agis?' appeared in *The Spectator* during the summer of 1916, the extent of his despair was evident for all to see. While the "shake of wind and earthquake and consuming fire" might well have been taken for the horrors of the Western Front, it was apparent that the greater horror for Tom was within. What was he doing, he asked himself, still alive in the wilderness when all he wanted to do was to "… shrink from sight / And desire the night."

Florence was disturbed at how their life had sunk so far. She felt very alone and even the decision by Tom that she and Sydney Cockerell, of whose motives she harboured some suspicions, were to be his literary executors did little to allay her fears of a creeping old age and death for both of them. She had begun to worry more since the death of Frank and it only took a little thing to set her off. Her perennial state of being was gloomy and pessimistic and while Tom could rally occasionally from his despair and even throw a witticism or two into a conversation, she most decidedly could not.

More disturbing to Florence, however, was the news that Edward Clodd was writing his memoirs, intended for publication later that autumn. For while Thomas had distanced himself a little from Edward over recent years, believing him to be rather too indiscreet, Florence had corresponded with him for several years without Tom's knowledge, often confiding in Edward in a manner she now regretted. Although they seldom exchanged letters now, Florence was deeply concerned about what he might write about them from those first excursions.

'Why are you not worried, Tom?' she would ask him. 'You know how indiscreet the man is.'

'He is a little casual,' Tom conceded, 'but I venture he will respect old friendships and confidences.' He looked directly at Florence. 'He has just remarried, remember, and his Phyllis is even younger than you. She was his secretary before becoming his paramour and I hear she cannot even write a good sentence. We might even claim some credit for giving him the idea.'

He chuckled. 'It is quite a thing, Edward getting remarried. I doubt that he will risk any parallels being drawn between the two of us.'

'You cheapen our time by saying what you do, Tom. I know I'd not trust him. Edward has been a good friend, and I don't say he would deliberately betray us, but unwittingly he might.'

'And I tell you he won't.' Tom looked at her, and she realised then he was not as confident as he sounded.

'So you say, Tom, so you say, but I will write to him still.'

He said nothing, but demurred, pleased perhaps not to confront his old friend with any such suspicions he might have. Far better Florence do it, he thought, for she would be more candid.

She wrote to Edward that afternoon and received a reply a week later. He was delighted to hear from her and reassured her that she had no reason to worry.

'My dear Florence,' he started, 'I would not betray either of you by writing anything indiscreet or that could in any way cast doubts upon you,' before airing some idle recollections of their times together in a way that made her feel she must destroy the letter immediately. He signed himself off as 'your trustworthy friend, Edward' – yet she was neither convinced nor reassured that he was all that trustworthy; but having pleaded her case there was little more she could do.

Thomas's intransigence led Florence to look at other means of escaping from Max Gate. In her wish for some respite, she was opposed by Thomas who, while wanting the privacy and solitude that was his due as a writer, insisted that she be at an arm's length so he could call upon her at any time, for support, for reassurance, sometimes for nothing in particular. For Florence, having to deal with his demand that she remain in and about the house at all hours to meet his needs was stifling and at times almost unbearable.

The illness suffered by her father over the winter months provided Florence with the excuse she needed, and having organised Kate to look after the household in her absence she made her way back to Enfield where she found her father ill and uncomfortable, but not in a way that would necessitate her being there. She minded not. Once she was there, she wasn't going to rush back to Max Gate while she had the sliver of a reason not to. She wrote to Rebekah and arranged to meet in London, to tell her "all sorts of things she could not write about" and to divest herself of the tragedy that was her marriage. Thomas had made a promise, she told herself, and had not kept it. Why could she not complain, even just a little bit, even though she knew by doing so she was being disloyal?

She spent her first few days at home in Enfield dutifully attending to her father as the family's roster required of her. She enjoyed seeing old acquaintances, but could not find it in her to visit Alfred's parents for which she chastised herself later. It did not take long, however, for her to become bored and to seek out her old acquaintances in the city, though London was a sombre and different place from that she had known before the war. Kitchener's posters, prodding any residual feelings of guilt, were everywhere, demanding ever greater sacrifices to be made by the besieged citizenry.

She had arranged to meet Mrs Henniker at the Lyceum for tea and relished the opportunity to talk about life at Max Gate. Lady Hoare held a special literary soirée for her, with a hastily assembled mix of personages, while Rebekah, who she soon recalled rather pensively had always been better company through the medium of print than in the flesh, met her several times and filled her head with any sort of nonsense. She managed to accumulate and then disperse any whiff of scandal that was part of the city, taking great pleasure when it related to people they knew or who, she felt, should know better.

Thomas was unhappy at her absence and told her so through a number of telegrams, each more urgent than the one before, questioning its purpose and reminding her of her obligations as a dutiful wife. Eventually, they had their desired effect as Florence felt she was required to return to Max Gate for the sake of propriety if nothing else.

On arriving home, she found him as terse and distant as before she had left. Summer was late and while she managed to get out more each day, she felt her ever more demanding husband was a millstone round her neck. Nor did her variable health help assuage her irritation and discomfort. She had been experiencing considerable discomfort with the mastoid bone of the left ear and by early April had already planned to return to London to seek an expert opinion.

When she returned, she was irritated to hear that George Bernard Shaw and his wife had visited Max Gate in her absence and, to her great consternation, had not even asked after her. They had had no visitors of note for so long and she wondered how much warning Tom had had and whether he had even thought to tempt her home by using the writer as an inducement. She was intrigued when he started to tell her of Shaw's support for the Easter Rising and how he had responded, by damning the Irish as untrustworthy and disloyal and blaming Gladstone for not sorting out the country when the opportunity had earlier presented itself.

The delight in which he told Florence of the conversation angered her, for she knew his views on the Irish were coloured by her own associations.

'Why this hatred, Tom? Why make Mr Shaw think you a bigot?'

'Because the Irish cannot be trusted, Florence. And I should know that, should I not?'

Florence left the room, angry beyond measure that, old man or not, he could invoke and tarnish the character of the dead in such a way, that he could be so obtuse and oblivious to her feelings by behaving so callously.

In April, Sydney Cockerell visited Max Gate. Florence was suspicious of the man, distrusting his nature, questioning his motives and finding his high-handed manner offensive.

'Why do you need this man, Tom?' she asked before he arrived. 'Do you not trust me with your estate?'

'Sydney is a very able man, Florence, and I have known him for a long time. I trust him. Work with him, not against him, for he is as determined as you but with greater purpose. I've known him from when Emma was alive,' he concluded, as if that particular link was in any way designed to appease her.

Despite her own original misgivings, Florence did make an effort to talk to Sydney, and against her expectations found her fears slowly diluted by the man's attention and his obvious devotion to her husband. Bullish and pragmatic, she could not doubt he cared for Thomas and his legacy, and putting her own mixed feelings on the matter to one side, that was enough for her.

Florence's pharyngitis showed little sign of improving and in May she determined to return to London for treatment. Thomas was sceptical of the symptoms she described and the proffered cures, and irritated that it was she who was meant to be healthy, looking after him, not the other way around. When she asked him for assistance in paying for her consultation and treatment, he refused, saying that she had her own means for such things, since she had refused to divest herself of the bequest she had been left four years earlier.

'I have used the bulk of that already, Tom, as you well know. It paid for my sister to become a qualified teacher, something she is good at and that I could manage for her. I don't have much left. Is it right for you to refuse to pay to look after the health of your wife?'

'It is as right as it is for a wife to keep money from her husband. What does it say of our marriage, Florence, that you have this separate money, especially as I know its origin?'

'You know nothing. You believed Bram Stoker because you chose to.'

'No, Florence, I believed Bram Stoker because what he said about you was consistent with what I know of you also. It is the way your head and heart work in parallel universes, but never in tandem, that gives you away, Florence.'

She stared at him, her dark eyes flashing.

'Then I will pay my own bills to repair the damage looking after you has incurred, Thomas. You forget how much I devoted myself to you when we first married, reading to you for hours on end. No wonder my throat gave out. And all that time, Emma's shadow lay there and people talked about us and you seemed to care for nothing but your writing.'

She left the room, Thomas being too tired to remonstrate with her or to consider retracting his words, although in the mood he was in he would hardly have been inclined to do so.

With Thomas refusing to relent, Florence travelled to London alone for the first of several treatments, further hardened against him, his cruelty, his capacity for exacting revenge and his meanness. She knew their marriage was becoming a mockery, a pretence, and that while she could not, would not, countenance leaving him now she had invested so much in the old man, she could see them leading separate lives, as he had known before.

Returning to Max Gate in late June, she was conscious of a change in atmosphere. Thomas was better than he had been when she had left, both physically and mentally. The weather, the soul's barometer, also contributed to her feeling of well-being, and a settled and enduring early summer permeated even the dark surrounds of Max Gate. Thomas had resumed his weekly visits to Talbothays and while relations with Kate remained strained, she enjoyed the time spent talking with Henry who had thawed a little towards her once more. Edward Clodd's memoirs had been published the previous month and to her great relief contained nothing about their time at Aldeburgh whatsoever, though that was tempered by the fact that while this particular mountain had been crossed they could still be undone by some future revelations. They had married in a clandestine manner and the anonymity of their marriage was bound to lead to speculation at some time in the future unless they somehow took the initiative and told their own account of all that had transpired as they wanted it known.

Following this time away, she began to feel a sense of equanimity, acceptance even, buoyed and encouraged as she was by Thomas's insistence that he pay for her treatment, albeit retrospectively. Later in the month, when a parcel came from an acquaintance of Thomas's, Arthur Quiller Couch, addressed to them both, she was intrigued to find a copy of the author's most recent book, *On the Art of Writing*, which they both read together and apart. As Thomas observed her, at first dispassionately and later with growing consternation, Florence's aspirations as a writer appeared to be sparked and flamed anew. He was right to be concerned. Even without his encouragement, she had determined to start writing seriously once again, whatever her husband might think and however little support he may give her.

They spoke little and when they did, viewed the other with sadness.

'You are quiet these days, Florence. Don't you have anything to say to me anymore?

'I have been thinking of Frank, that's all,' she would answer, 'Frank and all the others.'

'To think of them is understandable for those same thoughts abide within us all, Florence, but we should not let them deter us from thinking of ourselves sometimes.'

He hesitated briefly before returning to the conversation, as if measuring the effort that would be required.

'Where is all that joy we used to share? We used to talk once, Florence, about everything.'

'That is not how I remember it, Tom. I recall little joy and as for subjects, it was usually Emma as I recall.'

'Hush, Florence. That is not so.'

And she would just shake her head slowly, sigh, and try again.

'I'm sorry, Tom, I don't always feel so wretched. It is just that it has been such a long time since there has been anything to feel happy about.' She reached for his hand, all bone and cartilage. 'It has been a cruel winter,' she concluded, 'but it is about to end.'

Slowly, almost imperceptibly, as summer grew, Florence and Tom started to regain a little of their humanity. Although the outside world, which he now saw as starting at Dorchester, was still beyond them, they took the occasional walk traversing Puddletown Forest from Rainbarrows to Green Hill and back past the old home at Bockhampton, leaving Wessex at home for fear of the adders that were abundant at that time of year. Without the terrier to distract them, each walk became a therapy of sorts, a minor rehabilitation of the soul and spirit and both felt better for the exercise and the communion it provided them.

Back at Max Gate, little disturbed them in their shadowy enclave, where they had both taken to writing again with some of their old relish. Often now, after breakfast, they would toil at their own discrete labours, writing when they could, talking occasionally, each encouraging the other. Florence had started several articles and short stories, each one of which lay unfinished in a growing pile of papers and manuscripts.

Thomas, meanwhile, having finished his selected poems and the work he had undertaken some time previously on William Barnes, was assisting with a new dramatic production called 'Wessex Scenes' taken and adapted from *The Dynasts* to be produced first in Weymouth. As he worked hard to ensure he was happy with the script, it was more of an effort than it had once been. Florence had started to see him more as he was, a man about to turn seventy-six years old who depended on her and her alone. It was a love wrought of dependency should she want it, a love born of need, of sacrifice. And she remembered her mother defining love in much the same words and thought it not unusual. Thomas had taken some considerable time modifying the script, re-writing some parts and adding others until he was satisfied. One prescient addition was to allow for a young girl from nearby Beaminster, Gertrude Bugler, who Hardy had first seen perform as Marty South in a local amateur production of *The Woodlanders*, to take a leading role.

Chapter 17

THE (EN)TREATY OF MAX GATE

What precipitated the argument was not of great matter. It was, after all, as she knew it would be when it came, the product of a groundswell of resentment that had been building up in her for some time. Thomas had been tetchy and irritable since the death of his sister and that event and the horror and endlessness of the war had made him even more depressing and indifferent towards her. There had been times when some of the old affection returned, but they were fleeting. Nor had Florence been well recently, returning to her specialist in London for further treatment for her pharangytic complaint. He was unmoved by the vagaries of her health and while he had belatedly offered to pay for her medical care, she was still expected to pay for any personal luxuries – which in his mind meant anything other than her daily fare.

When Florence reflected on Thomas's marriage with Emma, she remembered that they had done little more than eat their evening meal together before retreating to their own private domains, two studies, one on top of the other, in the heart of the house and felt that four years on they were themselves no better.

She thought often of Emma, of Thomas's defence of her, of the pervasiveness of her presence which still unnerved her, often irrationally so. What had she written that upset Thomas so, beyond unearthing his obvious guilt? Surely she knew everything of his predilections and the vacillations of his spirit? Why should it – or anything – bother her?

She had only once before ventured up the steep flight of stairs from the first floor to the room that had been Emma's bedroom during the later years of her marriage to Tom. That she was moved to do so again was partly the result of boredom, partly a dark and brooding curiosity. Tom had wanted things left as they were, although he had overseen the burning of most of Emma's writing, her letters and her hateful diaries, and little else was touched. Polly Gale had left their employment not long after her mistress's death and her room had been used to store what remained.

On this occasion, Florence climbed the stairs with a sense of trepidation, surprised that she had willed herself to do so. With the stairway starting beside the entrance to Tom's spacious second study, she was made aware all over again of just how small and claustrophobic was the room where Emma had chosen to lock herself away. The angled ceiling with its diagonal struts and small cast-iron fireplace that looked as if it could manage no more than a single log, and that placed vertically in the grate, made the room feel even more oppressive. Only the view from the window facing northwards over the gardens pricked the bubble of despondency and gave her some fallow ground for the growing of an imagination, such as it was.

She stood in the room for some minutes just gazing abstractly, her arms pulled tightly across her chest. She drew in her breath and felt Emma's presence all about her, in the fabric, in the religious print still hanging on the wall, in her old clothes draped over the bed in Polly's bedroom. She leaned over the boxes of books that sat under the window and picked through them. Many were religious tracts, interspersed with books by Gaskell and Trollope, although none, she noted, by her errant husband. There was the copy of one of Emma's stories that Florence had corrected for her and she involuntarily pulled it from the box. The pages she had annotated and added to were as she remembered, but on one page her amendments were scratched out and the words "liar" and "Judas" written beside them.

Florence felt a chill pass down her spine. What was she doing, seeming to pretend to befriend her and then writing such vitriol? What did Emma know of her and Tom, after all? Reading on, it was clear the old lady knew a lot more than Florence had ever suspected, even from before the two of them had met. And she was so kind to me, thought Florence. What was she thinking? She asked herself when Emma first suspected that she was not as she seemed to be to her, that Thomas had instigated a deception not worthy of her or him. Or was this just a pattern in their lives, that there had been others before her, that Emma was well used to such "goings-on"? If I ask myself if I am a decent person, she thought, I would say yes, I am. It is not because I have no shame or that I am shameless, but because I have been true to myself in what I've done and tried my best to look after those I care for. Even if the truth of one person, she thought, leads to the unwitting betrayal of another. She had accepted to serve Tom and to care for him, for it was in her nature to be compliant, but only – and herein lay her anger – if he had kept his share of the agreement, which clearly he had not.

Florence had kept Tom's letter given to her on the night before they married in the false bottom of her jewel box, such as it was. She had looked at it often in that first month or so, but after that had left it where she felt it was safe. As she had been persuaded by some inner compulsion to look at Emma's room, to confront the spectre of her predecessor, so she took out the letter that had upset her so, in a similar act of contrition.

She knew each of his words, so carefully measured in his spidery script. It was not, she knew, a pre-nuptial letter, but what she now saw as a measured and cruel attempt to enslave her. She hated him for ever having written it, for its demeaning tone and numerous caveats. She hated the hint of blackmail when an appeal to her heart and sense of duty would have sufficed. Some of what he wrote then had not seemed clear to her at the time, but had become so as the months passed. He had wanted to muzzle her. He had wanted her to be his shield and companion, his housekeeper and secretary – these she had expected to be, but they were not at the heart of what he wanted of her. It came to her only after the poems had been published, after he had punished her, the realisation that he had in fact not sought her only as a bride, but as an accomplice. She sat down slowly, reading as she did so.

'Dearest Florence,' he had written, 'for so you shall always be. I know our marriage tomorrow is not as you want and I accept the responsibility for making it so. It will be strange for me to have married twice without any family present so at least you are better off than that. Simply, I could not have faced a public ceremony. Better by far to present the *fait accompli* and be done with it. I think in time you will see that I was right in this.

'Ours has been a long and complicated courtship, but you remain to me as when I first met you, a dear, dear woman, who knew how my life was and gave me the companionship I so sought. For that, I will always be most grateful.

'The realisation, in time, that there were others who meant more to you than me was, and still is, a great sadness. You were seduced by things above your station, if I may be so bold, when you are, like me, of these parts and company, of the same milieu as I. Stoker was your downfall and, to me, you were undone by that attachment. After mixing with their circle of friends, I sense you became frustrated by me. You were willing to compromise everything, not only between us, tenuous as that may have been at the time, but in your own soul. I cannot forget the betrayal I felt, although I will try to forgive you.

'You tried, I know, to link your absences with the fact that I said I could never leave Emma. She was mad, perhaps, even then I could have believed the fact and her writings told me as much, but she was not taken in by you, as you may have suspected. She was willing to allow you to co-exist, if you hadn't been so intent on deception. For that, I must accept some of the responsibility also and that I do.

'I know this sounds harsh, but it is best written now. We both are culpable in some ways and now have a duty to protect each other's reputations. I have decided that marriage is the best vehicle for that. Bram Stoker would have destroyed you, had I allowed him. Had I not been more cautious we both could have been uncovered many times, but friends chose not to do so. Marriage will blow away the residual gossip after a while and time will bury the rest. This alliance will be seen as a natural thing by those who look closely at such matters. You were a friend of Emma, remember, or so you presented yourself, and I, I valued you as my secretary, my helpmate and devotee. That will make our marriage explicable.

'I marry you, Florence, knowing I was your second choice, that had Ely Place been there for you, you would have taken it. I marry you in full knowledge that it is my reputation you crave to lie in the shadow of, not my presence. One day you may find out how it feels to be the second-chosen, for it is a hard yoke to bear, and I would not wish it on you.

'You may, of course, read this and decide that our marriage would be a mistake. I beg you to think carefully if you are tempted to make any such judgement and bear in mind, too, that I am old and the sentence will not be for your lifetime. Remember, also, that I can and will help you with the only thing I think you really care about and that is your writing. It is not for me to say how well you write or otherwise, for a spouse's word, even mine, counts for naught, but I will help you scribe and provide you with introductions. Remember, also, how happy we have been when we are on our own at Aldeburgh, on that weekend when Sydney and William stayed with us at Max Gate. It can be so again. The rest is up to you. You must remember, though, your writing is secondary to mine and this is no mere vanity. It is as it is. I do believe it is more than your name on the spine of a book you crave, for you have that already. So I pledge that I will support you as I can.

'I trust you will not abandon me in marriage. You are my handmaiden, my helpmate and my companion and although I don't know if it is in me to wholly trust you, I can offer you my love, limited and jaundiced though it may be. We both have skeletons in our cupboards, I know – even the righteous memory of your dear friend, Alfred, hovers over me as an example of all that I am not. I am not selfless. I am not forgiving. I am not patient or considerate. But you know all this. Thornley's money and his gifts still rankle and I intend to let you be a woman of independent means until you no longer can afford to be. Then you may be mine, alone.

'Meanwhile, when we marry, for I do not think this letter will surprise or deter you, I ask that you keep your counsel, that you keep distant from people, especially in these early months. Choose carefully who you write to and what you say, for you join the public domain as Mrs Hardy in marrying me. I intend to burn all our early letters that have escaped so far and I urge – nay, instruct you – to do the same. Most important, you must burn this letter, for once written, it is best to be filtered and absorbed, without a residue for others to find. Your loving companion and dearest friend, Tom.'

Florence folded the letter carefully and placed it back in the box. It was a judgement of all that had come to pass and she felt overwhelmed by it all. He had had no right to write of Alfred and Thornley and omit his own paramours. He had no right talking of her behaviour in such a coarse way when she had been so endlessly considerate. Yet she had married him the next day. She had read this and married him still. What did she expect? That something would change? He had warned her and she had experienced his vengeance. For a short while, Frank had served as a pacifier, a distraction to them both, but now life seemed to stretch out remorselessly ahead of her, grinding her down. Her only lifelines were her own sisters, who could not comprehend her life now and who would judge her harshly if they had known the passages of her life when she had veered away from what they saw as proper. She had trampled over their sensibilities, she knew, but she had not been sinful, not in her mind. Her other friends – Florence, Lady Grove, Rebekah – who knows what they thought of her? Mrs Henniker had been shocked by the speed of her marriage to Tom and had never been quite the same towards her since. Florence still counted her as a dear friend, but the relationship was compromised by degrees of intimacy. The others read her tittle-tattle and responded in kind, but she suspected it meant very little to either of them.

While the realisation had been slow in coming, Florence saw the impasse of their marriage could not continue and that she, they, could not survive as things were. Tom may have turned seventy-six, she thought, and may only have a year or so left, although – and she shuddered at the realisation – heaven knows, he might linger on like his mother had done, and what would be left of her at the end of that? What did she want, she asked herself? She could not leave him, not now, for where would she go? She wanted to write, she wanted to be someone else, and if she could have that she would be satisfied. But she would have to make Tom do what she wanted him to do, for once in his miserable life.

In early September 1916, Tom had rallied sufficiently, in body at least, to make another pilgrimage (as Florence described it) to Cornwall. She had known of the proposed visit for some time and had steeled herself to ensure he did not recede further into his maudlin self. Having agreed to accompany him out of some morbid curiosity to see the realm of his "late espoused saint" – as Florence had taken to calling her – she started to view the trip as a pilgrimage on his part and a penance on hers, and approached it with growing apprehension.

Having decided to make the long and circuitous journey to Cornwall by rail, they were required to change trains several times before eventually reaching Camelford, some fourteen miles west of Launceston. There they transferred to horse and buggy before completing their journey to the coast where they arrived late into the evening, tired and fraught and, in Florence's case, fervently wishing they had never left Max Gate.

Originally, Thomas had planned that they would stay with Emma's cousins in Launceston until Florence put her foot down.

'There is no way that I will sleep under their roof,' she told Tom bluntly, 'for I doubt they would let me see the next dawn.'

Nor would she abide staying at the Wellington Hotel in Boscastle for it was where he had resided when wooing Emma.

'I'll not have this trip turned into some pilgrimage for her,' she told him vehemently. 'I have agreed too much already just in being here.' And when

Thomas tried to reason with her, she would not countenance it, for she already saw the place as all granite and slate and full of an uncomfortable darkness. Eventually, he had relented and agreed that they would stay at the Castle Hotel in Tintagel for the duration of their time in Cornwall, though he resented the added expense and the extra distance to the places he longed to re-visit.

While somewhat appeased, Florence was nevertheless nervous at being ensnared within Hardy's mythological Lyonnesse and half expected Lilian Gifford to come round any corner. She was conscious, too, of the effect the trip would have on Tom and the multitude of memories that were inevitably stirring within him. Even on their first full day there, as they visited the site of the castle in Tintagel, he had become quiet and withdrawn, only remarking ruefully on the descent that it would be the last time he would visit there and that he must put an end to such longings.

He had been insistent that they both visit the church at St Juliot's where he took pains to show Florence the renovations that had been carried out following his first visit. She struggled to show any signs of interest. The main structural changes to the church, the removal of the tower and north transept and aisle, had already been decided before he had been employed, but it still irked him that he was implicated in the heavy-handedness of the project. He knew, also, that he had not taken much care with some of the original alterations, especially doing away with the original rood screen and the ornately carved pew ends and regretted his own part in the folly. It was probably, he reflected, his desire to spend time with Emma all those years ago that made him rush his drawings so.

When he insisted on pointing out to Florence the marble tablet that he had organised to be placed on the wall of the north aisle in Emma's memory, he spoke blithely about the fact that the memorial was one of which Emma's family would approve, until he was pulled up short by Florence who muttered, 'So this will no doubt draw another poem out of you, Tom' – a remark that in turn elicited from him the hasty contradiction that the stone was to commemorate her laying of the foundation stone for the rebuilt tower some forty-six years previously, not for her, but uttered, she felt, with all the conviction of an apostle.

'Perhaps if you had been a little more honest with me three years ago and told me of this then, it would make your protestations more credible, but you didn't tell me, Tom, for you thought it would never come to pass that you and I would end up here together.' She cast him a withering look before concluding, 'Especially as you and *she* couldn't manage as much in all the time you were married.'

'That is the point, Florence,' he replied. 'Time buries such attachments and I – we – can look at such things impassively now, can we not?' He looked at her, touching her hand as he did so. 'Please, Florence, believe me. It's your absolution I seek, not this constant reproach for things past.'

She grew silent, angry that he had bought her into this erstwhile shrine of his so he could wallow in his former life without a single thought for them and the short wisp of life they might have together.

Florence was unsettled by the visit to the church and her nervous sensibilities had been heightened. Even the land appeared animate as she remembered the poems that seemed to emanate from the very earth they walked over, each place name resonating in her mind. When Thomas decided to visit Emma's family at Launceston, she refused to accompany him.

'Why, Tom, why? They didn't want a churl mixing with their lot once before so why should they now?' He winced under her admonishment, though she gave him no time to answer before directing her ire at Lilian. 'And that niece of hers will be there and she is mad, quite mad. Visit if you must, but I do not want to know about it.'

Instead she decided to climb the dark granite path out to Penally Point to where she could look back at Boscastle harbour and outwards towards Meachard, the small island which guarded the river mouth. There she sat, enveloped in the curls of dark granite rock cut through by bands of hard white quartz, watching the brooding clouds gathering in the west.

She had brought a volume of Tom's poems along with her, determined to confront her demons in their native place. There was no reason she should feel threatened by his predilection for romancing the dead, she told herself, and she must be tolerant of his foibles. But it was difficult. When they were walking down from Beeny Cliff two days previously, he had started to extol Emma's horsemanship, describing how she would ride fearlessly along the cliff edge. Florence interrupted him abruptly. 'I do not want to hear any more of this "West-of-Wessex girl" of yours, Tom. She was never as you describe her; it is just your flawed imagination tinged with guilt that tells you so.' At the same time, she thought cruelly to herself, 'and would that she had been a little further west then rather than now.'

Tom's poems made for difficult reading. She could revel in his description of the Atlantic, the "opal and the sapphire of that wandering western sea", even though today it frothed and groaned and was altogether much less impressive, but reading of the woman whom Tom professed he once loved so and "who loyally loved me" made her squirm until, defeated by the intransigence of the words, she put the book aside and just stared into the distance, the silence interrupted only by the squawk of an imperious gull and the endless friction of sea working on rock.

She realised it was no use always revisiting what they had endured, singularly and together. Their lives had waned and dimmed, each being in some way a disappointment to the other, but she asked herself was that not to be expected? She had committed so much to Tom and would not allow herself to be found wanting on his behalf. Nor would she allow this place to consume her, and leaving her husband's collection of poetry resting on the rock for the coming tide to deal with, she made her way back down to the small township below.

The next two days they spent walking beside the Valency River and visiting Pentargon Bay. On the longer walks along the coastal paths, Florence found herself settling to the soporific rhythms of the coast and its immediate hinterland, fascinated by the kersey-waved hedges that ran down the seaward slopes through the fields full of heather and furze, sometimes forgetting in whose domain she walked.

Yet on Beeny Cliff, Florence could hardly bear standing there beside Tom, listening to the waves crashing on the rocks, not for his memories from forty-six years ago, but for the lines he had written but three years previously, no doubt standing close to where they were now.

For their final day, they had decided to walk along the cliff edge north of Boscastle harbour, first climbing Penally Hill before heading north to look out over Pentargon Bay towards the monolithic and craggy Beeny Cliff. Although Tom was feeling rather stiff and tired from all their earlier exertions, he was keen to see for the last time the dark and resolute cliff face that had so inspired him.

After a considerable struggle, they came over the brow of the hill where an onshore wind slapped brusquely at their faces. Clouds had begun to gather and Florence wondered which Cornish witch would dare threaten rain upon them, though she reasoned she knew but one.

They found a flat rock on the path's edge overlooking the bay and sat quietly, watching the patchwork of shower clouds coming together in the distance, like great heaped sacks of water imbibing and growing fatter still. The Atlantic itself was swollen and mobile and although the day was relatively calm, it exuded a brooding menace as it shimmered and ran. She thought how the ocean's waters changed, chameleon-like from black to green to blue as the clouds diffused the light upon its surface. Its great mass was as she felt at this very moment, endlessly changing and as inconstant as they had become.

'Tom,' she began, 'I hope we don't need to come back here again.'

He looked at her, his face sad and drawn.

'It is unlikely to happen again, but I cannot promise you that. I still have the family here, Florence, and I will not shirk my obligations to them.' Pausing briefly, he added by way of closure, 'One cannot just dismiss forty years of my life because you will it so.'

'They are not family, Tom, not to you and most certainly not to me. Not anymore. They are leeches. They want to do us mischief, of that I'm sure.'

He turned to her. 'Dear Florence. Can you not see that they are gone now, those demons that you feared. Can you not see it in me? That I am not weighed down anymore?'

She lowered her head. 'You may be better than when you came before, I grant you, but you have done nothing these three and a half years to make me feel secure.'

They sat, he with his hands in his lap, his hat and scarf about him although the day had started mild enough. Old. Old was what he looked. She should be careful.

He had taken off his crumpled hat and was teasing its rim through his fingers. The sharp call of a stonechat could be heard from the furze behind them. The air had cooled and she shivered a little. He waited for her to speak.

'Tom, do you remember when we married you said you would help me to be published?'

He looked up as if the words had awoken him. He hesitated for a minute then nodded and said quietly, 'And I will, Florence, and I will. Just give me time and I'll draft something out for you.'

'No,' she answered, 'I don't want you to draft out anything. That is the point. I am going to write something of my own. I have decided.'

'And what, pray, are you going to write about?'

She paused, aware of the gravitas of her next words.

'You, Tom. I'm going to write about you. And us also.'

He stared at her. 'You will not. I forbid you.'

'You forbid me? And why should I not? I have been waiting for two years for you to show any interest in my writing. Why should I not write of you?

'Because I would want it – that is reason enough. What is more, the Giffords would not welcome it, any more than would my own kin. Nor would it be done for people to start prying into our life, Florence. It is all too raw still.'

He wrestled with a piece of grass, knotting it smaller, tighter.

'I still remember being reminded that I was the son of a bricklayer when I first entertained the thought of becoming an architect. "Above my station," they said. "Insolent upstart. Does not know his place." It's always been that way with my writing too; always other writers waiting to flay me with their too clever words as some rustic who had the temerity to think he could write of anything that had any universal appeal. Even now, now I am famous, I don't trust them. I am not taken in by their approbation. Remember how they turned on me after *Jude*.'

He looked at her intently, as if to give weight to his words.

'You writing about me could open a can of worms. We don't want to encourage people to talk about us. Tongues can be sharp, Florence, and we have no need to stir up things now that people have grown used to us.'

'But they will talk, Tom, they will. If you wait, someone else will write of you as they have already attempted in the past. Sydney would agree with me, I know, for he has told me he has talked to you of it. At least I could write the truth.'

Tom didn't answer. The first hints of rain, the sudden drop in temperature, the fading light, the closing of the clouds, prompted them to stand up.

'The truth, Florence? The truth? What truth? Our truth? You and me?'

'It would be our truth, Tom,' she answered deliberately, 'the one we see, the one we want to be true.'

They started walking down the ridge as the first drops of rain started to fall, heavy, bloated drops that burst open upon contact.

'Then I should write it, Florence. I should write it. You know little of my early life and could not, I dare say, even write of us before we married without blushing.'

189

He paused, reaching out an arm to steady himself on the crumbling path edge.

'But it should be my book.'

'Your book, Florence?' He smiled at her, a small, tight smile.

He said nothing for some distance as they both concentrated on the descent. Florence walked behind him, waiting for what came next.

'You think it should be your book? Why your book?' He stopped and turned back towards her. How similar she was, he thought, how comforting that she feels it too, this distaste of his, this fear of belonging.

'Maybe you are right. Maybe it would make sense to have my life written by another. To remove myself. To let someone else say it for me and with greater conviction than I could muster. After all,' – and he smiled wryly as he spoke – 'I have never read an autobiography I could truly believe.'

He looked at her intently, life coursing back into his veins.

'Dear Florence, how inspired of you to think of it. Such a work would protect me from the charge – and they would make it, believe me – of making more of my life than was there. Whereas for you,' he paused for effect before saying without the faintest hint of false modesty, 'for you it would be the significant work you always want to write.'

He stopped again, gathering his breath, ruminating on the idea, looking across towards the next bay. A tree, bent almost in half by the ocean's tempests, reminded him again of how exposed they were to the elemental forces.

'Perhaps, just perhaps, dear lady,' he said, 'I have never given you or your ambition enough credit. As you say, people will write of me, of us, anyway and if we can dampen their curiosity, then that will be all to the good. And of course, it must be yours.' He paused, his ideas gathering momentum. 'Yes, it will be yours, Florence. It will be your great achievement, for we shall make it so.'

He took hold of her arm as they made their way down the hill, as if, by the President of the Immortals, their lives were aligned once more. The irony that it should happen here, moreover, in Cornwall on a pilgrimage to an earlier shrine, was not lost on either of them.

Returning to Max Gate the next day, they sat down together to flesh out their resolution. It was agreed that she would be the author of two volumes of Thomas's life, from birth to old age. Of course, he would help to tell her the details of the life, the anecdotes, the family, his many achievements and writings, but in the end it would be hers. And she was sure to add her bit, to use her censor's pen when she felt the need. They both agreed that discretion was all-important. Tom would write the text in his usual measured hand and Florence would type it before destroying the original draft. They would strip the letters and notebooks, those that remained after Tom's conflagration of two years earlier, and would systematically destroy them afterwards, ensuring only one version of truth remained.

In early December, Florence wrote to Rebekah Owen describing Thomas in a manner she had not done before. Rebekah was struck by the warmth in her words, her softness towards the husband she had so often railed against, and her finishing by writing, 'I wish people knew that he was really happy, for strangers must imagine that his only wish is to die and be in the grave with the only woman who ever gave him any happiness.'

At last, she, they, had achieved something from her misalliance. A common purpose. There was no denying that Tom needed her now as she needed him. Who cared for what end? They would be together. From this, perhaps, they could even grow a greater affection, even some happiness for the short time they would have together. And the book? The book would be a triumph and the triumph would be hers. She could now set about placing herself and Emma in the right order. This was what she had imagined and dreamt of. At last, there was a purpose. At last, she could become, for all the world, the mistress of Max Gate, the Mrs Hardy that would be remembered with admiration and affection.

AFTERMATH

Florence and Tom were to enjoy another twelve years together. While their lives would never be easy or straightforward, with their agreement on the writing of the biography they had reached a watershed in their marriage. There was now an understanding between them of how their lives together would work, how each would benefit the other and benefit from the other. In their relationship, such as it was, there was little passion, little intimacy left. The public would see Florence as the compliant and obsequious second wife, dedicated to spending her life looking after Thomas and his legacy and neither did anything to dispel the impression.

Florence appeared to grow into her role as consort and protector, building up her own coterie of friends and acquaintants, including T. E. Lawrence and Siegfried Sassoon with whom she developed strong and lasting friendships. But to many she was still a charlatan, a pretender, who had inveigled herself into Hardy's life for her own ends, and they treated her as such. In the eyes of locals, despite the many good and charitable works she did in later life, she was always an outsider. The gossip about her earlier liaisons with Tom never quite went away, especially of the years before Emma's death; whether at Aldeburgh or at Max Gate, the maids had watched and observed the couple with a good deal of morbid curiosity, missing little that went on, feeding their own suspicions and prejudices.

Thomas continued to treat her indifferently at times, sometimes cruelly so, but she put that down to creeping old age. He was approaching eighty now and while mentally as sharp as ever, he was less physically able, less tolerant, thought Florence, and with the passing of the years, altogether less appealing – except for his legacy and its residual benefits for her, which retained their attraction.

Tom died in January 1928. Soon after the funerals (for it took two to bury him), Florence went up to the top floor of the house and ventured into the two rooms wherein lived the spirit that had haunted her all those long years. She started with the clothes once worn by Emma, gathering up the dresses, the array of ridiculous hats, skirts and shoes, even old yellowing corsets, and stuffed them into boxes. These she handed on to the gardener who carried them downstairs for her and to a place near the pines where he had lit a bonfire to burn the household and garden rubbish. She sifted through envelopes crammed full of letters and dog-eared notebooks before indiscriminately throwing them into canvas sacks. There was an array of those tedious books that she had known she would find there, books of spirituality, even one or two of her husband's that had been inscribed affectionately for Emma. All sorts of paraphernalia were jammed into a jumble of boxes or drawers and it was more than she could bear to handle with her ungloved hands. The sky blue dress she remembered and she took care to throw it into the middle of the bonfire herself.

The flames could be seen from some distance. What had been a small bonfire smouldering near the edge of the lawn had taken to the new fuel with a renewed appetite as more was thrown upon it. Each box was met by a sudden explosion of ashes as smoke rose in a billowing cloud, as each in turn caught fire and crisply burned.

But burning would not extinguish the life that would continue to haunt her. Now that he had been laid on top of *her* in her sullen grave, she would never be able to supplant her memory.

In the years following Tom's death and before her own, Florence suffered a variety of ailments. More and more she turned back to her own family for comfort, especially to her sisters Eva and Margaret. Visitors to Max Gate would write of the sad lacklustre eyes of a childless woman and her great docility, wearing, as Virginia Woolf once described, "a sprigged voile dress, black shoes and necklace" and an overarching shroud of melancholy. They came to think her a nursemaid, a secretary whose devotion to her subject had merely spilled over, not thinking for a minute that she had had any other life. And she let them think so, for it was easier that way than to try and explain the convoluted existence she had once led.

In 1922 she confided to Siegfried Sassoon that having wanted it for so long, she had come to dislike being called Mrs Hardy because the name 'always seems to belong to someone else whom I knew for several years and I am oppressed by the thought that I am busy in her house, using her things and, worst of all, having even stolen her name.'

She was never to escape the shadow of Emma that had been cast, not by her life but by Thomas's memorial to it. Even in the few years left remaining to her after Tom's death the spectre of Emma loomed large and on November 27th, 1934, Florence wrote to Howard Bliss, 'Today is the 22nd anniversary of the death of ELH and she has been in my mind all day – and I have been up in the sad little attic where she died – still full of her presence.'

There was no escape, not here, not from the desk calendars caught on the anniversary of the date that Thomas and Emma first met, nor anywhere in this house that Emma and Thomas built as their own.

Yet Florence had resolved to live out the terms of her marriage despite Tom's fickleness, his vacillating ego, one moment name-dropping, seeking approval, the next indifferent and intolerant, vested as he was with a supreme belief in his own genius. She had endured his flirtatious obsessions whether real or imagined; that hurtful time with Gertrude Bugler in 1925 which severely tested the little confidence she had in her ability to hold the affection of her eighty-five-year-old husband – a commitment that she sometimes doubted she had ever enjoyed. All this for the promise of posterity.

And of course there was the debacle of the funeral, her hopes of marriage to James Barrie and the public identification of her as Mrs Driffield in Somerset Maugham's *Cakes and Ale*, and her subsequent public ridicule to navigate through.

And worse, when her authorship of 'The Life' was publicly questioned and the motives for such a complicitous deception by author and wife were aired and endlessly discussed, she realised she had lost the one thing she hankered for – her credibility as a writer.

Poor Florence. In October 1937, only a year after her father's death, she died of cancer at Max Gate with her sisters Eva and Margaret at her bedside. She was cremated at Woking before her ashes were buried in the now overcrowded plot at Stinsford Church, alongside those of Thomas. How death must have seemed a release for her from all the railings and ravages of life.

"Helpmate of Genius" – it was not the epitaph she ever wanted for herself. For in her own mind, she was always Florence Hardy neé Dugdale, writer and companion, mistress of Max Gate, who deserved to be known as much for her own subsumed talents as for her public role as companion to the grand old man of English literature.

POSTSCRIPT

While 'Florence, Mistress of Max Gate' is essentially a work of fiction, it is intended to sit, more or less, within the known parameters of her life as provided by the major biographers of Thomas Hardy. In some instances, actual events are taken out of the context of time and place and mingled with supposition on what may have been said or happened. For instance, Edward Clodd's first meeting with Florence almost certainly did not happen until four years after that described in the book, whereas Florence Henniker was probably already known to Florence by 1910; Lilian had left Max Gate in 1913 before Florence finally agreed to move in; and for convenience (although very much against her will, no doubt) Florence has been condemned to an extra year of teaching; and so on. The bulk of the story, however, keeps to the known chronology.

I hope that readers, especially adherents of Thomas Hardy, will excuse such liberties. While the majority of the characters are based on real persons, at least in name, and are in possession of some of their known personal traits, the story as told is very much a work of fiction which takes liberties in exploring the psychology of their relationships and the various "props", notably the marital letter and diaries.

To that end, I am indebted, first and foremost, to the major biographers of Thomas Hardy and the legion of other writers who have either written on aspects of Hardy's life, edited his work or collections of letters, or who helped develop the Wessex mythology. I have deliberately avoiding resorting to unpublished primary sources other than those cited elsewhere for the danger of swamping the fiction with too much superfluous detail and distraction.

I am grateful, also, to those who first read the novel in its draft form and offered encouragement, as well as to the custodians at Max Gate who allowed me to see around Hardy's private quarters, not then open to the public. I am especially grateful to my publishers and editors, Frank Kibblewhite and Anthony Head, for seeing merit in the story and choosing to publish it, as well as for guiding it through its latter stages.

195

Finally I am indebted to Thomas Hardy, both for the inspiration he provided in first drawing me to Dorset and for unwittingly giving the impetus for this book through the considerable steps he took to protect his privacy and reputation, even posthumously. The collective bonfires of Emma, Thomas and Florence, consisting of many letters and notebooks, and the subterfuge employed by Thomas and Florence in writing 'The Life' all served to fuel the speculation, the intrigue from which this novel is, at least in part, derived.